ABBAC1

PART TWO
of
THE JARDINE TRILOGY

&

BOOK TWO
of
THE FIBONACCI SERIES

by author and creator
Karma Lei Angelo

- - -- --- -----

For more information, contact:
KarmaLeiAngelo@gmail.com
www.karmaleiangelo.com

Facebook, Twitter, Instagram: @KarmaLeiAngelo

This book is a work of fiction. Names, characters, businesses, organizations, places, events and incidences either are the product of the author's imagination or are used fictitiously. Any resemblance to actual persons, living or dead, is entirely coincidental.

Book Cover:
Octopus charcoal drawing by Eugene Ramirez,
Owner of Revelation Tattoo Company
www.revelationtattoocompany.com
Aurora photograph by Jonathan Bean, Photographer
www.jonathanbean.photography
Adobe Photoshop support by Emily Jayne Snowdon, Creative
Consultant/Graphic Designer
emilyjaynesnowdon@gmailcom
Book spine photo by Dimitri Anikin and downloaded from
www.unsplash.com

All song lyrics used in the novel are the sole property of the band, Starset, and written permission to use any lyrics has been granted to the author by lead singer and creator, Dustin Bates.

All maps are copyrighted by Google. All illustrations are done by the author and are her sole property.

ISBN: 978-1-946385-06-2, paperback version

- - -- --- -----

DEDICATION

To my husband and kids:

You have put up with the restless days and sleepless nights; the hours-turned-days-turned-weeks of research, writing, revisions, and re-revisions to the exponential power; and the craziness which has ensued since conception of this project to the birth of this series.

You are my strength and pillars. Thanks for putting up with the madness. May it continue.

- - -- --- -----

TO THE READER

"Mathematics is the language of nature."
   ~Leonardo of Pisa

Abacus.
Calculations.
Shapes, designs.
Math and geometry.
The combination has endless possibilities.
They're found in flora, fauna, and all life.
From strands of DNA to the furthest galaxy, you'll still come across both.

That nature, that design—the imagery, symbolism, inner workings, outer mechanics, and thought-provoking ideas—breathe back and forth within these books.

The mathematics are elaborately stitched and woven, bringing together a solid skeletal frame for the stories unfolding now and those begging to be told as the series progresses. This design most definitely will continue.

- - -- --- -----

ACKNOWLEDGEMENTS

Kathryn Bax, co-founder of One Stop Fiction, for providing invaluable advice, help, and resources as I grow and learn. Her website and Facebook pages have taught me far more in the last several months than other websites have over the course of a year. I look forward to learning more!

Vivian Storms, CEO and Founder of Storms Publishing, Inc., for allowing me to use her husband's name and website (Jack Storms, www.jackstorms.com) in my books. I'm absolutely honored.

Richard Pini, for helping me discover my passion for writing when I was younger through his own talent in writing and editing *ElfQuest*, the longest-lasting and independently-owned comic series in the world (www.elfquest.com); and for being a mentor and friend for so many years. Words can't express this honor.

Dustin Bates, lead singer and mastermind behind the band Starset (www.starsetonline.com), for giving me permission to use his lyrics in my books. I've always felt your words enhance mine through your creative and intricate music. I hope to one day return the favor. Thank you!

- - -- --- -----

ANCILLARY

See Book One (MODI INDO0RUM) for the explanation of the Ancillary section.

Book Two assignment:

"Dark on Me"
STARSET, *Transmissions*

- - -- --- -----

MAPS

Location, location, location.

Whether it involves places where dead bodies are found or murders are committed, the locations within THE JARDINE TRILOGY are significant. Since there are several towns and locations mentioned across several states, maps will be provided to help the reader better understand where events transpire.

These Google maps will be provided at the beginning of each book. Color versions of these maps will also be provided on the author's website.

A full set of maps will be available in the complete Appendices section of Book 3, ZEPH1RUM.

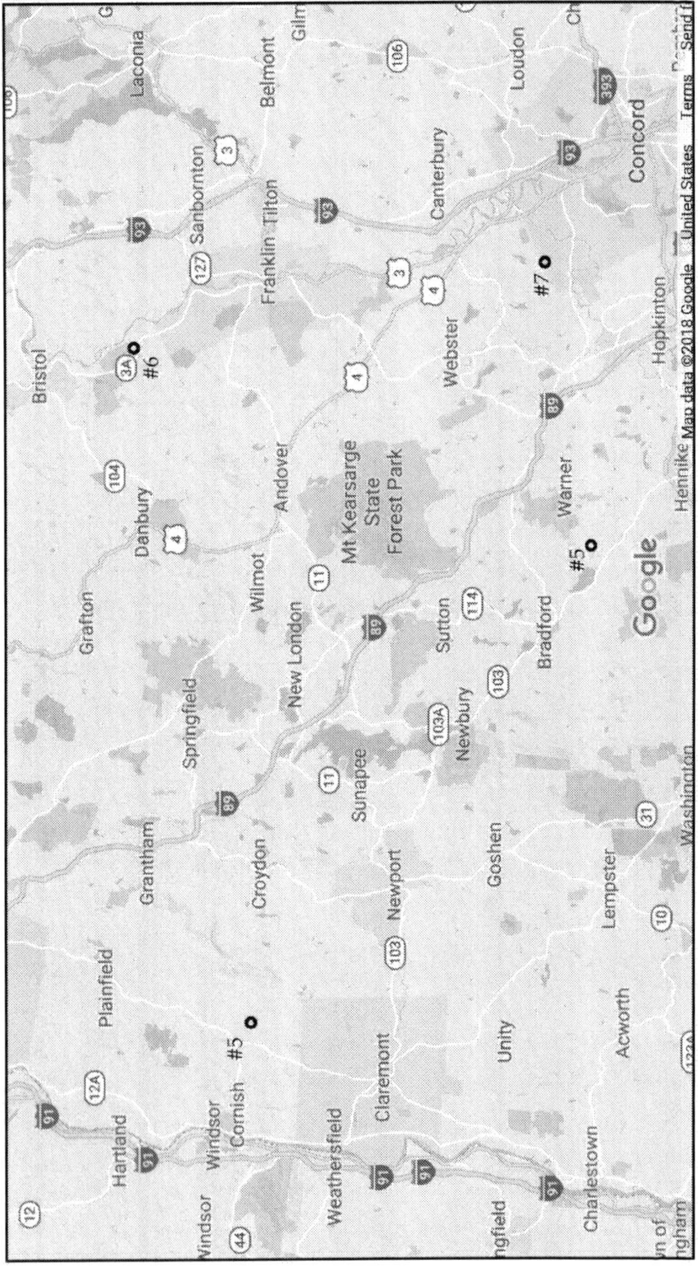
Laconia
Belmont
Sanbornton
Bristol
#6
Franklin
Tilton
Canterbury
Loudon
Concord
#7
Webster
Hopkinton
Danbury
Andover
Mt Kearsarge State Forest Park
Warner
#5
Grafton
Wilmot
New London
Sutton
Bradford
Springfield
Sunapee
Newbury
Grantham
Croydon
Newport
Goshen
Lempster
Washington
Plainfield
#5
Cornish
Windsor
Hartland
Claremont
Weathersfield
Unity
Acworth
Charlestown
Google
Map data ©2018 Google
United States
Terms

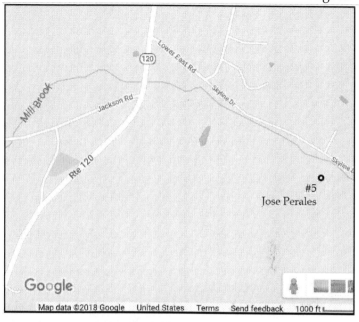

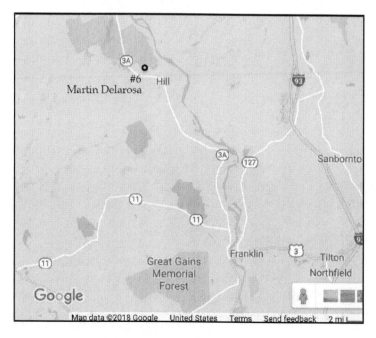

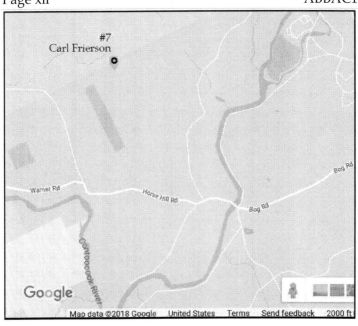

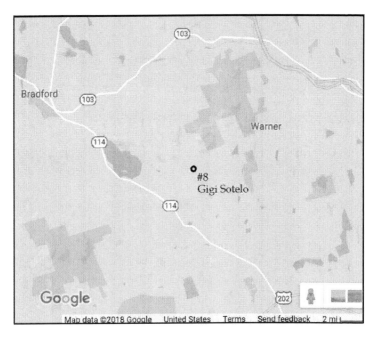

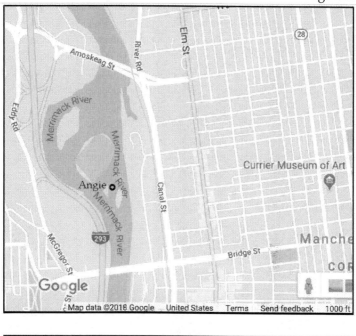

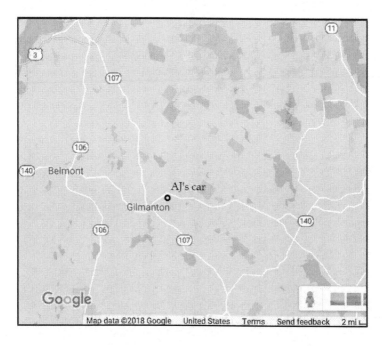

- - -- --- -----

CONTENTS

- - -- --- -----

ABBAC1

CHAPTER THIRTEEN: THANKSGIVING

Tuesday, May 24, 2022

She tried Tony's phone again. Straight to voicemail. "COPERNICUS!" she yelled in the car, hoping he was listening. "PLEASE! Don't hurt Tony!"

For fuck's sake! "ANSWER ME! ONE of you!" she yelled at her phone.

Only stark silence answered. Her anxiety increased, and she held her breath until her stomach ached.

BREATHE, dammit! Stay calm! She repeated the words to herself over and over.

Her mind raced as she pieced together the two men's last few days with her.

She glanced at her phone.

A dead zone.

No bars.

HOOOOONK!

"SHIT!"

The barreling sound of a construction truck snapped her eyes back to the road. She overcorrected the steering to avoid the truck, and her vehicle spun into the oncoming lane. The car skidded into the shoulder and sloping ditch. It was only then she saw the intersection. And the stop sign she flew past.

"FUCK!" She slammed her hand into the steering wheel.

She looked at her phone again. Still no responses. Still no cell phone service in the sloping valleys of her route. Still no way of knowing exactly what was happening to either man.

"Proceed to the route," her phone demanded.

"Shut the fuck up!" she screamed at it. "You aren't helping!"

She kicked up pebbles as her car lunged out of the ditch and she spun back into her lane. She quickly flew back down the rough road to her ultimate destination.

She looked at her G.P.S. again.

Thirteen fucking more minutes too long! Goddammit to every possible hell imaginable!

She could not calm herself as the fear and adrenaline took over her body, something she had not felt since her abduction and Aggie's brutality from a couple of months prior.

She could not imagine what the next few minutes would hold when she would pull into the mansion's driveway, the same mansion she visited the previous year.

How did I miss signs?!?

She could not imagine losing either man, especially one to the other, especially after their confrontation at Cassie's wedding and the secrets they kept from her.

She could not imagine what would have happened if she had not solved the last clues Copernicus left, the ones in her possession the entire duration of her investigation: the clues that pointed to a war fought with ones and zeroes.

- - -- --- -----

Tuesday, November 24, 2020

AJ sat slumped in her chair and stared at Conrad from across his desk. She studied his face and prayed he just lied to her. Her mind numbed at the information.

"Can you repeat that, please?"

"Tony's a double agent. He's been working with the Fasciata for a number of years now."

"He's a double agent?" Her voice crawled in a whisper. He nodded.

She stared at The Desk Scar again and her mind took off down a familiar, deep path. "He knew about the car then."

"We don't know that, Jardine."

"He knew my son would be in the car." Her voice slightly louder, she continued to stare at the nothingness in front of her.

"Jardine, we—"

"He almost killed my dad and my son!" Manic undertones overtook her voice. She stared at Conrad. She felt lost and could feel her hands turning cold as her stomach knotted.

"Detective Jardine!"

The firm voice pulled her back from her mind's edge. She sat quietly and waited for him to say something next. She rubbed her clammy palms against her thighs to calm her nerves.

"AJ?" His voice held a fatherly softness this time.

"Yes, sir?" She stared at him, trying unsuccessfully to read his thoughts.

"Go home."

"But, sir?"

"No arguments, no buts." Slowly and carefully, he repeated, "Go. Home. Be with your family. They need you right now."

He reached over and grabbed her hands. She stared at his dark skin against hers. She never noticed how young his fingers appeared; they contradicted the decades of experience the man had. They were frighteningly warmer than hers and it helped calm her. She looked back up at him as a tear forced its way out.

"Take this week off. Save a plate for me and Mr. Yates. We'll be there for Thanksgiving."

"Hunh?!? Sir? Did you just invite yourself and Peter to my parents' house for Thanksgiving?"

"Yes, Jardine. I did. Give me two days. I need a couple of days, and then we'll talk more about this. In detail."

His eyes remained stoic, and she nodded in compliance. Though she did not understand what to expect, she knew to trust him.

She always knew to trust him.

- - -- --- -----

<u>Thursday, November 26, 2020</u>

Ameena shut herself away in her office the better part of the morning avoiding all her family and the chaos in every other room. She sat on the floor refreshing her brain with all the case files.

She heard the doorbell ring.

"I'll get it!" She jumped up and ran to the front door, hoping to intercept the entrance before her mother.

"Welcome, sir! It is so good to see you again," she heard her mother, Jamilla, say.

Shit. She beat me.

Ameena opened the office door and saw her mother usher the Deputy Director in the house. Then her mother squeezing Conrad in a big hug. The detective was slightly mortified until she saw Conrad smile.

"Mom!"

"Thank you, Mrs. Andrewson."

"Please, call me Jamilla!" Her Middle Eastern accent fluctuated with excitement and randomly inflected words. "Ameena is always talking about you! She loves you, you know. She admires everything you have done for her."

"Mom!"

"What, habibti? It's the truth!"

"Mrs. Andrewson, she's the best detective on my team. There's little I wouldn't do for her."

"That's good, sir! And it's *Jamilla*! Please, let me get your coat. And remove your shoes. I can take them as well."

"Yes, ma'am."

Jamilla shuffled off with Conrad's effects, leaving him and Ameena standing alone in a moment of awkwardness.

"Sir, thank you for coming here."

"My pleasure."

The awkwardness continued.

Finally, Ameena said, "Sir, would you like a tour of the house and to meet the rest of the family?"

"That would be nice."

"This is the dining room and kitchen." She mentally

chided herself for stating the obvious when she saw her boss grin.

She watched as his eyes scanned the open floor plan. The dining room was reorganized with one large elongated table and a smaller, shorter table. The latter was set with placemats and napkins for five young children; the former, fine china for a more elaborate Thanksgiving dinner. A drape blocked the wide doorway connecting the dining and living rooms. They could hear the TV playing on the other side.

Conrad stared at the curtain. "What's behind the drape?"

"We converted the living room into a temporary bedroom for Mom and Dad. He'll be in a wheelchair for a while, so that's why the rooms have been shuffled around. I'll introduce you later. I think he's sleeping right now."

Conrad nodded and turned his attention to the kitchen. Relish trays were set out, and several dishes were in various stages of finalization. The smell of turkey and cranberry, with a hint of pumpkin and pecan pies, permeated the entire house.

Ameena saw him stare at a dish on the stove and she watched his curiosity with her own. He walked over to the strange diamond-sliced meatloaf to inspect it.

Jamilla walked back in.

"That is called *kibbeh*."

"It smells wonderful, Mrs. Andrewson."

Ameena's mother walked over to the kitchen drawer and pulled out a wooden spoon. She glared at him and waved the spoon in his face. "If you call me that again, I'm going to beat you with this spoon, do you hear me?"

Mortified beyond imagination, she watched the interaction between her work boss and home boss. Conrad froze. Her mother stood firm. Ameena needed to use the bathroom.

"Mom!"

"What? I'm only joking, habibti! I could not do such a thing to the man who has watched over my daughter and taken good care of her."

Ameena watched Conrad and saw him grin from ear to ear. He appeared to enjoy the banter. Relief washed over her.

"*Jamilla*," Conrad emphasized, "please, tell me about this kibbeh dish."

"Of course! It is a meatloaf with a type of wheat mixed inside. We add spices such as cinnamon and nutmeg to give it a distinct smell."

Then she leaned into him, close to his personal space — which seemed to surprise him — and made a palm-up gesture with one hand, her fingers pressed and cupped together, as if for more emphasis.

"The bottom of the dish is coated with caramelized onions and raisins! The juices from the meat and the cooked onions give it this incredible flavor."

And with the last word, she popped her fingers open like a firecracker, exposing her best-kept culinary secrets.

"I can't wait to try it."

"We have so much food for you today! We have marinated kabobs, the kibbeh, the turkey, relishes, tabbouleh, dates, salads — everything for our honored guests!"

"Mom," Ameena interrupted, "I would like to take our *honored guest* and introduce him to the rest of the family."

"Of course! Of course! Go!" She shooed him out of the kitchen before he could say anything.

Ameena smiled weakly at Conrad and escorted him away. "Let me introduce you to my sisters-in-law upstairs."

"Sounds good. Is Peter already here?"

"Yes, sir. He's with my brothers, somewhere."

As they walked up the stairs, Conrad said, "Your mom's a fierce woman, Ameena."

"Yeah, wait 'til you meet the rest of the family. I should warn you, my brothers are a lively bunch. We're close-knit, and my family's pretty hands on. And passionate. I promise everyone's harmless, though."

"Understood."

"Except maybe my mom. She really might use that spoon." They both chuckled at the veracity of the tiny cook. "I hope we aren't intimidating you."

"Ameena, I'm enjoying this. I promise. I'm glad to be here."

"I hope so, sir. Everyone will treat you as part of the family."

She opened the child gate at the top of the stairs. They heard video games and children to their right and women's voices to the left. They walked into the master bedroom on the left. One woman sat on the bed; another stood, changing a diaper on a struggling toddler.

The sitting woman had sandy blonde hair, hazel eyes, and appeared to be in her late twenties or early thirties. Her hair was pulled straight back in a ponytail, elongating her neck and oval-shaped face.

The other woman appeared Middle Eastern and wore a royal blue hijab over most of her head and chest, slightly exposing her front forehead. Her curly hair was nearly the same color as her eyes: near-black.

"Kat, Ghada, I wanted to introduce you both to my boss, Deputy Director Conrad McMillan."

"It pleasure to meet you. I am Ghada." The Middle Eastern woman carefully pronounced each English word. "My English not good. I apologize."

"Your English is perfect, ma'am."

"Hi! I'm Katherine. Everyone calls me Kat." The American woman held her hand out to Conrad's. "It's a pleasure to meet you, Mr. McMillan. We've heard a lot about you."

"The pleasure is mine to meet you both. Please, call me Conrad."

"I'm showing Conrad around the house and introducing him to the family," Ameena said. "Where are Nabih and Dana?"

"Brother and girlfriend in your room," Ghada said.

"Dana has a headache and needed to lay down for a bit," Kat added, "and I think Nabih is taking a nap after their long drive up here."

"And what about Ari and Faruq?"

The two younger women looked at each other, then Kat answered. "We think your brothers are in the basement."

"Um, how you say? They want to shoot guns?" Ghada asked shyly.

"Yeah, they may've gone to the pond in the back to target practice. I haven't heard the guns go off yet." And then, as if on cue, shots rang out. Kat grinned. "Yes, they're at the pond."

"Is Eoghan okay with his arm?" Ameena worried about her son's injury and a possible accident while walking in the iced-over woods.

"Ameena, he's *fine*," Kat emphasized the last word in a nonchalant manner.

"Mr. Conrad, would you like meet daughter?" Ghada picked up the two-year-old and placed her on her hip. "This is Houda."

The toddler clung to her mother and shyly watched the Deputy Director. She had her mother's curly dark hair and dark eyes. Conrad smiled at Houda. The little girl dug her face into her mother's chest, playing a bashful game of hide-and-seek with him.

Ameena could tell Conrad enjoyed it; his fatherly nature showed.

"Lizzy! Will! Come here!" Kat yelled.

"Hakim! *Ta'ala hon.*" Ghada added.

They heard the video game in the other room go quiet then what sounded like a stampede of little footsteps come running into the room.

"Hi!" "Hello!" "Hi!" came three responses out of the three children. It was evident which curly, dark-haired child was Ghada's son; the other two children—a younger boy with blondish hair and a taller, thin girl with reddish hair— were Kat's children. One of the boys tried to run back out of the room.

"William Ernest! Get back in here!"

The son sighed big and rolled his eyes as he stomped back in the room reluctantly.

Kat looked at Conrad. "I'm sorry about that. They're so excited to play that racing game in the other room."

"No need to apologize. I have young ones myself."

"You have children, sir?" Ghada asked.

"Yes, ma'am. I have a thirteen-year-old son and a twenty-one-year-old daughter."

"Beautiful! This is Hakim. He is *khamsa*—eh, five years old." Ghada struggled with the English translation for the number and held up five fingers on her hand. "He is, eh, named after my brother. Daughter named after sister."

"Nice to meet you, sir." Hakim extended his hand out.

"Nice to meet *you*, Hakim."

"This is William. We call him Will for short," Kat said.

William mimicked his cousin, even though he appeared less impressed with Conrad's presence. "Nice to meet you, sir."

Conrad shook his hand. "It's a pleasure to meet you, Will."

"May I go now, Mommy?" Will danced impatiently in place, unwilling to stop moving.

Kat saw Conrad smile, then nod slightly in approval. "Yes, go play." Both boys ran off immediately. "This is Elizabeth. She goes by Lizzy."

Elizabeth appeared tall for her age. "It's nice to meet you, sir." She extended her hand.

"And it's nice to meet you as well, Lizzy." Conrad shook her extended hand.

"Mrs. Jardine?"

"Yes," both replied. They looked at each other and giggled.

"Please. Call me Ghada."

"And call me Kat."

"Ghada. Kat." Conrad emphasized the throaty Arabic

pronunciation of the 'g' and 'h' together. "You both have beautiful and respectful children."

"Thank you," Kat replied.

"*Merci*. Thank you," Ghada said.

Conrad perked at the French word. "*Parlez vous français?*"

"*Oui!* Yes!"

Kat smiled. "*Le français est la troisième langue de Ghada.*"

Ameena added, "French is actually the second language in Lebanon. Arabic is the primary language, but almost everyone knows French and English as second and-or third languages."

"Impressive. I learned French when I was stationed overseas decades ago. But, that's a story for another time."

Ameena walked out of the bedroom and searched the other rooms for her daughter. When she could not find the eight-year-old, she walked back in the master bedroom. "Have you both seen Jenna?"

"Jenna is with Papa," Kat said.

She turned to her boss. "Ready to head downstairs and see my dad?"

He nodded. "It's a pleasure to meet you all."

Ameena and Conrad both went back down the stairs and walked toward the make-shift curtain. She held back the drape for Conrad to walk through. Two air mattresses leaned against the wall, ready to be laid flat for resting bodies later in the evening.

Ernest appeared to be sleeping, propped up on his side of the queen-size bed. He had a cast on his leg and another on his arm; bruises polka-dotted his entire body. Jenna rested near her grandfather and watched TV.

Every time Ameena saw her dad, her heart sank into a broken mess. The day of the accident played over and over in her head as she overanalyzed every event, both before and after she found out about Tony's involvement. She grew angry at those thoughts and wanted to torture information out of her partner and whoever tampered with the car's computer system. Before her mind delved into that dark analytical path again, Jenna saw them and sat up.

"Hi, Mommy." Jenna tried to whisper the words and not wake Ernest.

"Hi, baby." Ameena tried to be equally quiet, but Ernest stirred awake.

"Jennie-Pennie?"

"Yes, Papa?"

"Can you get me a glass of ginger ale, please?"

"Yes, Papa."

Careful not to move too quickly on the bed, Jenna got down and went over to her mom. She held Conrad's stare and put her fists on her hips in a defensive stance, standing between him and Ernest.

"Deputy Directory, you can't see my Papa right now. He needs his rest."

Ameena saw Conrad cover his smile from the mispronounced word.

"Jennie-Pennie, it's fine," Ernest said.

Jenna glanced behind her at her grandfather, then turned back to face Conrad. She took a step towards him and touched him on the arm. She held his gaze and whispered, "You need to tell Mommy the truth about Daddy."

"Jenna!" Ameena scolded, shocked at the reaction. "Go get Papa the ginger ale before he gets too thirsty and starts hurting again."

The little girl let go of Conrad and walked off to the kitchen.

Stunned, Ameena looked at Conrad. "I'm so sorry! I don't know what—"

"It's okay, Jardine. She's perceptive and bold, I give her that."

Before she could respond, they heard Ernest grunt in pain as he tried to reposition himself. Ameena walked over to the bed. Conrad followed.

"Dad, how are you feeling?"

"I'm okay, just tired a bit. But I'll be fine."

"Dad, do you remember my boss, Conrad McMillan?"

Ernest glanced over at Conrad and did not move. "Nice to see ya, Conrad. Apologies, but I'll have to. Shake your hand. Another time. I'm afraid."

"Not a problem, Mr. Andrewson. It's my pleasure to see you again."

"Like. Wise." His voice sounded labored.

"Dad, we'll let you get more rest. I'm about to show Conrad the office where we'll have our meeting later after dinner."

"Okay, darling." Ernest took a long pause from the pain in his chest. "Think. I'll rest. Some more."

"It was nice to see you again, sir." Conrad's words fell quietly as Ameena escorted him out of the room.

As they held back the drape to exit, Jenna walked past the pair with a full glass of soda.

"Jenna?"

"Yes, Mommy?"

"Set the ginger ale next to Papa and let him get some sleep, okay?"

"Okay." She disappeared behind the curtain, but not before she gave Conrad another long glare.

Ameena gestured. "Here, I'll show you the office. We won't go down to the basement. It's a disaster." As the two walked into the office, she shut the door behind them. "This is where we'll have our work meeting after dinner. It's secure, but I'm sure you want to take some precautions."

"It'll do just fine."

"Sir, about what Jenna said earlier, I'm sor—"

"No apologies, Jardine. I understand," he interrupted. Then Conrad changed the subject. "How *is* your dad doing?"

"He's okay. In a lot of pain, as you can tell. He's a fighter, though."

"He is. If your family needs anything, you ask me. Understood?"

"Yes, sir. Do you need me to prepare anything prior to

our meeting?"

Conrad studied the room then locked eyes on the fireplace. "If you have any logs to start a fire, I'd like the fireplace going. And a few towels."

"Yes, sir."

"Otherwise, I think this is good."

"Thank you, sir."

She opened the door.

"Oh, fair warning, my family is a bit, uhh, passionate. Dinner can get pretty lively at times."

He smiled. "AJ, you already told me that."

"Oh. Yeah. Sorry, sir."

- - -- --- -----

After a couple of hours of small talk and commotion with an almost over-cooked turkey, everyone finally settled in for dinner. An overabundance of food poured off the countertops. Jamilla assumed it would be completely gone before the end of the night; Ameena knew her brothers would let nothing go to waste.

She noticed the difference the last couple of days made for her mother. When Ameena told her about Conrad's visit on Thanksgiving, the Lebanese mother began preparing the meals and dictating chores to everyone. Her love of hosting parties and having guests relit the passion in her eyes. This — the celebration of Ernest being home, the celebration of all her sons and their families in attendance, and the honor of having the Deputy Director and Peter in her home — made her happy again.

With the exception of Jamilla's teenaged grandson, Eoghan, all five of the small grand-children sat at the small table as each of their moms fixed their plates and served them first. Kat made sure her two children, Will and Lizzy, did not sit next to each other; her son tended to make jabs at his sister which would sometimes escalate into a food fight.

Hakim and Houda were more well-behaved, so Will sat

between them. All the mothers hoped Ghada's children would have a calming effect on Kat's son.

Jenna wanted to sit at the adult table and help her grandfather, but Jamilla insisted she spent some time with her little cousins.

William was still being rambunctious, but with a quick stare from Jamilla and a shake of her spoon, he settled down quickly.

The adult area consisted of two large tables placed together to accompany the crowd. Peter and Conrad sat at one end, while Ernest, in his wheelchair, sat at the other end with Jamilla. The long sides of the table were shared by two pairs each: Faruq, Ameena's oldest brother, and his wife, Ghada, sat next to Arif, the middle brother, and his wife, Kat; opposite of them and on the other side were Nabih, the baby brother, and his long-time girlfriend, Dana, next to Eoghan and Ameena.

Peter was no stranger to the family, and he had much in common with all Jamilla's children. With no siblings of his own, he welcomed every opportunity to visit the Andrewson's home when Ameena's brothers were in town.

However, from the studied look on Conrad's face, Ameena knew her boss still attempted to put names and faces together. She knew for any stranger that remembering who was who in her large family — and keeping any names straight — could be a difficult task.

It did not help matters that all three of Ameena's brothers looked the same: none appeared Middle Eastern and all had the same fair skin, brown hair, and hazel or green eyes. All three brothers were stout in stature and dwarfed their sister in comparison. Each served in a different branch of the military, but this still did not help Conrad with the who's who of siblings at the table. Faruq did appear slightly taller than the other two, and he still carried a buzz-cut hairstyle. Nabih was quieter and reserved, while Arif — or Ari as he preferred to be called — seemed to be an instigator with a wicked sense of humor.

Dana, the newest addition to the family, mirrored Conrad's demeanor. She and Nabih met the year prior and this was their first Thanksgiving together with the family. Her hair matched Nabih's, and she had stunning green eyes and olive skin. Dana remained quiet, but Ameena knew once she felt comfortable around the crowd, she would open up and be more talkative.

While Jamilla finished the plates for each guest, conversations continued on many tangents:

"What do you think of the new president?" "They said it would be another harsh winter." "Biomechanical engineering, Momma." "You soak the meat in olive oil and yogurt." "Yes, the Cowboys will make the playoffs!" "No way the drone can fly to the pond in the back." "Fresh basil, that's the key!" "Our vice-president, though." "Forget about it, the Giants are in this year!" "Look at all of the snow we've received so far." "I'll bet you your Star Trek collection it can!"

Finally, Jamilla sat down and everyone went silent.

"*Bismillah al Rahman al Rahim,*" Jamilla held her head down in prayer. Faruq and Ghada did the same.

Dana, unaccustomed to the Middle Eastern culture, leaned over to Nabih and whispered, "What did she say?"

Nabih politely whispered back, "She said 'In the name of God, the Beneficent, the Merciful.' We always do a prayer and blessing before eating."

"Were we supposed to say that, too?"

"Dana, sweetheart," Jamilla said, "You may say what you like at the dinner table to bless the food and family. All beliefs are welcome in our home."

To make his girlfriend feel more comfortable, Nabih put his head down and added, "Lord, thank you for your protection in our travels and allowing us to be home this holiday with all our family. In Christ's name, amen."

"Thank you, your Holy Noodle, for your pasta sacrifice. Ramen," Ari quipped. Ameena kicked him from under the table. "Ow! What'd I say?"

A few snickers reminded every one of the light-heartedness in the home.

Jamilla smiled. "Please, everyone. Eat! Enjoy!"

"Momma?"

"Yes, Faruq?"

"Ghada and I wanted to share something with the family." They both stood up. Faruq motioned to his wife. "Go ahead and tell them."

Shyly, and hoping her English correct, she said, "We are pregnant with third baby."

The news caused an uproar.

"Congratulations!" "*Mabruk!*" "*Alhamdulillah!*" "Two months along so far." "Due in the summer." "We're having another cousin!" "We don't know yet." "Wow! That's amazing news!"

Exchanges of delight and joy ensued after many hugs and handshakes later. When everything and everyone settled down again, Ameena saw the puzzled look on Conrad's face.

"Sir, is something wrong?"

"No, AJ, everything's fine."

"AJ?" Dana asked.

"Ameena changed her name when she became a detective," Faruq said.

"She didn't really *change* her name. She took her maiden name again," Ari said.

"I thought by using my initials, it would make me stand out more as a detective," she told Dana.

"She's the one who caught the Rune Killer," Faruq chimed in.

"That was you!?" Dana sounded surprised.

"Yes." She blushed slightly.

"Yeah, Mom's name made the national news," Eoghan said.

"She's an ass kicker," Ari added.

"Don't say those words at the table, habibi," Jamilla scolded.

"Detective during the day, Super Mom at night!" Faruq teased.

"Tony is her kryptonite," Ari also teased, singingly. He jumped from another kick to the leg. "Ow! What'd I say?"

"How is Tony doing?" Ernest did not say much in the line of conversation until then.

"Tony's fine. He's been busy working another case recently and I haven't seen much of him." She glanced at her boss.

Conrad changed the subject. "Jamilla, this food is delicious. I'd love to get some of the recipes from you."

"Of course, of course! I love sharing the family recipes."

"Mom, Will hit me again!" came Lizzy's voice at the kids' table.

Before Kat could say anything, Jamilla turned around in her chair and gave her grandson a stern look. Will quietened down immediately.

While an attempt to change the subject and a distraction by the children were welcomed, Ameena's brothers could not help being themselves and stirred the fire more.

Nabih leaned over to his date. "My big sister will kick your ass — I mean butt — if you steal anything."

"No, I won't. Don't listen to him, Dana."

"She'll interrogate you to death, that's all," Nabih said.

"Or she'll toss you in prison and lose the key," Faruq added.

"Be careful, she may waterboard you," Ari teased.

"If she won't, maybe I should if you don't mind your manners! Don't make me grab my spoon!" Jamilla added the threat to the conversation.

Eoghan and Peter laughed, while the siblings kicked each other immaturely under the table.

"Stop that or I'll get the spoon!"

"She'll do it, too!" Ernest gave his wife a wink before kissing her hand.

"I'll say I am proud of my Ameena in her new career."

"When did you become a detective?" Dana seemed

curious to know more.

"I think it was almost three years ago now."

"Yeah, it was," Eoghan said. "Mom graduated the Fall semester of 2017."

"That's an impressive memory," Conrad said.

"Thank you, sir."

"Eoghan's brilliant and quick-witted, like his mom," Kat said. "Aren't you about to go to college soon?"

"Yes, Aunt Kat. I'm a senior now in high school."

"Any ideas where you'd like to go to college?" Nabih asked.

"U.N.H. all the way, baby!" Peter, a University of New Hampshire alumnus, remained quiet until then. He said it so quickly, it made everyone laugh.

"I haven't decided yet. I applied for several scholarships, but if I don't get any, I may take some basic classes here at the local college first."

"Oh, that's smart!" "Very good idea!" "You should do that." Multiple replies encouraged him to remain at home for his first few semesters.

"What will you major in?" Nabih asked.

"I may follow Mom's footsteps and do forensics. Or go into law enforcement like the F.B.I."

The room went quiet.

Ameena felt an immediate change in the energy around her. She could tell there were mixed feelings about the topic, especially considering her background. She felt her heart beat harder and took a deep breath.

Finally, Nabih broke the tension. "Nah, you watched too many *X-Files* reruns! Ow! What'd I say?"

"More like father, like son. Let's hope he does better, though," Ari said.

The table fell silent and eyes went wide.

"What did you say, Ari?" Ameena's smile faded.

"That's not what I meant, Ameena. He won't die like Michael." Then, realizing he said the wrong thing again, he rolled his eyes and mumbled, "Fuck…"

Ameena remained calm and focused on the plate in front of her. She did not see everyone glancing at each other in uncomfortable silence. She never thought of Eoghan becoming an F.B.I. agent like his father, but now those thoughts flooded her mind. She stared at the kibbeh on her plate, and suddenly, she had no appetite. She felt the emotions changing as depression and sadness overtook her.

"Ameena, I didn't mean it that way, I promise!"

"It was an innocent comment." "Ari doesn't have a filter on his mouth." "He meant it runs in the family." "He's not surprised Eoghan would want to go into law enforcement." "Habibti, baby, it's okay!" "Michael was an amazing detective."

"No, it's fine. Promise," Ameena lied. She could still feel her heart racing.

"I'm sorry, I didn't mean to say that, Mimi." Ari made another futile attempt at an apology and used her childhood nickname to lighten the mood.

"Ari, stop. It's fine. It's not easy for a mother to think about her child going off to college or going into a dangerous profession. Is it, Momma?" She tried to divert the conversation.

"Look what your brothers put me through! Each gray hair is their doing!"

The tension lessened, but before the conversation continued, Ameena stood up. "Thank you, Momma, for the dinner."

Jamilla also stood up. "Habibti, hand me your plate. Do you want more?"

"No, Momma, maybe in a bit for dessert. I need to get ready for our meeting. Excuse me."

She quickly excused herself to the restroom, then shut the bathroom door and leaned her body forward against the sink, her arms propping her up. Though they tried to be quiet at the table, she could hear them talking about her from the other side of the door.

"Ari, what the hell were you thinking?" "You dumbass,

don't mention Michael, ever!" "I said I was sorry!" "No, they haven't found the killers." "Still a cold case." "She'll never get over it." "Yeah, three bullets, two in the gut. It took her a long time to recover." "That's why she changed careers at her age."

She played whack-a-mole with her memory as glimpses of Michael — and the night they were both gunned down — kept pushing their way back up from the depths of where the monsters were buried. Her stomach hurt. She closed her eyes and pushed the mind demons back down again and again.

Not now, not now, not now! It won't happen to Eoghan. It won't happen to Eoghan. Deep breath. It'll be okay. Focus on Conrad. Stay focused, Jardine.

All it sometimes took was a simple trigger for the P.T.S.D. to shoot from the depths of her mind. She loved having her family together, but the darker side of the brotherly combination and over-excitement was the brashness which would pop up from idiotic banter and loose lips. Her family witnessed it many times before and knew why she was in the bathroom. They knew to give her space and change the subject to football or the weather or the latest technology — anything but what the subject was before.

It's okay. You can do this. Take another deep breath. Take another deep breath.

She stayed there for several minutes, inhaling and exhaling, until the memories and visions faded. She opened her eyes and stared at herself in the mirror. She would stand there for as long as she needed, and her family knew she needed to stand there for a while.

- - -- --- -----

She led both Conrad and Peter into the office and shut the door.

"The towels you requested are over there on the desk,"

she motioned while she lit the logs in the fireplace.

Conrad nodded, grabbed the towels, and positioned them at the base of the door and around the windows to muffle the sound. He looked at Peter.

"Did you bring the device, Mr. Yates?"

"Yes, sir."

She watched, slightly confused, until she saw the objects Peter pulled from his backpack. Then she nodded in understanding.

Peter took the scanner and swept the room. After a few minutes and all corners later, he shook his head. "Nothing, sir."

"Good. Continue."

Peter grabbed another small electronic part and attached it to the device in his hand.

"AJ, you did tell your family there would be Wi-Fi and phone disruptions, correct?"

"Yes, sir. The kids are watching a DVD movie upstairs and the guys are going back outside in the woods to target practice. Dad'll be napping, and Mom brought some board games up from the basement as an extra precaution."

"Good."

A simple nod to Peter and the technician pushed the button. An initial buzz, low hum, and steady blinking light indicated the E.M.P. was activated. All internet, Wi-Fi, and cell phone service within a dozen meters were completely disrupted.

"Nothing I tell either of you leaves this room. Understood?"

"Yes, sir," both subordinates replied.

"Jardine, since you left my office two days ago, I contacted Agent Aserbbo's supervisor, Larsson Clancy. I told Mr. Clancy about my concerns, your hypotheses. I explained the accident and the photo to him. Mr. Clancy gave me more background information on the Orders and Hapalo. And, he assured me Aserbbo is not *directly* responsible for what happened—"

"How is that even possible after what you told me?" she interrupted.

"Jardine, I'll get to that. Mr. Yates, what you have not been informed of yet is that Agent Aserbbo has been working as a double agent for the Fasciata."

"Oh, shit!" Peter's face went white. He turned to AJ. She nodded. Then he looked at Conrad again, stunned at the news.

"Aserbbo's under a highly secretive directive which few people outside his immediate circle know."

"Sir, was he the one who tampered with Ernest's car?"

"No, Mr. Yates." Conrad focused on AJ. "Jardine, we'll discuss this in detail in a bit. Understood?" She nodded. "First, let me explain to both of you some background I discovered.

"The U.S. government has been fighting a war on drugs and cartels for decades now. Everyone knows this. Bureaus have sent seasoned agents undercover to infiltrate these criminal organizations. Many of these cartels have been brought down and eliminated, but not all. Hapalo's is one such organization.

"Years ago, on two occasions, the government was able to get close to a couple of Knights. But each time, the undercover agents were discovered. Good men and women were mutilated, massacred, and murdered. I cannot begin to tell either of you how many agents were lost.

"After one brutal assignment resulted in multitudes dying, the strategy changed. Instead of sending in older and experienced agents, the government sent fresh college graduates with little training. The logic behind this had to do with all the government leaks. Hapalo had insiders feeding him information on who the established agents were. So, instead, they sent in the ones with no records or history in the government just yet. It was a risk they were willing to take.

"Aserbbo was one of those agents. At the time he graduated, there was a new operation—called Operation

Borel—ready to deploy. A total of thirteen agents were sent undercover, and Aserbbo has been there ever since.

"All of the agents were instructed to infiltrate—by any means necessary, and I mean *any means*—the organization and move up in the ranks until he or she could locate and learn of Hapalo's whereabouts. They all knew the risks going in.

"Aserbbo was inside the Fasciata Order for a brief time when his cover was blown. To this day, he still has never told us the full details. And until he finishes his assignment, we can't press him for what happened. All we know is his and his partner's covers were blown, and they were captured.

"He and his partner were both taken in front of the Fasciata Lord and all eight Octave Knights on 'trial'. Somehow, he convinced them to spare his life. He told them every detail of his assignment, including the identities of all thirteen undercovers. He did eventually tell the government he was forced to kill his own partner."

"Oh my gawd," she whispered.

"Remember, he was instructed to go as far as he could by *any means necessary*. The Order decreed that he was to kill or help kill every other undercover before he completely regained their trust. How many he personally murdered, he's never said.

"It was weeks before Aserbbo could reach out to the D.E.A. and let them know what happened. By then, only a few agents were put in witness protection or pulled from their assignments. And even then, the Bureaus were not successful in keeping most of them alive. Out of the thirteen, only two still live. Aserbbo and one other, a woman living in Dallas now.

"Aserbbo was instructed to transfer to the D.T.F. here in New England. He reports to the Boston Knight regularly, so the strange phone calls he receives are probably connected to that. It's possible some of his confidential informants are actual Fasciata members, but he's never said. Larsson's been unsuccessful in tapping his phones—the Order makes Tony use burners which change constantly. And, Larsson's only given information that Aserbbo's allowed to give him.

"We must be extremely careful with how we handle Aserbbo's assignment. *No one* has ever been undercover *this* long in the organization or been able to get so close to a Knight or Lord. No matter what happens—to his family, his friends, *you*—he must finish the mission. Hapalo has to be stopped, by any means."

"Sir, what do I DO? I'M his partner now. How do I protect my family and myself from another attack?" Fear fluctuated in her voice.

Conrad turned to Peter. "Mr. Yates?"

"Yes, sir?"

"Please give us a moment."

"Yes, sir."

Peter stood up and walked out of the office. When the door closed, Conrad secured the towels back in place and waited a few seconds before continuing.

"AJ, this is a dangerous web you're tangled in. With Aserbbo so deep undercover for so long, Larsson has had, on numerous occasions, concerns on where Tony's actual loyalties are. The D.T.F. doesn't have any checks and balances with what information he gives the Order. He walks a very fine line with his undercover work, and we don't know if he's responsible for some of the leaked information leaving our buildings.

"Larsson and I had a long talk a few weeks ago when you first came to me with the Fasciata information. He briefed me on what he could, and we both agreed making you Aserbbo's official partner was a smart move. My intentions with this was for you to completely gain Aserbbo's trust before I informed you of the ultimate assignment here."

"Ultimate assignment?"

"You're the only person Aserbbo has ever let into his personal circle since he's been undercover. I watch how both of you interact, and he's obviously attracted to you. Even after your personal involvement together during the Rune case, you both still have chemistry together. There's no easy way to say this." He sighed. "We hoped Tony would fall in love with you."

"What?"

"Men in love do strange things, and those strange things are what we need him to do."

"You what?" She glared at him.

"I didn't stutter, Jardine."

Her anger boiled over. "How could you?! This — this is a betrayal of MY trust!"

"Lower your voice, detective," Conrad commanded in a firm, authoritative voice.

She turned away.

He continued, "Listen to me, Jardine. You're a damn good detective. You're my best, and there's no betrayal there. You were *always* meant to be assigned to Aserbbo, but when we realized we had the opportunity, we jumped on it. We are briefing you now instead of a few months or years down the line, when it may already be too late emotionally. The initiative you took with Copernicus, and even coming to me about your suspicions of Tony, told me you're ready for this."

Emotions flipped and rolled in her mind. "Sir, what am I supposed to do now? Someone came after my dad! And my son!" The panic mounted in her voice.

"I'm putting you on administrative leave right now. Stop!" Conrad held up a hand and halted her interruption. "It's paid leave and I'm assigning you a fake case. It's a pedophile project I've called 'Operation Godel'. If anyone asks, you're posing online as a teenage girl to catch an elusive sex predator. It's a high-priority case and you've been pulled until further notice. You'll be on this case for a couple of months or so until I deem you ready to be back in the office.

"We'll provide you a new secured and encrypted laptop

which you're to start using. We've designed the backstory and fake accounts of an imaginary sex offender and have a detective from the West Coast posing as the pedophile. He'll communicate with you through online chat rooms. We're doing this so if anyone—especially Aserbbo—comes around, you'll have a solid paper trail to fall back on. No one will suspect anything out of the ordinary unless you tell them, and you won't. Understood, detective?"

"Yes, sir."

"This isn't a punishment. It's the best we can do to protect you and your family and pull you away from Agent Aserbbo, at his request."

She looked up at him. Confusion replaced all other emotion. "What do you mean at *his* request? I thought this was *your* idea? Why would he want me pulled from the case?"

"The pedophile backstory was my idea. But Aserbbo requested you be pulled from the Fasciata case, at least for now."

"But, sir, why?"

"When I contacted Larsson Tuesday evening, word somehow already got back to Aserbbo about your accusations. Larsson insisted it did not come from his department, but somehow Aserbbo already knew."

"So, we also have a mole in the department?"

"That, I don't know. What I DO know is Aserbbo approached me yesterday and gave me details on the accident. He didn't find out about the malware until after the fact. It appears the Boston Knight is not telling him everything. We don't know if this is a sign Aserbbo's work is compromised or not.

"What he did tell me is the Fasciata felt threatened with this investigation and caused the accident to distract you. He told me he didn't want to see you or your family hurt, so he offered this idea, this administrative leave, as a peace offering—his 'olive branch' to you."

"Honestly, he can take his olive branch and shove it up

his—"

"Jardine," Conrad chided, the fatherly tone evident in his pronunciation.

She took a deep breath. "Sorry, sir. But fuck a goddamn duck, I'm *pissed*!"

"Are you pissed because of Aserbbo's involvement in the accident and the Fasciata? Or are you pissed because Tony kept these secrets from you?"

She paused and thought about it. "I don't know, sir."

"Do you remember when I asked you if your personal relationship with Tony would interfere with the case?" She nodded. "And do you remember what you told me?"

"Yes, sir. It wouldn't interfere."

"How close did the two of you get, detective?"

The question caused her to blush slightly. "Sir, that's no one's busi—"

"Jardine, answer the question!"

"We've kissed, but we've never been intimate, sir."

"No, how *close* were you?"

Her cheeks flushed in solid crimson. "Tony told me he cared deeply for me. But I told him I can't love him right now."

"Why?" Conrad stared at her intently, and the silence lasted almost more than she felt comfortable.

"Because I still love my husband, sir." Her voice was barely audible.

"Ameena, you will never stop loving Michael. You will never get over that. But—and I tell you this like a father to a daughter—whatever happens, do NOT fall in love with Tony. It's too dangerous. Do you understand?"

"Yes, sir."

"Now, more than any other time, you cannot allow emotions—whether it's love or hate or something in between—to get in the way. You must be rational and analytical of everything. You must be logical."

"I'm human, not Vulcan," she muttered without thinking.

"What was that, detective?"

"I said I'll try, sir."

"Good," he replied. He stood up and put his coat on. "Do you have any more questions for me, Jardine?"

"No, sir."

"If you do, ask." The statement concluded their conversation as he put his gloves on and wrapped the scarf around his neck. Before he opened the door, he held her eyes with his and added, "One more thing, Jardine."

"Yes, sir?"

"Don't contact Aserbbo. The Fasciata Lord pulled him to another Octave for a while. I'm not sure which location or when he'll be back. He told me he'll try to reach out to you before Christmas. Wait for him."

"Yes, sir."

"Are you clear on these instructions? Do you understand your assignments here, the real and fake?"

"Yes, sir."

He opened the door and motioned for Peter. Without words, Peter went into the office and disconnected the E.M.P. device, putting the pieces back in his pocket.

Conrad scanned the dining room one more time before he grabbed the front door handle. The house was oddly quiet, and no one appeared downstairs.

"Jardine, please give your mom and family my regards. I don't do goodbyes."

"Yes, sir."

"Even for the ones I love."

He opened the door to step out into the snapping wind. "And Jardine?" he added, as he pulled his keys out of his pocket and secured his coat closer around his neck.

"Yes, sir?"

"Stop saying 'yes, sir.'"

There was a hint of approving affection in his voice as he walked off and disappeared into the dark.

- - -- --- -----

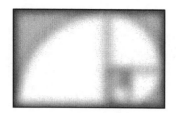

CHAPTER FOURTEEN: CONTACT

Tuesday, December 22, 2020

*U**gh! This fucking disgusts me!*
She continued her sexual conversations in the private message room. Several individual screen names cycled through various levels of teenage talk. She had been on the pseudo assignment for nearly a month, and she did not know how much more of her assignment she could stomach.

Her brothers and their families finally left the week after Thanksgiving, and a sense of normalcy almost returned to the household. However, the home remained in disarray with temporary sleeping arrangements everywhere.

Eoghan's best friend, Derek, now stayed with them for an indefinite amount of time. His mother, Nancy, became addicted to methamphetamine months prior; and, before summer ended, she transgressed into a new black heroin.

The heroin overdose happened the day after Thanksgiving, on Black Friday. Derek came home and found his mother unresponsive. He called paramedics, and she remained in the hospital for three weeks. All the toes on her right foot and two of her fingers on her left hand were amputated from the gangrene and side effects she developed.

When Nancy was finally discharged, she was taken to prison for child endangerment and aggravated assault. The latter occurred while her body detoxed. She went into a rage and stabbed a police officer in the leg with a hypodermic needle. The only reason she did not get slapped with a felony possession charge was due to the Good Samaritan Overdose Immunity Law, a controversial law that protected addicts seeking medical help from being arrested or prosecuted for the drugs.

Derek was immediately swept into the Andrewson home and welcomed as one of Jamilla's own grandchildren. While AJ knew it to be necessary and was happy Derek was safe with them, she secretively wanted privacy from all the warm bodies in the house. She could only hole herself up in her bedroom for so long, and she finally could not take it anymore.

She set up her laptop in a little nook of a popular bookstore in the City of Manchester an hour south of Belmont. Her work phone served as a secured Wi-Fi hotspot to minimize snooping eyes from the store's free service; no one needed to know the particulars of her online chats.

A couple of hours into her assignment, she noticed the other screen names slowly disappeared without warning. She saw a flicker, and a new screen name appeared. She verbally choked on her coffee from the message.

```
NCPoland1543: Hello
```

The cursor blinked by her screen name, waiting for a response.

Be calm! This could be a trick of some sort.

```
Roar317811: Hi
NCPoland1543: How is your father?
Roar317811: My daddy is @ work
NCPoland1543: Are you sure?
Roar317811: Of course Y wouldn't I B?
```

```
NCPoland1543: Because he was in a
serious accident several weeks ago
Roar317811: No he wasnt hes a banker
Roar317811: U must have me confused
w/ SE
NCPoland1543: No
NCPoland1543: You can drop the
disguise, Ameena. I know about
Operation Godel. There is no need for
the act.
```

Her face flushed. *How does he know that?* Before she could respond, he answered her thoughts.

```
NCPoland1543: I know you're on
administrative leave, Ameena. You're
on a fake sexual predator assignment.
I've been monitoring your progress.
Roar317811: Copernicus, who are you?
NCPoland1543: Someone who is
protecting you
Roar317811: That's hard to believe...
NCPoland1543: Why?
Roar317811: Because you won't tell me
who you are!
NCPoland1543: When the time is right,
I will. I promise.
Roar317811: How did you know I was
undercover?
NCPoland1543: I know you were given a
fake assignment as a ruse
NCPoland1543: I know you want answers
NCPoland1543: I know you're sitting
in a bookstore in Manchester
```

She slammed the laptop shut. Her eyes scanned the store studying last-minute shoppers. Dozens of patrons flipped through books aisle after aisle. The coffee shop was packed with individuals on laptops, tablets, and smartphones.

There were murmurs of dozens of voices around her.

No one appeared out of place. No one looked suspicious. No one stood out.

She grabbed her things and made a beeline to the restroom.

- - -- --- -----

She sat in one of the stalls for well over half an hour, lost in ethical turmoil.

What the hell do I do? Do I tell Conrad? No, I shouldn't tell him. He's on vacation with his family. I can't interrupt that. Shit, do I tell my partner? Fuck, I'm still pissed at Tony, the bastard. Wait, is this a joke he's playing? Is he Copernicus? No, his grammar sucks. It can't be him. Is this someone I know? Could it be Pinick? I haven't talked to him in a few weeks. Maybe I should keep Copernicus talking. Is this guy someone I can really trust, though? What do I do?? It can't be worse than Tony's deception, can it?

"Excuse me! My daughter needs to potty. Are you almost done in there?"

The voice on the other side of the stall snapped her out of her thoughts.

"Yes, just a second!"

She exited the stall and gave the waiting mother an apologetic look before washing her hands. As she ran the water through her fingers, she closed her eyes and splashed her face. She took a deep, long breath, then stared at herself in the mirror. She knew what she wanted to do.

- - -- --- -----

She went back in the chatroom.

```
Roar317811: Are you still there?
NCPoland1543: Yes
Roar317811: I'm going to be honest
```

here
Roar317811: *I don't know if I can trust you*
Roar317811: *Or should*
NCPoland1543: Understandable concerns
Roar317811: *Why should I trust you???*
Roar317811: *And don't tell me because you have to protect me*
NCPoland1543: Because
Roar317811: *I've already heard that and it's horse shit*
NCPoland1543: Fair enough
NCPoland1543: What would you like to know first?
Roar317811: *I don't know*
Roar317811: *Everything*
NCPoland1543: Let's start with how I know you're in the bookstore
Roar317811: *Fine.*
NCPoland1543: Look around. What do you see?
Roar317811: *Last minute shoppers. A bunch of people everywhere.*
NCPoland1543: What else?
Roar317811: *People standing in line to check out, others reading books from the shelves*
NCPoland1543: What else?
Roar317811: *...*
Roar317811: *People on laptops. Others using their smartphones*
NCPoland1543: What else?
Roar317811: *WTF else do you want me to tell you???*
NCPoland1543: What. Else. Detective?

She glared at her monitor. He wanted her to think, to analyze, and to dig deeper into the details. He wanted a calculated and analytical answer. And she would give it to him.

*Roar317811: I see employees walking
around keeping an eye on possible
thefts. I hear scanners beeping. I
smell a burned bagel.*
NCPoland1543: Good. And?
*Roar317811: I see devices being
removed from toys before shoppers
walk out the door.*
NCPoland1543: Yes. More?
*Roar317811: I see surveillance
cameras in the ceiling*
NCPoland1543: And what of the cameras
looking down at you?

She peered upward and studied the black hemispheres
around her.

*Roar317811: Most likely they're
monitored on multiple screens and the
video feeds are recorded digitally*
NCPoland1543: What else do you know
about the digital recordings?
*Roar317811: They're probably stored
on physical servers within the
building or in cloud services through
multiple servers*
NCPoland1543: Good. And what do you
know about the security of the
security?
*Roar317811: The security of the
security???*
NCPoland1543: Yes
*Roar317811: Nothing's ever 100% safe
from being penetrated. If it's
digital, then it can be hacked
eventually*
NCPoland1543: Yes
*Roar317811: And my guess is you're
not in the back of the store watching*

me
NCPoland1543: Correct
Roar317811: I know you're a hacker
Roar317811: And you're monitoring me
from a distance
NCPoland1543: Yes
NCPoland1543: What else, detective?
Roar317811: If you're a hacker, you
appear to be a sophisticated one. I
would guess these messages will
disappear and leave no trace
NCPoland1543: Correct
Roar317811: Is that how my
screenshots of your emails
disappeared last time we chatted???
NCPoland1543: Yes. If you take
screenshots or photos with your
phone, I can and will wipe your
devices clean before the data can be
transferred. There is nothing you do
digitally that I will not know.
Roar317811: Are you threatening me???
NCPoland1543: Never. I'm threatening
to those who threaten you.
Roar317811: Do you know who would try
to harm me and my family?
NCPoland1543: Do you know the harm
they would face for harming you?
Roar317811: You answered a question
with a question
NCPoland1543: And you avoided the
answer with an answer
Roar317811: I don't assume anything
about you
NCPoland1543: Then don't assume. Go
with your instinct, detective.
Roar317811: You want my assessment?
NCPoland1543: Yes.
Roar317811: You're highly intelligent
and incredibly secretive. You cover

every trace of yourself and you're
always slightly out of reach from
being discovered. You like games. You
know intimate details of my life, so
we either know each other or you are
a highly adv
Roar317811: OMG
Roar317811: Michael?????

She held her breath and felt her heart bounce past two beats. She felt as if seconds stretch into hours while she waited for the response.

NCPoland1543: No, Ameena. Michael is
in fact dead.
NCPoland1543: He was murdered.
Roar317811: How do you know that?????
NCPoland1543: I can't tell you right
now
Roar317811: Bullshit!
Roar317811: You don't want to tell
me!
NCPoland1543: I'm still learning of
all those involved
Roar317811: How dare you bring my
husband into this!
NCPoland1543: You mentioned his name
first.
Roar317811: You want to keep playing
games, asshole???
Roar317811: I'm done playing this
one.

She shut her laptop and stared at the surveillance camera. She hoped he watched as she flipped him off, furious at whatever cat-and-mouse game he tried to play with her. She simmered over the information as she drove home, analyzing everything she had read and learned, which turned out to be very little.

- - -- --- -----

Darkness crept into the late afternoon when she finally pulled into the driveway and hit the garage door opener. The empty house welcomed her.

She walked in through the garage and up the basement stairs where Abbott and Costello eagerly waited for her at the top. They then ran to the front door, tails slapping each other, again eagerly waiting for her. She dropped her stuff on her bed and went to the door to let them out.

When she opened the door and the dogs flew out, her eyes caught sight of something unusual. She saw footprints in the snow leading from the front porch to the driveway. She never noticed them when she pulled up.

Then she saw a glint of porch light reflecting off a small gift-wrapped box. She picked it up and examined it. It sparkled with reflective and holographic silver snowflakes in a royal blue background. It was no bigger than a business card box, and it was heavier than she expected. A typed label was addressed to her.

After she let the dogs back in, she opened the box. The object inside was wrapped in tissue paper, save a black ring sticking out above. She held the ring and pulled it from the container. She first thought it to be a wind chime, but then realized she held a kinetic mobile.

Each branch of the mobile perfectly balanced with a corresponding branch. Each branch held a specific number of reflective glass beads ranging from one to eight in sets. The glass beads all appeared similar in shape but unique in color and design; they caught shimmers of light and made prism shadows on all surrounding surfaces. When she placed the beads carefully back down in the box, they echoed with crystalline vibrations.

It mesmerized her, this simple yet complex piece of art.

She peeked in the box for a card but found none. The gift-giver did not leave a name.

Moments later, after she finally settled into her bedroom and started to work on a report for Conrad, she heard her phone ping.

It was a message from Tony:

> Hey you, tried calling a few days ago never heard back wanted to say hi and say Merry Xmas hope to chat soon after the holidays hope you aren't mad at me I miss you more than you know please don't ignore me I'm sorry for how things turned out–Tony

Damn you, Tony. Not today. You can sit on that text for a while, asshole.

She placed her phone down and returned to working on the report. She heard another ping from her phone.

Hell's bells, what does he want now?

She glanced at the phone number but did not recognize it. She tapped on the message:

> I hope you enjoy
> the gift ~nc

That fucker. Her anger increased again. She replied:

> You have the
> wrong number.

She blocked the unknown number before thinking. She set her phone down for a second time when she heard a third ping. She became irritated at the constant interruptions. Frustrated, she looked at her phone again: another phone number she did not recognize. She tapped on the message:

FYI, you cannot block
me. Please, Ameena, chat
with me a bit longer.
I'll wait for you. ~nc

Why should I?

I need you,
now and always ~nc

She tossed her phone across the bed. She had little to no
desire to talk to the mysterious Copernicus. As she climbed
out from the covers, her phone pinged again. She ignored it,
went to the kitchen, and poured herself a glass of water. She
stood at the kitchen counter and stared out the window for
several minutes. Curiosity replaced her anger, and she went
to retrieve her phone.

I will share what
I've learned of the
Fasciata and their
designer drug ~nc

That caught her attention and made her pause.
*Maybe I should give him a chance. Maybe he really is trying
to help, even if he's as elusive as a Sasquatch.*
She finally replied:

Later this evening.
When things settle down.

Again, her ethics fought within her mind like two sumo

wrestlers juggling her brain.

There's no easy solution. No matter what I do, it's always the lesser of two evils.

- - -- --- -----

She leaned back against the headboard and took a deep breath. Minutes later, she logged into the familiar chatroom. She watched her screen flicker and a message pop up.

> NCPoland1543: Hello
> *Roar317811: Hi*
> NCPoland1543: How are you this evening?
> *Roar317811: Fine.*
> NCPoland1543: The family sounds well. Your father appears to be on the mend.
> *Roar317811: How do you know that???*
> NCPoland1543: You look tired

"That sonofabitch! He must be using the webcam," she whispered to herself. She got up, left the room, and several minutes later, came back with a piece of paper and tape. She flipped off the webcam and then taped it.

> NCPoland1543: Ah, you don't like being watched
> *Roar317811: What do you think???*
> NCPoland1543: If anything, I'm showing you how easy it is to do surveillance and spy. Imagine if this were the Fasciata
> *Roar317811: Your cartel can go fuck yourselves*
> NCPoland1543: I am not part of the Order
> *Roar317811: I thought you were*
> NCPoland1543: No, quite the contrary

Roar317811: Ok. Prove it
NCPoland1543: What would you like to know?
Roar317811: Honestly? I have so many questions for you.
NCPoland1543: I'm sure you do. I will answer what I can.
Roar317811: How do you take over the message room?
NCPoland1543: It's a cloned window, a copy which mimics the data of the old chatroom. By all outward appearances, you're still in the other chatroom, in case spying eyes are watching. Think of how magic tricks work: people focus on the object and not the slight-of-hand trick to fool them.
Roar317811: You're proving an interesting teacher
NCPoland1543: Who is teaching whom?
Roar317811: Perhaps each to the other
NCPoland1543: You have a wit with words

She stared at his words. She found she enjoyed the banter and play with language. He seemed a skilled opponent in the game, and she wanted to play.

Roar317811: And you, an enigmatic air
NCPoland1543: Your pen is cocked, I see
Roar317811: The ink is in the chamber
NCPoland1543: You have already pierced my heart with your bulletin
Roar317811: Wait, you love me???
NCPoland1543: And you hate me?
Roar317811: You answered again question for question
NCPoland1543: Love and hate are

forged of the same metal.

Roar317811: I'm indifferent to you. I don't know you, nor do I trust you.

NCPoland1543: Then allow me to gain your trust. Allow me to explain what I can, for now.

Roar317811: Let's start with the Order. Tell me about the drug they use. Prove to me you know about the Fasciata. For all I know, you could be some kid living at home, locked up in his basement playing games with government officials for thrills.

NCPoland1543: Fair enough. Understand there is still much to discover. This is what I know:

NCPoland1543: Regular heroin is a strong diamorphine and gives euphoric effects to the user. It is primarily made from the resin in poppy plants. The sap from the pod of the poppy flower is refined to create the opiate. In and of itself, it's highly addictive. (more)

Roar317811: I know this already…

NCPoland1543: My explanation is thorough and will be long. I will let you know when I am done.

"A polite reprimand? Hmmm."

She left her computer to grab a pencil and notepad. When she settled back down, she took notes as each message appear, then disappeared.

NCPoland1543: Heroin made cartels rich around the world—especially for the drug king, Hapalo—until roughly two decades ago. A couple of things happened. 1) Prescription drugs became popular and easily accessible.

And 2) Governments around the world
started a war on drugs and began
cracking down on importers and cross-
border suppliers. Producers were
plucked off by law enforcement.
(more)

NCPoland1543: Hapalo tried his hand
with carfentanil, the elephant
tranquilizer. For a drug thousands of
times stronger than morphine, he
thought he would profit easily from
so little. However, it proved
extremely detrimental to his
business. The drug was highly
dangerous and killed too many
customers. He lost more money than he
made. He knew other cartels ruled the
cocaine and marijuana industries and
therefore, did not consider those
drugs. For Hapalo to make a profit
again, he went back to the very
product that made him a king: heroin.
He needed a resurgence in the heroin
trade to be king again. (more)

NCPoland1543: Over a decade ago,
Hapalo finally found a solution to
the monetary problem. They hired a
chemist to create a new and more
potent, exotic heroin. He/she was
tasked with discovering various
compounds which could be added to the
opium during the refinement process.
They wanted a drug more addictive,
more valuable—something which could
not be refused (more)

NCPoland1543: They knew Mexico had
experimented with scorpion,
rattlesnake, and viper venoms. The
latter two caused instant death from
the coagulation of blood in the

circulatory system; it was a useless product and was abandoned. Scorpion venom did nothing to increase the euphoria. So, the original chemist knew not to use those venoms, but instead, began searching the globe for other venoms: species of spider, various invertebrates including caterpillar, wasps, and ants. They even extracted venom from Komodo dragons. Each failed to produce the effect desired. (more)

NCPoland1543: Several years passed as the chemist continued to experiment with insects and plants until finally, they gave up those pursuits. They kept looking again and turned to marine life. That's when they discovered a potent neurotoxin, called tetrodotoxin, COULD produce the hypnotic euphoric effect wanted. The blue-ringed octopus—along with its cousins the blue-speckled, the blue-lined, and two others—were the perfect producers. This specific octopus was the mere size of a tennis ball but could produce enough tetrodotoxin to kill twenty-one adult humans within minutes. The venom was far deadlier than cyanide and had to be handled with extreme care. Just holding an octopus could result in the venom seeping through the pores and killing a person. (more)

NCPoland1543: By extracting and diluting the octopus venom through a highly-guarded and secretive method, and then combining it with the opium in an equally unknown process, it became the perfect addiction. A

FRACTION of the heroin was needed for many times the euphoric high. Imagine how much profit Hapalo could now make. And, it was easier to conceal from law enforcement because smaller batches could be produced in smaller locations, less needed to be transported, more could be hidden and stashed away. (more)

NCPoland1543: Hapalo tested his heroin in the German market. It became hugely profitable and was given the name Prussian Black. The cartel began marketing it across Europe, and then eventually branched out to other continents, including North America. This Prussian Black, the Fasciata's designer heroin, is the most sought-after drug in several key cities across the U.S. While it is not responsible for all drug overdose deaths in the epidemic sweeping the country, it is growing in percentage. (more)

NCPoland1543: Users are more likely to become addicted to Prussian Black than any other opioid. Some addicts don't realize how little is needed, and therefore, overdose and die. Those who have been careful discover the sheer euphoria and immediate rush to the brain. The drug is quickly converted to morphine and binds rapidly to the brain's opioid receptors. The user's arms and legs feel heavy, breathing slows, and sometimes they feel drowsy or mentally incapacitated. (more)

NCPoland1543: Shortly after the initial euphoric effects, the tetrodotoxin begins to take control. It prevents the nervous system from sending messages to the rest of the body and can prevent muscles from responding. In low quantities, it slightly paralyzes the users, allowing them to feel as if they are flying or floating in the air. They hallucinate. They feel as if they can travel through space and time. They are completely oblivious to the world outside of their bodies. (more)

NCPoland1543: In larger quantities, it kills. Some die from a fraction of a syringe-full. Some require much more. The opioid part of the overdose can be treated with naloxone, but the venom cannot. And there is no antidote, no cure. Yet. The only way to prevent death after an overdose is to manually help the victim breathe (CPR, mechanical ventilator, or valve bag mask is commonly used) until the involuntary muscles can begin to work on their own again, which could take hours. And only if they survive the first five hours of the overdose. (more)

NCPoland1543: The exact methodology Hapalo's Craftsmen use is a highly-guarded secret. There are no computer records I have found. And I have not discovered all the key players involved with the Boston Octave. Yet.

Roar317811: OMG, but how do you know all of this???

NCPoland1543: I cannot reveal my sources now. I am still doing research.

NCPoland1543: I'm sure your partner

has already briefed you on the
cartel's history?
*Roar317811: What do you know of
Tony's involvement with the Fasciata?*
NCPoland1543: That, I cannot tell you
Roar317811: Can't? Or won't?
NCPoland1543: I cannot say where his
loyalties lie at the moment. However,
I do know your professor is innocent.
My photo you found on his wall: it
was planted there.
Roar317811: You took the photo?
NCPoland1543: Yes
*Roar317811: Why were you there? Were
you stalking me???*
NCPoland1543: I was tracking several
Fasciata members and knew they were
connected to the tattoo shop. I had
hoped to talk to Mr. Mahoney and
monitor his involvement with the
Order, especially after they brutally
beat him.
*Roar317811: Was Loki part of the
Fasciata? Was he dealing drugs?*
NCPoland1543: No. On the contrary, he
was trying to prevent others from
getting harmed. He tried to protect
his employees, customers, and even
you, the best he could.
*Roar317811: What about Angie's
involvement?*
NCPoland1543: She's innocent as well.
I had no idea they would harm Ms.
Carmicle.
*Roar317811: Do you know where Angie
is?*
NCPoland1543: I know she went into
hiding and is safe, for now. But she
is not my priority. You are.
Roar317811: But WHY are you trying to

protect me? And WHY do I need protection???
NCPoland1543: After your visit with the professor, the Fasciata discovered you were looking into information on some of their members from the Boston Octave. You were beginning to get too close. They hacked your father's vehicle and staged the accident to scare you and slow down your progress with the case.
NCPoland1543: Ameena, I cannot let them harm you or your family. You mean too much to me.
Roar317811: Which members?
NCPoland1543: I cannot tell you right now
Roar317811: Bullshit. How can I trust you if you won't tell me?
NCPoland1543: And how do I know I can trust you?
NCPoland1543: Fair question, before you say otherwise
Roar317811: You don't
NCPoland1543: Then why risk trusting the person who won't trust in return?
Roar317811: I don't have an answer for you
NCPoland1543: Then you understand why I don't answer
Roar317811: You gave me the gift today?
NCPoland1543: Yes. It's a kinetic sculpture.
NCPoland1543: Do you like it?
Roar317811: It's beautiful, yes. Why did you give it to me?
NCPoland1543: Because I know you better than yourself, at times. I

know the holidays are hard for you
some years. I know you are missing
your husband more this season. I know
the hurt.

*Roar317811: Michael is this you? Is
this some sick fucking joke?????*

NCPoland1543: As I told you before,
Michael is dead. He was, in fact,
gunned down and murdered. I'm so
sorry, Ameena.

NCPoland1543: I am not cruel or
heartless towards those I care for

*Roar317811: You don't know what it's
like*

NCPoland1543: I do, Ameena. I've lost
those dear to me. I know the loss as
equally as you, if not more. I know
the pain which doesn't ever go away.
I know the hurt and despair, the
desire for closure of some means, by
any means.

*Roar317811: I can't stop crying. I
can't stop remembering…*

NCPoland1543: And that's why you keep
pushing forward. You bury the
memories and try to leave them
behind.

Roar317811: Yes

NCPoland1543: And that's why I move
forward. You feel as if the road is
ahead of you, so why would you want
to go back the way you came?

*Roar317811: And that's why you don't
want to get caught? You don't want to
be prevented from getting closer to
the Fasciata?*

NCPoland1543: We are the same metal
and sharpness, detective.

Roar317811: But on different sides

NCPoland1543: Sided differently. But

of different forges, no.
*Roar317811: I need to tell my boss
about this conversation.*
NCPoland1543: And I trust you will
*Roar317811: And I know this chatroom
is encrypted and I won't have any
proof this occurred.*
NCPoland1543: And you know any
attempt at taking photos or
screenshots will result in immediate
deletion on any device.
*Roar317811: What should I tell my
boss then?*
NCPoland1543: Tell him what you must
NCPoland1543: Tell him the
information I gave you about the
heroin
NCPoland1543: Tell him to look into
the A.T.F. agent your professor knows
*Roar317811: The A.T.F. agent is
involved somehow?*
NCPoland1543: Yes, as is a man named
Martín Delarosa
Roar317811: Who is Martín?
NCPoland1543: A person of interest
*Roar317811: Are you not a person of
interest as well?*
NCPoland1543: Interesting, perhaps,
but you will not find a digital
record of me. I have removed myself
from databases and searches, though
you are welcome to look.
*Roar317811: You trust me enough to
give me all this information?*
NCPoland1543: I would trust you with
my heart if yours could be trusted
with me.
*Roar317811: Your heart is fond of
me???*
NCPoland1543: Is yours not?

The screen flickered.

He was gone.

Her cheeks flushed slightly from the emotional and mental game she played with the hacker. The conversation was enlightening.

She had more detailed information for Conrad and she felt, for the first time in nearly two months, she made progress towards finding Loki's killers. She also felt the gentle touch of compassion and kindred-like feelings from Copernicus. The name—and day's dialogue between the two—churned in her mind until she eventually drifted to sleep.

- - -- --- -----

<u>Tuesday, January 5, 2021</u>

"And you couldn't find *anything* on this hacker?" Conrad asked.

"Correct, sir. Again, there was no way to take any screenshots, copy-paste the conversation, or take photos with my phone. He prevented me from doing anything electronically. And he said if I did, he would delete them."

Conrad stared at her in an uncomfortable silence. Finally, she could not take it.

"Sir, while he explained the Prussian Black, I hand-wrote everything down. There was NO way I wanted to risk him intercepting an email or remotely deleting any text file. I wrote every detail I could remember."

Every detail relevant to the Fasciata.

"And why didn't you come to me the next day?"

"Because you were on vacation, sir. I was *not* about to bother you and your family. And before you say anything, you know how important family is to me, so I assumed it was equal for you."

"Fair enough."

"That's what Copernicus said a couple of times."

"Jardine, I'm not a hacker."

"I know, sir. You can't even navigate a browser window on your laptop." She turned away as he glared at her. "On another note, I looked through the national and international databases for any reference to a Copernicus and there weren't any. I even checked Interpol, other state databases, and all international databases I could find. Again, nothing."

"And you don't know who the hell this guy is?"

"No, sir. The only thing I did find was a possible explanation to his email handle, the NCPoland1543. I explained it in October during one of our meetings. Do you remember me telling you about the mathematician named Nicolaus Copernicus?"

"Vaguely."

"He was a mathematician who died in 1543. Was from

Poland. I think our hacker has some affection for this guy. I also double-checked various spellings of the name based on the regions of Europe he was associated with, and nothing popped up either. For all we know, 'Copernicus' could be a fake name."

"Have you received any more messages from this guy?"

"No, sir. He hasn't contacted me since then and I haven't reached out to him."

Conrad continued to stare at her, deep in thought, and tapped his fingers on his desk. "What about the lead Copernicus told you about?"

"Which one? The A.T.F. agent?" He nodded. "I haven't followed through with that, sir. I didn't know if you wanted me to work with Agent Aserbbo yet."

"Did Aserbbo ever reach out to you?"

"Yes, sir. He sent me a few texts."

"And what did he say?"

"Wishing me Merry Christmas. Apologizing for upsetting me. Begging me not to ignore him. Pleading for me to respond."

"And, did you?"

"Eventually. He apologized for not being there for me. He told me he'd been undercover on a new assignment and couldn't reach me until closer to Christmastime. He wants to see me, but I told him it wasn't a good time yet, with my dad and all."

"And how do you feel about coming back to work and continuing your investigations with him?"

"Once bitten, twice shy, sir. You mentioned needing checks and balances, and I honestly think that's what's needed here. I've had time to process everything and think about it. I'm ready to come back and continue."

She locked eyes with him. He tapped his fingers on the desk.

"Very well. You can start back next week after I close out Operation Godel. Call Agent Aserbbo and set up a time and day to meet with the A.T.F. lead. I also want you both to find and interview this Martín Delarosa."

"Yes, sir." She stood up to leave.

"AJ?"

"Yes, sir?"

"If you find it difficult to work with Agent Aserbbo for the duration of this case, I need to know."

"I understand."

"And do NOT tell him about Copernicus or what you've found out. Until we know more about this hacker, let's keep this information to ourselves for as long as we can."

She nodded, then left.

- - -- --- -----

Tuesday, January 12, 2021

They were in the car headed to the A.T.F. office in Manchester. Tony avoided the interstate, and instead, took some back roads to make an unscheduled stop with an informant.

AJ avoided looking at him or even saying more than three words to him for most of the drive. She hoped to make him as uncomfortable as she could the entire car ride together. The only enjoyment she had was staring at the gray skies, monotone landscape full of snow, and meandering river parallel to the road. She was slightly glad they were not on the interstate.

Without warning, he pulled into an open space off the road, put the car in park, and turned it off. The vehicle sat precariously close to a guardrail, enough so she could not open the door and get out. The lack of an escape route made her apprehensive.

Tony repositioned himself closer and stared at her. She pulled back slightly, not knowing what to expect. He continued to stare at her in silence. His blue eyes elicited care and sorry. For a brief instant, the fluttering in her stomach stirred; she swallowed the feeling back in its hidden place.

"How long are you going to be mad at me?"

"We need to get going."

"No, we are staying here—"

"We can talk about this later, not—"

"No." He cut her off. "I want to talk about this right now. You've been ignoring me for weeks, and I'm sick of it."

"I don't care what you want."

He sighed. She saw his eyes turn rigid. "Give me your phone."

"What?"

"Give. Me. Your. Phone." They locked stares until she finally reached into her coat and pulled out her phone.

He lifted himself from his seat, pushing his body into her personal space as he reached for his phone in the back pocket of his jeans. Her eyes went down to his neck, his collarbone, and the toned skin teasing her underneath his shirt. Another fluster; another deep breath to push those feelings back.

He sat back down and grabbed her smartphone, placing it with his. He opened his car door and dropped both phones on the ground outside before shutting the door again.

"If you want your phone back, you have to talk to me."

She shifted her body to stare out her window, knowing she was cornered. No flight, only fight. She was angry at him for being put in such a position. Then she changed her mind and faced him.

"Fine. You wanna talk? My son blames himself for the accident. My dad almost died because of your involvement! And you didn't try to stop it! YOU fucked up, asshole!"

"I know I did," his voice equally raised with hers. "And I told you, I'm sorry. What else do you want me to say right now?"

"Tell me the truth, Tony! Did you know it was going to happen? Why didn't you try to STOP it?"

"I couldn't!"

"Wanna know why I've been ignoring you, you piece of shit? Because all you are is a fucking pathetic memory of what I DON'T need in my life!"

His lips pressed firmly together. "Keep going."

"You're an evil bastard. A-a two-timing snitch who hurts anyone and everyone around them. You don't care for anyone else except yourself because if you cared for me or my family, the accident would NOT have happened!"

"HEY! YOU wait a minute!" He matched her anger with his own. "I've been protecting you! The accident was NOT supposed to be that severe! It was supposed to be a minor fender-bender, THAT'S ALL! And I was NOT the one who caused the accident!"

"But you KNEW about it, TONY!" She yelled back. "You knew the E.C.U. had been hacked. And you did NOTHING to prevent it!"

"I COULDN'T!"

"BULL SHIT! You could have told me!"

"I wasn't allowed to, AJ! If I told you ANYTHING, they would have found out and it would have been MY ass! I couldn't blow my cover."

"Which one, Aserbbo? Your D.T.F. cover or your cartel cover, you worthless ass?"

"That's NOT fair!"

"Like hell it is! You almost had Eoghan KILLED! My father almost DIED, you fucking asshole!"

He lowered his voice and stared at her. "You have no idea what these people are capable of. They *kill* everyone who gets in their way, and those are the lucky ones."

"You should be so lucky then. You're pathetic and make me sick."

She turned her body and head to look outside again, almost pouting. Suddenly, he grabbed her and forced her to face him.

"Look at me!" he demanded.

She pulled her arms up to stop him from touching her, slapping his hand from her.

"Don't touch me!"

"Cut it out, AJ!"

He grabbed her right arm with one hand. Angry, she landed a hard punch to his face with her left.

"You bitch! Grrr!"

He squeezed and twisted her right arm, causing her to yell in pain. When she tried to use her left hand to pry his off, he grabbed that arm. She struggled relentlessly with him, but he easily pinned her against the glass window of the passenger door.

"LET GO OF ME!"

"NO!"

"LET GO!" She screamed in desperation and fear, but he did not release her.

She tried to claw at him, but he kept her pinned against

the cold glass. She could not bite him. She could not head-butt him. She continued to struggle, but her arms weakened quickly. She was pinned against her will, and there was nothing she could do, except succumb to his strength.

Several minutes later, she finally tired and stopped fighting him. He was much stronger, and she hated herself for being so weak. He kept her in that position until her fingertips tingled from the lack of blood circulating. She lost the battle and turned away, baring her neck to him.

In defeat and frustration and anger, she cried. Finally, she let the weight of her muscles give up as her upper body relaxed. Only then did she notice he released his grip slightly, but still held her against the window.

"Look at me," he said calmly.

She refused.

"Look at me!" There was more force and authority in his tone.

Still, she refused.

He softened his voice in a begging plea. "*Please*, Ameena. Look at me."

Finally, she turned back towards him. She noticed the additional grays in his beard and studied the details of his lips before her eyes finally rested with his. She saw the pain and remorse glossing in his eyes as wrinkles tightened in his lower lids.

"Please forgive me. I fucked up. I know this. I'm sorry." He leaned into her, pressing his chest against hers and whispered in her ear, "I still care about you, Ameena. And I haven't stopped wanting you."

She felt the warmth of his breath on her earlobe and the softness of his beard against her jaw. She could smell the bath soap, his aftershave. His words brought the flutters back again. She rotated her jaw into his, pressing skin against skin.

She leaned closer to his ear and whispered, "How can I trust you after this?"

Several seconds later, he pulled himself slowly back from

her ear, letting his mouth brush against her cheek to her lips before pulling back to stare at her again. They held each other's eyes for longer than she realized. She could see the tenderness and pain on his face.

"I don't know. You may never be able to," he whispered.

The tension continued between them for a few more moments. Then he slowly released her arms and sat back down in the driver's seat. She watched his mannerisms and saw the inner turmoil he fought within himself. He grabbed the steering wheel with both hands, knuckles going white from the grip, as he looked down.

"I'll never forgive myself for what happened, Ameena."

"And if *I* never forgive you?"

She watched him sit up with his eyes closed, swallowing deep. His eyelids changed into a pastel pink. She stared at him and wondered what his next move would be. Finally, he took a deep breath and focused on the road ahead of them.

He cranked the ignition without looking at her. "We need our phones now."

He opened the door, retrieved the devices, then shut the door again, handing her phone back.

She was cold after being pressed against the window for so long. She was cold because the car had been shut off in the middle of winter. She was cold because she and her partner might never feel the warmth between them again.

- - -- --- -----

They pulled up to the A.T.F. location in downtown Manchester. An old mill building housed the government branch. It was one of many built in the 1800s along the Merrimack River. As she stared at the massive size of the building, she could only imagine the scenic view from the top floor.

After checking in and being shuffled to a conference room, two men eventually walked in to greet her and Tony.

"Hi, Taylor Rion, Carl's supervisor." The incredibly tall man shook hands with both. His smile was warm and inviting.

"Carl Frierson." The thinly framed man stood a head shorter than his boss. His fair skin and distinctive hair color revealed his Irish roots.

After introductions, they all sat down at the table. AJ pulled out a couple of folders of information while Tony started the conversation.

"Mr. Frierson, we discovered you may have given someone information regarding cases we're working, and we wanted to clarify a few things with you."

"Sure." AJ noticed he picked at his cuticles.

"Do you recognize this man?" She pulled out a photo of Raymond Pinick.

Carl glanced at the photo. He hesitated. "Yeah, I do."

"How do you know him?"

"He's—he's a friend of a friend. He came to me a while back about some drug overdoses, including his son's. The old man has kinda lost it if you ask me."

"We didn't ask you," Tony said.

Carl picked at his fingernails.

She put the photo away. "Mr. Frierson, Dr. Pinick has been given a lot of information about some of these victims, but a couple of them are from cases Agent Aserbbo and I are working. We want to make sure sensitive information hasn't been leaked."

Carl chipped away at another finger, tearing more of his cuticle. She could tell his energy was nervous as he appeared to barely be holding it together.

"Look, I thought I was doing a friend a favor. Dr. Pinick had some questions regarding his son's death, and I directed him where he could go for help. Then, he started asking me about another drug overdose he discovered, and then a couple of others. I didn't think anything of it."

"Agent Aserbbo," Taylor said, "Carl's been reprimanded for his indiscretions. He's on a probationary period with us now and has been informed he's to no longer provide any information to anyone else."

"Honestly, I'm sorry I did it. I wasn't thinking."

"There's a lot of *that* going on." She knew only Tony fully understood her meaning. "Mr. Frierson, do you recognize this photo? It was taken a few months ago."

She showed him the photo from the day of the tattoo shop fire, the one from Pinick's wall. He glanced at it, then at Tony, then back to her.

"No, I don't. Am I supposed to?"

"We're trying to discover the source of this image," Tony said.

"It was found in the professor's home, but he has no knowledge of it, and we know he didn't take this photo," she said.

Carl glanced back at Tony. "Sorry, can't help you with that."

"Can't or won't, Mr. Frierson?" AJ pulled another photo out. "Do you recognize this person?" She slid the photo of Jose Perales over to Carl. He studied the mugshot and shook his head.

"What about this person? His name is Martín Delarosa?" She slid the file towards him. Again, he shook his head quickly.

"And what about her? Her name is Angie Carmicle. She worked at the House of Skulls Tattoo and Body Piercing Shop in Laconia, the same place the other image was taken."

When she slid the photo towards Carl, his demeanor changed. He immediately pushed it back to her.

"Look, I don't recognize any of these people."

"Are you sure? Maybe you need to take a *good* look."

"We're done." Carl stood up to leave. "I told you, I don't know anything about any of these people. I admit to helping Dr. Pinick with information he needed, but I don't admit to anything else."

A quick thought crossed her mind. "Carl, one more thing. Do you have any tattoos?"

He stared at her and she watched his cheeks tighten. "I'm not answering that. That's not relevant and none of your business."

He offered no hesitation in his departure. Taylor turned to the pair after the door closed.

"Carl's been with us for a couple of years now. He's had a not-so-normal approach to things. He's been effective at what he does, but we don't know how ethical his operations have been. If I had any information to provide you guys with, trust me, I would share it." He smiled at AJ.

"We believe you." She smiled back.

With no other information to learn, the pair left the office. When they finally got in the car, she asked, "Did you notice how nervous Frierson seemed to be?"

"Yeah. He's hiding something."

"He really changed his demeanor. I have a gut feeling he's involved with Angie somehow. Did you notice how he wouldn't answer the tattoo question?"

"Yeah, but it doesn't mean he's hiding anything. Could only mean he doesn't have any tattoos or thought the question was too personal."

"True…" Her voice trailed off.

She mulled over the information from the meeting. With her mind so focused on the discussion, she did not hear Tony asking a question.

"AJ!" he finally yelled.

"Huh? Sorry, I was lost in thought."

"More like checked out. I was asking you if you wanted to grab a bite to eat."

She tensed. "No, I need to get back home soon. I didn't tell my mom I'd be out late."

"Past your curfew?" He tried teasing her with his usual charming stabs, but she was not in the mood.

"No. I need to check on my dad."

"Oh." He paused. "Will we have a chance to catch up soon? I'd like to visit your parents."

"I don't know, Tony. This is my first week back in the

office, and I'm behind on a lot of things. You know the red tape is never-ending."

"That's an understatement." He paused for another moment. "AJ, are we okay?"

She thought for a little bit. "We're as okay as we're going to be for now."

"Have you said anything to your family, about the cause of the accident?"

"No. It would tear my mom apart. I told them the E.C.U. malfunctioned and the accident wasn't Eoghan's fault. He's been taking it hard and still blames himself."

There was another long pause.

"Ameena?"

"Yes, Tony?"

"How do I make things right between us?"

She paused to think. "I don't know. We may not be alright right now. Will we be one day? I don't know. Maybe. Maybe we won't. But we take this one step at a time and one conversation at a time. That's the only thing I can promise you."

He nodded again and did not say anything else.

She knew he wanted more, but she kept her emotions in check. She still found him attractive, but she told herself she did not love him. Her heart still belonged to Michael, and she lost herself in those thoughts again. She needed closure. She needed answers. She could not rest—or allow herself to love again—until she found Michael's killers.

She stared out the car window and noticed the vastness in the naked landscape. Her mind drifted to New Hampshire's famous poet, Robert Frost, and one of his poems. She finally understood the words:

> The woods are lovely, dark and deep,
> But I have promises to keep,
> And miles to go before I sleep.
> And miles to go before I sleep.

- - -- --- -----

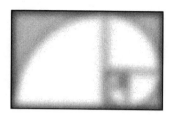

CHAPTER FIFTEEN: LEADS

Tuesday, February 2, 2021

❞ What did you find out?" Conrad sat down across from Tony and AJ in the conference room.

AJ could see the exhaustion in his eyes and knew his European trip the previous week weighed on him. She wanted to ask him about it, but from the look on his face, she thought it would be better to wait a few days.

"Sir, the week after we met with Frierson, we got a hit from one of Angie Carmicle's other bank accounts. She'd withdrawn all of her money and closed out the account."

She slid a bank report over to her boss. He studied the amount and then glanced up at her above the rims of his glasses.

"That's not good."

"No, sir. It's not."

Tony added, "This was done in downtown Manchester—blocks from the A.T.F. office. We had the bank pull the surveillance tapes for us." He opened his folder and pulled out screenshots from the video feed. "She was alone and appeared to be hiding her appearance. She's running. I have eyes and ears watching out for her, but I'm not sure we'll find her anytime soon."

"Agent Aserbbo, did she ever go to the hospital after her injuries the night of her rape?"

"No, sir. We double-checked all the hospital records and

even cross-referenced her name with urgent care facilities across New England. Either the injuries weren't that severe, or she took care of it herself. But there's no record anywhere."

"Other than the bank video, she disappeared again," AJ said. "Her cell phone's been disconnected, and she hasn't registered a new one. We checked utility companies, the post office for forwarding addresses, anything we could think of. It all came back negative. She's vanished again."

"That can't be good." Conrad paused. "We need to find her and get her into protective custody. As soon as either of you have any leads, you contact me immediately. Understood?"

"Yes, sir," they said in unison.

"Any leads on Perales yet?"

"No, sir," she replied. "He hasn't popped up anywhere for anything. Still no hits on bank records, toll roads with his vehicle, no facial recognition at any government sites — nothing. We even went back to his last known address, and there's been no sign of anyone living there for a long time."

"We also checked out-of-state and out-of-country databases in case he'd left the states, but nothing came up there either," Tony said.

"So, Ms. Carmicle has vanished in thin air, and Perales is still missing." Conrad's thought was more of a statement than a question. "Is there any good news?"

"Yes, sir."

"We were able to interrogate Martín Delarosa last week," Tony said. "He was picked up on New Year's Day for public lewdness and drunk and disorderly conduct. He was found on the side of the road in his car with a known prostitute. Both were passed out with needles still in their arms. The arresting officer found heroin on the woman and she's doing time for intent to sell. When Delarosa went to court, the judge threw the book at him."

AJ tagged in. "His lawyers — and somehow he has damn good ones — did get the sentence reduced and he gets out of jail over the summer. August to be exact. He's only serving eight months. But with him incarcerated, we took advantage of it and questioned him about everything we could. He has the same octopus tattoo as our overdose victims. We asked him about it and the connection with our missing persons."

"What did he say, Jardine?"

"He's swimming in the river denial, sir."

"Say again?"

"He's denying anything and everything about anyone."

"We showed Delarosa pictures of Perales and he said he didn't recognize him," Tony said. "But when we showed him the pictures of Angie, he stared and smirked. Then he denied knowing anything about her."

"And your gut is telling you otherwise?"

"Yes, sir," she said. "We also showed him a picture of Frierson to see if he would have a reaction, and nothing but more denial."

"Other than Mr. Mahoney's statement, do we have any hard evidence tying these octopus tattoos to the Fasciata?"

"Loki only vaguely mentioned the tattoos were for specific clients. He never said directly they were for the Fasciata. He only wrote the name down on her business card and gave it back," Tony said.

"Sir, other than the research I did online, there's no hard evidence yet. I mean, we know Fasciata means 'bound' so I think the octopus tattoo is like an initiation for cartel members. Each member 'binds' themselves to the Order by getting the tattoo."

They paused between the conversation.

"Wait! I have an idea. What if we went back and re-interviewed Frierson and Delarosa about the Prussian Black heroin? Maybe we can make a connection to the Fasciata that way?"

She saw Tony stiffen. "Prussian Black?"

"Yeah, that's the name I was given. Basically, it's more addictive and only a fraction is needed."

"I know what Prussian Black is, AJ. How did you find out about it?" She noticed the crow's feet tighten between his brows.

"You aren't the only one with connections, Tony."

They stared at each other.

Before Tony could question her more, Conrad interrupted them. "Jardine, did you ever get the autopsy report on Mr. Mahoney?"

"Yes, sir. I thought we went over it a couple of months ago?"

"No. We were waiting for the dental confirmation to come back and then shortly after that, you were on leave."

"Oh."

She forgot about Loki's autopsy report and the meeting she had with Cassie. The car accident and her father's injuries distracted her. As did her chats with Copernicus.

She realized she blushed and then noticed both men staring at her. Before either could ask, she reached over the side of her chair, grabbed her binder, and flipped through it. She found the stapled papers she wanted.

"Here's the autopsy report, sir." She slid it over to him. As he scanned it, she summarized, "Cassie could not I.D. the body visually or through DNA. There's no record of his DNA in the system. She sent off for his dental records and made a positive I.D. that way.

"There was no evidence of soot in his trachea or smoke inhalation in his lungs. She confirmed he died prior to the fire starting. His skull had been hit repeatedly, and he died from blunt-force trauma."

"And we're left looking for five murder suspects with our only witness, who can identify any of them, on the run now?" Conrad asked.

"Yeah," Tony said.

"I've also been looking into the police databases for anyone booked with the same tattoo," AJ said. "We came across a few names—Delarosa among them, but that's it. The other names are scattered across the U.S., so there's nothing we've been able to connect with the arson or Loki's murder. I've found similar tattoos of full octopuses, but not the single tentacle that appears to be the Fasciata's signature."

"Is there any information you can give me on the Prussian Black?" Conrad asked Tony.

"The production is a highly-guarded secret. Each Octave makes sure only their Craftsman and Knight know the location of the labs. Sometimes a Merchant or Farmer will know since they provide the supplies and deal with distribution of the drug. But Serfs and Peasants almost never know the locations."

"Sir, they have to get the tetrodotoxin from living octopuses. I can try to track down aquariums and pet shops to see if I can find someone who owns one. Maybe if we find an octopus owner, we find the supplier for the venom used in the heroin."

"Interesting." Conrad looked at the clock. "We'll continue this discussion next week. I have a lunch meeting to attend to."

He stood up. Tony and AJ followed.

"Keep me informed on your progress."

"Yes, sir," they both said.

He walked off, leaving the pair standing by the conference room door. Tony tried to walk out, but she grabbed his arm, pulling him back in the room. She shut the door, keeping her body between it and him.

"Something wrong?"

She studied his eyes. "Did you know Hull and Fay personally?"

"No, I didn't."

"But you're part of their organization. How can you *not* know them?"

He rolled his eyes at her. "Do you know the names of everyone in this building?"

"No, but—"

"That's what I thought. You can't know everyone. Each

team functions separately. Every team member is assigned certain tasks. The same goes for them. Never is the entire Octave in one location. And never do they all know about each other. The only way to know is by the tattoo."

"What about Delarosa? He has the tattoo."

"I don't know him either."

He reached for the doorknob and she slid over to block his hand. She continued to study his face and knew he was keeping something from her.

"You're lying."

Frustrated, he snaked one hand around her waist to the doorknob and placed his other palm on the opposite side of her. He leaned in.

"Delarosa is dangerous, AJ," he whispered. "He's gone after one of my C.I.s. That's all I can tell you right now."

"Why won't you tell me more?"

She stared into his eyes and saw them soften. She wanted to know more than what he wanted to tell.

"Not today," he whispered.

He planted a tender kiss on her forehead. Then he twisted the knob, carefully opened the door, and left.

- - -- --- -----

"Hiii," came the annoying, unmistakable voice of Tiffany.

AJ's thoughts of Tony were interrupted and that fouled her mood.

"Hi, Tiffany."

"How are you doing?" Her voice slithered softly with the telltale indication she wanted information.

"I'm okay. Can I help you with something?"

"Suuure. I was wondering if you will be seeing Tony in the next couple of days?"

"Why do you ask?" AJ did not hide the annoyance in her voice.

"Well…" Tiffany provided a dramatic pause before continuing. "You see, Brenda broke up with her boyfriend not long ago, and she thought Tony was attractive. And — "

"Tiffany, stop. I know you have Tony's phone number. If you or Brenda or *any*one else in the office want to date him, then you can call him. I don't care. But I am *not* getting involved in any rumor factors, and I won't be the middleman passing information back and forth."

Tiffany gasped and huffed slightly. "Well, that was *rude* to say, don't you think?"

AJ rolled her eyes. "No, that's not what I think. What I think, I can't say, and you don't want me to say what I think. I'm busy right now in the middle of some research."

She turned her back on the woman standing there.

"I was only trying to be nice and ask you how your dad was doing. You don't have to be a rude priss and prune about it."

AJ slapped her palms on her desk and stood up. She glared at Tiffany in such a manner, the woman quickly took steps back and out of range of a potential sucker punch.

"Let's get this straight, Tiffany. You don't give a fuck about my dad or me or my family or even anything to do with me. You only care about yourself and your ulterior motives. And 'priss and prune'? Seriously? Who's the pussy priss who started the goddamn name calling?"

"Uh! You don't have to use any vulgar language!"

AJ walked away, not wanting a confrontation. Tiffany, on the other hand, did.

"Must be nice to have favoritism to take a month off from work."

AJ stopped. "If you have an issue with the assignments given to me by OUR Deputy Director, take it up with HIM."

"Maybe I should take this up with Human Resources. This sounds like harassment to me."

"Do whatever the fuck you want, Tiffany. I don't give a shit what you do or what you think."

"Rude bitch," Tiffany said under her breath.

"I hope your uterus punches you in the ovaries." AJ blurted the words out without thinking twice and walked down the hall.

"At least I have a uterus."

The last insult hit its mark. AJ kept walking beyond the tofu-colored walls and elevators and into the illuminated laboratory-half of the building. She walked into Peter's processing lab, shut the door behind her, and purposefully banged the back of her head on the door several times.

Peter looked up from his computer monitor. "Hey, AJ!" When she did not respond, he frowned. "Let me guess. Tiffany?"

She nodded. "I just need a breather."

"Take your time."

She stood there for a few minutes with her eyes closed and focused on her breathing. Peter continued to swab several pieces of evidence on his table. Then she sighed, "Fuuuuck..."

"What did she say now?"

"Same old bullshit, different smell. She wanted to find out more information about Tony again."

"Oh, brother. Better him than me." Peter chuckled.

"Yeah, you do have a point there."

"What got you so upset?"

"We threw uterine jabs at each other."

"Oooooh, never mind! I don't wanna know!" Peter laughed. His infectious laughter caused her to relax.

"How's work on this end?" She quickly changed the subject.

"Not bad, not bad. Haven't really been too busy lately, but my right eye's been twitching, so it could change quickly."

"True."

"Any word from Cassie or Nadine about the wedding yet? Did they set a date?"

"Oh, I'm not sure. I haven't spoken to her in a few weeks. We texted on Christmas and New Year's, but that's been about it. I've been neglecting my bridesmaid duties."

"Nah, Cassie loves you to death. She's been giving you

plenty of space with all the family drama going on. How's your dad, by the way?"

"He's slowly getting better." She let out a deep sigh. "I should head back now. Thanks, Peter."

"*Mi lab es su lab,*" he laughed, as he combined his Spanish and English.

Several minutes later, she reluctantly walked towards her desk. As she walked down the hallway, she saw Conrad exit the elevator.

"Jardine? My office."

"Yes, sir."

She followed him into his office and he shut the door behind them. She could tell something was wrong.

"Have a seat."

"Sir, is something wrong?"

"Becky in H.R. stopped me downstairs. Care to tell me about the conversation you had with Tiffany?"

She reiterated the conversation in detail, including the reproductive organs.

"Do you realize Ms. Devry put a formal complaint in?"

"No, sir, but I did dare the—*her* to."

"It's your word against hers, and right now, detective, you don't have too many friends outside of my office walls."

"I'm not here to make friends."

"I know."

"And I don't put up with someone's bullshit. I'm not wired that way."

"I know."

"So, what should I do then?"

"Becky will call you in sometime this week to get your statement. I recommend you tell her about any other altercations you — or anyone else you know — have had with Ms. Devry."

She sat back and crossed her arms. "And you wondered why I wanted to leave this place after the Rune murders?"

Conrad sighed. "Jardine, I understand all too well. Ms. Devry has been a thorn in my side from time to time."

"At least she's not an ass cactus like she is for me."

Conrad facepalmed and covered his face with his hands as he muttered something under his breath. She could only imagine what he thought sometimes. Finally, he looked up, a serious expression on his face.

"What was one of the first things I taught you?"

"If you want to eliminate problems, come up with solid solutions, sir."

He nodded. "Same goes for office encounters. Understood?"

"Yes, sir."

"Good. Now, let's talk about Agent Aserbbo."

"Sir?"

"I need to know what the hell you were thinking with your comment about the Prussian Black. It caught him by surprise. That wasn't a smart thing to say, Jardine."

"Sorry, sir. I blurted it out before I thought about it. But we're fine, I promise."

"AJ?" He gave her his paternal do-not-lie-to-me glare.

"Sir, we hashed out the tension in the car a few weeks ago. We've been working fine since then." She left specific details out.

"And how are you feeling about all of this?"

"We're as okay as we can be right now, sir. There was — and is at times — tension, and we're handling it. It isn't and won't interfere with the casework. But I don't trust him yet and don't know when I will. I haven't told him anything about Copernicus."

"And don't. Now, tell me about your personal observations with the Frierson and Delarosa interviews."

"Do you want to know about my observations of Tony or the interviewees?"

"Everything, detective."

"Yes, sir. Starting with the first interview, Frierson was quite nervous. He was tearing his cuticles frequently. I also noticed his foot constantly moving up and down under the desk, almost vibrating. He was anxious, nervous. He kept glancing back and forth between everyone. Frierson immediately ended the interview when he saw a picture of Ms. Carmicle. My instinct is telling me he knows a lot more than what he claims, and he knows Angie. He may even know where she is."

"Good, but we need more than gut instinct. Do you think he knows Agent Aserbbo?"

"I'm not really sure. But I didn't want to ask just yet."

"That's a smart move. What about Delarosa?"

"He gives me some serious creeps. He's a cocky sonofabitch, for sure. He was bragging about how he'd be out of jail later this year and can't wait to fuck girls again. He has no respect for any women, so I wouldn't be surprised if—" She stopped.

"What is it, AJ?"

"What if Delarosa was one of the five who raped Angie? He has the Fasciata tattoo and smiled when he saw her picture, so couldn't it be motive?"

"That's possible. Is his DNA in C.O.D.I.S.?"

"Doubtful, sir. His lawyers pushed the fourth amendment on the state attorney. And, Angie never reported the crime. There's no record of a rape kit being processed or collected."

"So, we have nothing to connect him to Ms. Carmicle, except that he grinned at her picture?"

"That's correct, sir. Maybe instead of asking him about the *missing* persons, we should question him about the *deceased* involved."

"Explain."

"With your permission, I'd like to go back and interview both Frierson and Delarosa by myself, without Tony. I want to take the photos of the individuals Dr. Pinick believes are connected with the Fasciata Order. Granted, Frierson provided some of the information to Pinick and could recognize the names, but I want to see his reactions."

"Who are those people again?"

"Dr. Pinick believes three others—besides his son,

Chris — were murdered and have ties to the cartel. He thinks Chris was the first. Damian Winters, Nathan Hull, and Mary Fay are the other individuals. If you remember, Nathan Hull and Mary Fay were married, and both were heroin overdose victims. The *only* things tying all these individuals together are the tentacle tattoo and the fact they all overdosed on Prussian Black. And, Delarosa has the tentacle, so there must be a connection."

"That's an interesting approach. I would prefer you went with a partner, Jardine."

"I know, sir," she argued, "but I believe Tony would be a distraction. I want to see Frierson's and Delarosa's reactions without anyone there, in case there's a conflict of interest. I can say I have a few follow-up questions and it won't take long."

Conrad sat back and thought about what she said. "Fine. Schedule a time to meet with both Frierson and Delarosa. I want an update later next week."

"Yes, sir."

"And, Jardine?"

"Yes, sir?"

"Be. Extra. Careful." The concern and command in his voice was unmistakable.

She nodded and left.

- - -- --- -----

<u>Tuesday, February 9, 2021</u>

The wind howled, stinging her cheeks as she quickly walked to the A.T.F. building. The temperatures dropped into the single digits, and this was one of the few days she wished she was in her cubicle. But she had several leads to follow up on, and she refused to let the weather discourage her.

"Detective Jardine, how are you?" Taylor smiled down at her as he extended his hand.

He greeted her in the lobby and escorted her to the conference room.

"I'm good. How are you?"

He continued to smile at her. "Not bad. Carl will be down in a second." As they walked into the conference room, he shut the door, then touched her on the shoulder. "Between you and me, he's been on edge since last week. He's also scheduled a three-week vacation starting next week, which is strange."

"How's that?"

"He *never* takes a vacation. He takes a day or two here and there, but that's it. And, we haven't found anything connecting him to the people you're searching for, but it could change."

"Thank you for letting me know."

He nodded. They chatted for a few more minutes until Frierson finally walked in, taking a seat opposite of her. She studied his mannerisms. His hands were together on top of the desk; his cuticles, freshly torn.

"Mr. Frierson, I have a couple of follow-up questions from last week."

"I told you," Carl protested, "I don't know anything about those missing persons."

"I believe you, sir," she lied. "I have some other photos of individuals I wanted to show you."

"Oh," he replied, pausing slightly. "Okay."

She put several folders on the table. She opened the first one and slid it over to Carl. "Do you recognize this person?

This is Chris Pinick."

"That's the professor's son."

"Did you know him personally?"

"No, ma'am. The professor showed me pictures of him. That's all."

"Okay." She opened one of the other three folders and slid it to him.

"This is Damian Winters. From what we know of him, he had a long criminal record and may have had ties to the Fasciata Order, an organization responsible for spreading Prussian Black heroin. Mr. Winters had part of a blue-lined octopus tattooed on him. This specific tattoo may be the Fasciata's signature, but we're still investigating the connection."

She noticed Carl's complexion fade into a whitish hue. She opened the next folder and slid it over.

"This is Nathan Hull, an overdose victim we found on Starr Island. He also had the same type and style of tattoo on him. He also died of a Prussian Black overdose."

Carl's foot started to tap. She slid the next folder over.

"And this is Mary Fay, Mr. Hull's wife. She was another overdose victim. Guess what she died of? Prussian Black heroin. And she also had the same tentacle tattoo."

"Wh-what does this have to do with me?" She noted the sweat near his temple.

"Do you recognize any of these people?"

"No, I mean, yes. I mean—Chris looks familiar, but I don't know those other three."

"Are you sure?"

"Ye-yes. Positive."

She noticed his hands under the table in his lap. She could faintly hear him picking at the cuticles.

"Not even since you're the one who provided Dr. Pinick the information he requested on all these individuals?"

Carl glanced at Taylor with a silent plea for help.

"Carl, answer the question."

There was continued silence. Then, suddenly, Carl

blurted out, "Look, I don't know anything! The professor asked me to find some people for him, and I-I did. I didn't know this would turn into an interrogation. I thought I was helping a pathetic, sad, old man."

"That's fine, Mr. Frierson. I wanted to know if you knew anything about these people. That's all. We think our missing persons may be connected to these deceased ones, but we aren't sure yet."

"I-I'm sorry, but I can't help you." He stood up abruptly. "Taylor, man, I gotta get back to those reports and get them filed before I leave on vacation."

"Sure, man, no problem." Taylor dismissed him then stared at AJ. They both stood up. "I really hope he hasn't done something stupid."

"I hope not either. Other than being on edge this last week, how's Mr. Frierson been?"

"Honestly, it's almost as if a fire is lit under his ass now. He's been a perfect role model and has been getting his shit done."

"I guess that's a good thing then."

"Let's hope he continues the new trend. Sorry he couldn't be more helpful."

"No problem, thank you for your time."

AJ felt disappointed as she walked to her car.

Well, shit, other than seeing Taylor, that was a bust. Maybe Delarosa will provide better results.

- - -- --- -----

She pulled up to the prison on Route 3. The short-lived interview with Carl Frierson produced no solid results, and she hoped the second interview of the day would be more productive.

She sat at the table and waited for Delarosa to be escorted into the private interviewing room. From down the hall, she heard the thick rattling of barred doors sliding open and shut followed by the jingling of chains getting louder.

Finally, the escorted inmate came in and sat down in front of her. Martín always grinned wide when he saw her. She studied him, noting he appeared much younger than she first remembered: near-hairless, smooth skin with a healthy tan complexion, fit upper torso, and bright brown eyes. His dark hair was parted and slicked back. Even in the prison pink jumpsuit, he still looked like an over-confident and cocky banker.

"Blues." He raised one eyebrow and cocked a crooked smirk. He fixated on the color of her irises. "Couldn't get enough of me, could you?"

"How've you been, Martín?" She remained un-phased by his disgustingly flirtatious demeanor.

"Better, now I see those beautiful eyes of yours."

"Want something to drink?" She gestured to the plastic cups of soda on the table.

He grabbed a drink and took a sip. "We don't get this pop inside. Tastes good. Like you, I bet."

She ignored the come-on. "Have you thought of any more details you could provide us since we last talked?"

"Only how much I can't wait to get out of here and have some fun again. Maybe you and I can go on a date." He continued to smile, hoping to entice her into his foreplay.

"I need to ask you a few more questions and show you some photos."

"Oh, you don't wanna go on a date with me? You too good for someone like me?" He acted hurt, but she did not fall for it.

"Martín, I'm here to ask more questions about my cases, not flirt with you."

He sat back, his lips pursed. He appeared pissed he did not get more of a response from her. He crossed his arms best the handcuffs would allow.

"I'm not in a talkative mood, *detective*. Guard," he called out with a nod of his head.

She stared at him and watched one of the guards approach. The prisoner wanted to play games. She wanted answers. He wanted to push his boundaries with her, and she needed more information.

He stood up.

"Will you please answer some of my questions, Martín, *por favor?*"

"What do I get out of it, Blues?"

He peered down at her and seemed to enjoy the angle of his view as she stared back at him between sips of her cup. She thought of a compromise. She set her cup back down and leaned against the chair, arching her back slightly.

"Tell you what. You answer my questions, and I'll take my coat off for you."

She had his attention. He gestured for the guard to go away as he sat back down. She nodded to the officer, and he stepped back against the wall. Martín's fingers interlaced and the handcuffs around his wrists clanked on the metal table.

"Fine, what're your questions? I got time," he smirked.

She pulled out several of her folders and showed him a picture of Chris Pinick.

"Do you recognize this person?"

He glanced at the photo, then turned his gaze back to her.

"Yeah, he looks like a cool kid. Looks like someone I've partied with before."

"Do you know what happened to him?"

"Nah," he shook his head. "He disappeared a while back."

"Can you tell me anything about him?"

He shook his head again, relaxed with the questioning. "Nah, Blues. He was some college punk. Really smart, into books and science and shit."

"But you may have partied with him?"

"Eh, maybe. I don't remember much when I party, if ya know what I mean."

She pulled another picture out: Damian Winters. "What about him? Do you recognize this man?"

"Eh, maybe, he used to ride with the other kid, the

science guy. Acted like a head-banger. Both were college brats. That's all I know."

"Do you remember partying with him also?"

"Nah, like I said, I don't remember much."

She took the pictures back and pulled out Nathan Hull's photo. "What about him?" She slid the photo over.

"Unh uh." Martín motioned at her. "Take your coat off first."

"No, you have to answer questions first."

"That's not our deal, Blues."

"Did I put sunglasses on? Answer these questions, and the coat comes off."

Martín studied her and then glanced at the photos. "Nope, I don't know 'im."

She sighed. She knew he played the game hard to win and would not give up the information easily. He knew more than he let on.

"Coat."

She knew she needed to give him something in return. She stood up slowly. Without her eyes leaving his gaze, she slowly unzipped her coat and slid one shoulder out at a time. She purposely pushed her chest up while she slid her arms out of the sleeves. Martín continued to stare. She continued to be disgusted.

"Now we're talkin', Blues."

He wet his lips. She grabbed another folder and pulled an image of Mary Fay out. Before she sat back down, she leaned over the desk, watching Martín's expression as he peered at her chest, and slid the photo to him. Then she sat back down.

"What about her?"

"Heh. Yeah, I recognize this chick."

"What do you know about her?"

"She's Mudo's thing on the side. Some trashy *weta*."

"Mudo? Who's Mudo?"

"No, you owe me something else before I answer." He stared intently at her.

"Fine." She reached for her blouse and placed her hands on the button between her breasts. Martín smiled more until he realized she began buttoning the collar all the way up. Then she reached for her coat again.

"No, no, no, Blues! Mudo's a friend of mine."

She stopped, put her coat back down.

"And?"

"That chick's old man O.D.'ed a while back, so Mudo said he wanted to start hittin' it."

She put her hands back on her collar.

"Mudo had been bangin' her for a while. He would give her the Prussian so he could get favors from her, know what I mean?"

She unbuttoned the collar. "Keep talking."

"One day, Mudo just disappeared. Then the next thing we know, the news said his old woman was found in the woods. An overdose. Gigi was pretty upset."

She slid her hand down and undid the next button. "Who's Gigi?"

"Dunno. Some mutual friend of ours."

"Not good enough, Martín." She fastened the second button back.

"Wait! Gigi's a friend of ours."

She flicked the button away from the fabric to expose the skin underneath.

"He's tight with Fr—. I mean, he's a good friend of our crew. That's all I know about him, I swear!"

"And who's Mudo?" She went down to the third button on her blouse and seductively pulled apart the material.

"He goes by Jose."

"Jose Perales?"

"Yeah, that's it." His eyes never left AJ's breasts. "Jose Perales."

She stared at Martín in disbelief. She leaned back over and took the photo from him. Then she opened her last folder and pulled out another photo. She leaned over again, slid the photo to him, and gave him a clear view of her bra.

"Is this Mudo?"

"Yeah, that's him!" He made no effort to hide the excitement in his voice.

"You're telling me you lied about knowing Jose Perales when we asked you before?"

"What can I say, Blues?" His eyes never left her breasts as his mouth curved in a crooked form.

"And you're saying Jose Perales is Mudo, and he dated Mary Fay, then disappeared before Fay's body was found?"

He nodded repeatedly. She took the photos back and stood up straight, taking away his view of her chest. He snapped out of the sexual trance.

"Thank you. We're done." She rebuttoned her blouse.

"Blues! Aww, come on!" He made no effort to hide the irritation and anger in his voice.

"What else can you tell me?"

"Unbutton the shirt again."

"No, you had your fun."

"That's fucked up, Blues!"

"I know. So are you." She fed on his cockiness and served it right back to him.

"You played me!" His voice pitched with anger.

"Of course, I did. We had a — mutual — agreement. You gave me what I wanted, and now I don't need you anymore."

Martín stood up quickly and aggressively. It did not phase her but caused the guard to move forward and grab him on one side. It only incited Martín more.

"You *puta!*"

She understood the insult. Instead of acting rational and ignoring it, she pushed Martín a little more.

"Sticks and stones, love. But it's a good nickname for you. I hope they're really taking good care of you on the inside. And *inside.*"

Martín jerked forward. The violent force caused the guard to lose his grip, falling backward. The inmate flipped the table on her, spilling the cups of soda across her stomach as she fell to the ground on her back. He threw the table across at the guard. Even though his hands were shackled, he jumped on top of her, futilely reaching for her neck. The guard scrambled back up and grabbed him before he could hurt her. Martín kept yelling and screaming at her, then spit on her before a couple of other guards came in and restrained him.

"Wait until I get out of here! I'll show you what a fucking *puta* you are, Blues! I'll show your momma! I'll show your whole fucking family!"

She quickly got up and dusted herself off. Her hands quivered, but she hid them before anyone saw. She looked at the spit on her chest, secretly pleased. She kept her composure and returned the smirk. "See you soon, Martín."

She watched as the guards dragged him out.

"Ma'am, are you okay?" one of the guards asked her.

She nodded her head. "Oh, yeah. He's probably not, though."

- - -- --- -----

The wind howled and slapped with rage as she walked to her car. It made her wet blouse that much more uncomfortable, regardless of the winter coat covering it. When she reached her car, she popped the trunk and dug through some spare clothes she kept in the back. She quickly grabbed an I.S.B. t-shirt and got in the car, changing shirts while the car warmed up.

Got you, you bastard! Assault on a government official and DNA collected from the assault! Now we can put you in C.O.D.I.S. Maybe even add some time to your sentence. Fucker...

She placed her wet shirt in an evidence bag, labeled and sealed it, then tossed it in the back seat.

I'll take it to Peter tomorrow.

She sat in her car for a few minutes as it continued to warm up. She pulled her smartphone out and checked her emails: miscellaneous tasks, company meetings coming up, and other inter-office memos filled her inbox.

She saw an email from Conrad and clicked on it:

> From: C McMillan
> To: A Jardine
> Subject: Fwd: Carmicle found
> Date: Today at 08:34 a.m.
>
> Jardine,
> See below.
> -CM

She scrolled down to the forwarded email. It was from Larsson, Tony's boss:

> Conrad,
> Tony just reached out. One of his CIs ran into Angela Carmicle. He's picking her up this afternoon and taking her into police protection.
> -Lars
> P.S. See you at the range Saturday.

She reread the email and hit 'Reply'.

> From: A Jardine
> To: C McMillan
> Subject: Re: Fwd: Carmicle found
> Date: Today at 08:55 a.m.
>
> That's good news! I'll text Tony in a bit.
>
> Update this AM:
>
> Carl Frierson: no luck. Denied everything. Extra nervous after seeing pics. Knows more than what he claims.
>
> Martín Delarosa: Recognized all overdose victims. Said

they all partied together. Said Pinick was a science nerd. Perales is bf of Mary Fay, disappeared before she was found. Mentioned someone named Gigi. Almost said someone else's name. Will look into further.

Octopus: Called around to several New England pet stores yesterday. Found one store with info on someone who specializes in the blue-lined. Heading there now to check it out.

Be back in office later this PM.
~AJ

- - -- --- -----

She never expected the structure at 6765 Granville Road in the Town of Warner to be a massive mansion cut from the picturesque mountainside. Nor had she expected to see such a spectacular view overlooking the western horizon as she pulled up in the paved driveway.

She parked next to a couple of expensive cars, walked up the stairs to the oversized front doors, and rang the doorbell. As she waited, she peeked through the glass side panels to study the interior of the home. The mansion appeared immaculate, marble, and worth more than her town's police department were allocated in a decade. She felt intimidated by the luxury.

She heard the locks click and watched as a housekeeper opened the door.

"May I help you?"

"Hi. Yes, I'm Detective Jardine with Major Crimes from the Investigative Services Bureau. Is the owner of the house available?"

"Yes, please come in." He motioned for her to come in and then shut the door. The bangs and clicks of locking mechanisms echoed loudly everywhere. "Follow me."

AJ scanned the foyer and double spiraling staircase. The

entryway opened into a massive space filled with rich artwork and sculptures. Sounds continued to bounce off hard surfaces.

She followed the housekeeper. His shoes clopped across the floor, the sound echoed from all directions. Her thoughts conjured uncomfortable mind demons.

Not now! Don't think about that. Don't think about Michael. Take a deep breath! Focus on your task.

"Please wait here, detective."

The man's voice startled her and brought her back to the present.

AJ stood in the entryway of a large atrium and heard the housekeeper walk away. Cathedral-style bay windows soared three stories above her. She counted eight elongated glass panels which created a swooping arc and view of the mountainside. She could only imagine how beautiful the sunsets were from that location.

She continued to study the rest of the atrium. More fine art and sculptures lined the walls. More marble flooring reflected natural light in every direction.

In the center of the atrium stood eight fifty-five-gallon saltwater aquariums which formed an octagon. She stared at them, then walked around each, investigating the creatures. Black lights illuminated the multi-colored aquatic life within.

She stopped at the last aquarium and bent in to inspect the contents. She saw a tiny blue-lined octopus hiding in the sand. It glided over to her and appeared as curious about her as she was of it. Its small tentacles suctioned to the glass, and she touched a finger on the opposite side. She watched the octopus pulse with color.

"Her name is Lady Lusca."

The woman's voice caused AJ to jump, spin around, and stand at attention facing the direction of the sound. She saw a beautiful woman standing in the entryway. Her tanned skin glowed and contrasted the expensive white pantsuit she wore. Her hair was pulled back in a bun; her persona, flawless. She was stunning, as if she stepped off a red-carpet event. AJ would not be surprised if the woman had a home in Hollywood, not New Hampshire.

"My apologies, Ms. Jardine. I did not mean to startle you." The woman's Latin accent flowed effortlessly from her lips.

She walked closer to AJ and held out a hand, giving the detective a firm handshake.

"Valda Bigollo, Vice-President of Casa Fait Research. How may I help you?"

"Ms. Bigollo, I apologize for bothering you, but I was given your name from a pet shop in Boston. They said they sold you some venomous octopuses, particularly the blue-lined. I'm assuming these are the ones?" She pointed to the aquarium.

"Yes, of course. I bought those. This is where we house our cephalopods."

"They're gorgeous creatures." AJ continued to admire the marine animals, leaning in to play with Lady Lusca again.

"I grew up in the Dominican Republic. My blood flows with the Caribbean. That's why I only have saltwater aquariums. I've grown fond of octopuses over the years and have spent half my life dedicated to them." AJ was oblivious to the woman studying her.

"Does the natural light in this space affect the water quality of the aquariums? I'd assume the extra sunlight would be detrimental to temperature and algae content?"

Valda smiled again. "All the atrium windows are tinted, helping to minimize the UV rays coming in. We tinted the aquarium windows as an added precaution. We even control the humidity levels and artificial temperature in this space to ensure the quality of our marine life."

"Wow! They're stunning creatures. It's hard to believe something so small can kill over twenty-one people."

"Did you know the blue-lined octopus and her cousins are typically nocturnal, shy little creatures? They only envenomate prey *or* when they feel threatened." Valda paused. "Detective, may I ask what your visit is about?"

She stood back up. "Have you heard of a designer heroin called Prussian Black?" Valda shook her head. "We suspect octopus venom is being used in the drug. We're trying to track down the source and that's what led me here."

Valda smiled softly. "Oh, I see. I understand where perhaps some confusion is coming from. My companies *do* extract the venom from our octopuses. Please, follow me."

She led AJ to a private, spacious library. Each wall was adorned with paintings of octopus erotica. A computer and research station occupied a corner of the room. Valda searched for, then grabbed, a thick folder and handed it to the detective.

"My company works with several research facilities from around the world. Our mission is to find and develop antidotes to various venoms and poisons, both natural and manmade. I'm personally involved with research for a tetrodotoxin antivenom specific to the blue-lined octopus and her cousins."

"I thought there's no antidote?"

"Yet," Valda added, smiling. "That's what we're trying to help create. My scientists extract the venom, study the chemical makeup, and then try to find other chemical compounds to counter the effects. They study octopuses like other scientists study venomous snakes or insects."

"How do you extract venom from an octopus? They're so small."

"The blue-lined uses bacteria to create its venom and releases it one of two ways. One, they can discharge saliva into the vicinity of their victim. The saliva can get absorbed into the skin. Or, two, they use their beak and inject the venom. Bites are typically small, painless puncture wounds.

"We have better results by extracting through the second method. My researchers are trained to handle the octopuses with care. They have a pronged instrument which allows the tentacles to be gently moved out of the way and expose the beak. They then utilize a method similar to the way a snake's venom is extracted. None of my octopuses are ever harmed."

"What can you tell me about TTX?"

"I can tell you we've found TTX in several parts of the octopus, including the eggs. I can also tell you that the neurotoxin contains various amines such as serotonin, dopamine, tyramine, and histamine."

"What is tyramine?"

"That's a compound that can be found in foods, like aged cheeses and chocolate. It can sometimes cause migraines and high blood pressure. We're researching cheese and chocolate allergies at the moment."

"And what happens to the venom after it's extracted? Do you study it here?"

"Not always. My scientists do most of the extraction here and my researchers will then transport the vials directly to the universities in need of the venom. It's too dangerous to mail the samples, so I only allow hand-delivery. My company has other extraction facilities across the United States."

"Have you noticed any samples missing? Do you think someone's using your specimens for heroin production?"

Valda shook her head. "No, that's highly unlikely. My company has several checks and balances as the venom is processed. I keep highly detailed records of everything and only employ people I personally trust. Casa Fait Research has a solid reputation for quality which *must* be upheld in this industry. Here." Valda grabbed a pen and notepaper. She scribbled something down and then handed the paper to AJ. "This is my accountant's name and phone number. He can pull all the details for you, including a list of all the facilities we do business with as well as a list of our employees. We want to help in any way we can."

"Thank you, Ms. Bigollo." AJ handed the folder back, but Valda stopped her.

"Please, you can keep it. It's an extra copy and goes into

detail about what we do. The information may help in your investigation."

Valda led AJ back to the front door.

"Thank you again, Ms. Bigollo."

"It's my pleasure, Detective Jardine. Please contact me if you have further questions. Good luck with your investigation."

AJ walked to her car and got in. She thumbed through the folder, then set it down on the front seat next to her. Her mind mulled over the information. Valda seemed genuinely helpful. AJ had no reason not to trust her.

- - -- --- -----

She hit the garage door opener as she drove down the driveway and parked. She grabbed everything from the front seat and went into the house. Before she could set everything down on her bed, her phone pinged with a text message. She glanced down to see Tony's name.

> Heading to Laconia
> to find Angie. Not
> far from you now.
> Can swing by and
> get you. Wanna join me?

She thought about it for a few seconds. It was still early in the day.

> Sure. Text me when
> you get here. ~aj

> Be there in 5

- - -- --- -----

"What do you mean she's disappeared again?"

"That's exactly what I mean. My C.I. was confident we could find her at her aunt's house in Nashua, but when I got there, they said she was gone. The aunt's step-son thinks Angie was headed up to Laconia to visit her mom. Have you had better luck than me?"

"Actually, yes." She smiled. As she told him about the events of the day, she noticed Tony's expression change. He became quiet with uncharacteristic anger. "Tony, are you mad at me?"

"Do you have ANY idea how DANGEROUS and STUPID that was?"

"Why are you yelling at me?"

"AJ, you were attacked by an inmate! It could've escalated into more violence!" He glanced back and forth from the road and her as he drove north and continued to lecture her. She grinned more, and it appeared to confuse him. "WHY are you smiling?"

"Because I have his DNA now. He spit on my shirt and I'm giving it to Peter tomorrow. I'm filing an assault charge on him with the evidence. If he has anything to do with raping Angie, we can keep him locked up for a long time."

"Dammit, Jardine, that's not a good idea."

"Why? Martín's an asshole. He deserves to stay locked up."

"You know his lawyers will get him out and they will dig up shit you don't want made public."

"I don't care. I don't have anything to hide."

"You say that now, but you don't want to try them. It's a bad idea."

"I don't care if it's a bad idea."

"You're too goddamn stubborn sometimes! Fuck!" He slammed his hand on the steering wheel in frustration.

She stared, confused and wondering where the anger came from. Then she became defensive, pissed at Tony's reaction. She looked out the window as the car drove past dirty snow.

"I know what I'm doing."

"No, you DON'T, Ameena," he argued. "That was fucking stupid to tease him. What the hell got into you — opening your shirt up to provoke him?"

"Tony, calm the fuck down," she countered. "I was fine. I knew exactly what I was doing. I wanted him to attack me. I wanted his DNA and I got it!"

Tony bit his lip and remained silent the rest of the short trip. When he parked the car, he leaned over the center console and grabbed her by the shoulders.

She stared at him. She noticed more gray hairs peppering his beard.

"Don't go after Martín. I'm *begging* you."

She saw fear as his eyes pleaded with her, and she felt the stirrings in her stomach again.

"Why, Tony? What aren't you telling me, because you're keeping a lot from me."

He shook his head. "I — I can't tell you."

"That's not good enough. You don't have to worry about me."

Without warning, he leaned in and kissed her, then pulled back to take in her eyes. Her stomach leaped from the unexpected excitement. He leaned in again with another kiss and she reciprocated the movement.

He let go of her shoulders and pressed her body between his and the passenger seat. He kissed his way to her chin and ran his beard against her jaw, pressing his cheek into hers. The sides of their faces enjoyed the intimate touch. His mouth rested near her ear.

"You want me to let you in?" he whispered.

Her hands felt his body. Her teeth grazed his earlobe. Her thoughts solely focused on him as she lost her senses in the moment.

"Yes." Her answer lingered before he replied.

"I love you," he whispered. "I *always* will. No matter what happens."

She froze, stunned. She held a breath. "I…"

In all the time they had known each other, he never said he loved her until then.

"I…" She did not know how to reply.

He quickly pulled back and planted a final kiss on her lips before sitting back in the driver's seat. And as suddenly as it began, it was over. He took a deep breath and recomposed himself.

"Let's see if Angie's here."

- - -- --- -----

The car ride back to her house remained quiet. Tony did not appear to be in a talkative mood. Angie never arrived at her mother's home, and no one had seen her since she left her aunt's house in Nashua a few hours prior.

Tony drove down her road. She stared at him in the darkness, hoping for any light to read his face.

"Tony? Are you okay?"

"No. No, I'm not."

He pulled into her driveway and snaked downhill to the house. He parked and waited for her to exit, but she did not move.

"Please talk to me, Tony."

"I think I said enough earlier."

She leaned in to kiss him on the lips, but he held rigidly and did not return the affection. She pulled back and studied him again, hurt from the rejection. He grabbed one of her hands and squeezed it.

"Not today," he whispered. The porch light caught the reflection of a tear in his eye.

She nodded, then exited the car in silence. She left him in the driveway as she walked into the house.

- - -- --- -----

Ameena laid in bed, staring up at the ceiling. The house was still, save the oil furnace and clinking pipes of the wall heaters. She could not fall asleep; her mind still processed the day's events. Each time she focused on all three interviews, her mind found an excuse to think of Tony. She suddenly felt swept away in the emotions and realized she was holding her breath again.

Damn him! Why did he have to tell me he loved me? He's NEVER said that!

The left and right sides of her brain played tug-of-war with her emotions and logic. She still distrusted him and hated him for her father's accident, but she still found him attractive.

"Love and hate are forged from the same metal." That's what Copernicus said. Why, then, do I feel like I'm holding a sword in each hand?

The push-pull of emotional thought kept her awake longer than she cared.

- - -- --- -----

CHAPTER SIXTEEN: ANGIE

<u>Wednesday, February 10, 2021</u>

She grabbed her phone off the nightstand and stared at the overly bright screen. A phone number with a New Hampshire area code appeared, but she did not recognize the number.

"Hello?"

"Detective Jardine?"

"Yes?" she answered, trying to place the familiar voice. "Who's this?"

"Angie Carmicle."

"Angie!" AJ sat up in her bed, more alert. "We've been looking for you for months."

"I know," the woman whispered.

"Are you okay?"

"No. No, I'm not."

"Where are you?"

"They're going to kill me." She could hear Angie crying on the other end.

"Angie! Where are you? I'll come get you right now!"

"The Fasciata. They have me. They have a message for you." The unmistakable fear in the woman's voice sent chills down AJ's neck.

"Angie, let me talk to them. Let me—"

"No! No no NOOO!" AJ heard a thud as the phone dropped. She heard more screaming, then—

BOOM!

"ANGIE!" The screaming stopped and the only thing she could hear was faint crackling noises. Then footsteps. Then a deep disguised voice.

"De-tec-tive. Jar-dine. That. Was. A. War-ning."

"Who is this! Where's Angie???"

"You. Know. What. Hap-pened. To her. Back. Off. The Fa-sci-at-a. Or. More. Will. Die."

Click.

- - -- --- -----

She arrived at her office shortly before five o'clock and started contacting law enforcement departments across several towns. She scoured databases and news sites for any mention of a woman's body or murder. Conrad exited the elevator sometime after five that morning and she updated him on her progress.

"Should I call Angie's mom and let her know what happened?"

"No, Jardine. Until we have a body to go with the name, we don't contact the family. We don't even know if the phone call was real or a ruse. Keep checking. Contact the hospitals and fire departments and see if anyone's been brought in for a shooting."

"Yes, sir." She turned to leave.

"And Jardine?"

"Yes, sir?"

"That stunt at the prison? Careless, detective."

"I know, sir, but I got his DNA. We can process it and use it as evidence against him if he's raped anyone else. You did say we have cold cases—including serial rapes and assaults—needing to be worked."

"Where's the evidence?"

"The bag's in my car. I'll go get it and bring it up to Peter."

She left his office and went down to her car. After several

minutes of searching, she gave up and went back in the building.

"Sir?"

"Yes, Jardine?" He continued to study his computer monitor.

"I can't find the evidence bag. I checked everywhere in my car and it's not there." He stopped and looked up at her from above the rims of his glasses. "I might've left it at the house."

"We'll deal with it later, Jardine. Focus on Ms. Carmicle for now."

"Yes, sir."

"And, AJ?"

"Yes, sir?"

"Find Tony. We need him today."

- - -- --- -----

"Sir?"

"What is it now, Jardine?"

"Got the call from Tony. They found her body."

"Shit." He took off his glasses and rubbed his eyes.

"Tony's almost here to pick me up. We're heading to the scene, and I'll document what I can, sir."

"Who found her?"

"Tony said one of his C.I.s contacted him. It was a body dump in Manchester along the Merrimack."

"Keep me posted on your progress, Jardine."

"Yes, sir."

She quickly grabbed her things and headed down to the lobby when she saw Tony pull up by the front sidewalk. She got in the car, and before she could say anything, he said, "Don't ask why it took me so long to get back to you this morning."

"Tony, FIVE hours before you could get here?" She stared at him.

He rolled his eyes. "You did anyway. I'm sorry. I had to

go to Boston last night to run a lead down and didn't get back home 'til two. I've had little sleep and my phone's been ringing off the hook this morning."

"Fine. What did your C.I. tell you?"

"That the body's in bad shape, AJ." She studied him and noted the extra distance in his eyes. She knew he was tired and sleep-deprived.

"About yesterday in the car..."

"Don't. Not today." His eyes never left the road. "Let's have this conversation under different circumstances. I'm exhausted and not able to think."

The rest of the car ride was in silence.

- - -- --- -----

It took several minutes before they could push through the crowds gathered and get to the police barricades. Reporters were camped out in their vans as close as they were allowed. An occasional journalist recognized AJ and questioned her—live, on camera—about her involvement with the body. A news helicopter roared above the scene. Several spectators took video and photographs on their smartphones. A media circus ensued around her.

The pair stood near the shore of the Merrimack River, south of the Amoskeag Dam. Angie was found floating face down near the shallow, downstream bank of the river. Her body was stuck between a few rocks. Her extremities twitched in the rapids.

Officers erected plastic fencing and a tent to conceal the sight of the body and wait for the medical examiner. When they finally made it to the scene, AJ gasped and froze at the horror she did not expect to see.

She had seen something similar before—the mutilation at the Rune Killer's dump sites—and it always unsettled her. She fixated on Angie's body and tuned out all the noise around her.

"AJ?" Tony's voice snapped her out of her thoughts.

"Sorry," she whispered. Her eyes never left the corpse. She took a deep breath and proceeded for a closer examination.

Angie floated in the icy water, naked and stripped of any dignity or decency. Her frozen hair stuck to the side of her body, matted and tangled with dead leaves. A large bloodless hole opened the back of her head. AJ knew the woman watched her own execution.

Think of her as a random victim. Desensitize yourself from this like all the others. Don't focus on her as a person. Focus on the work. It's only another body. She repeated the words to herself several times.

She processed and collected what she could. She hoped some of the trace evidence would help them pinpoint where upstream the body was dumped in the river. She doubted — given the amount of ice and slush — Angie would have been dumped too far north.

The M.E. finally arrived and assessed the body. She watched as he and another officer flipped the body over. Her stomach gripped her intestines at the worsened condition and depravity of the crime.

Angie's face was swollen from multiple beatings; bruises were fresh, recent before death. Thin ligature marks wrapped around her wrists and ankles; she was restrained while being beaten. She saw the single bullet hole in the woman's temple; given the exit wound, she doubted the bullet would be found at all.

There were deep cuts across Angie's body. Her breast tissue was pulled back as if someone tried to remove her areoles and nipples but peeled the skin back instead. AJ saw more lacerations across her stomach, inner thighs, and shoulders. She assumed Angie had also been sexually assaulted; the wounds were too personal and intimately inflicted.

And the more she stared, the more her mind pulled her into her own near-death experience. She felt her face flush and her blood pressure rose. She started feeling dizzy and quickly excused herself before she threw up. She walked several meters away and stared at the rapids coming from near the dam. The watery noise helped muffle the commotion behind her.

"Hey," she heard Tony's voice say. He touched her shoulder. "You okay? You started turning green back there."

She peered up at him and saw the tenderness and concern.

"I'm fine. I needed to catch my breath. I wasn't expecting to see her in this bad of a condition."

"I'm sorry."

"For what?"

"I shouldn't've brought you here. I didn't think this would have such an effect on you."

"I'm fine, Tony. I promise."

He reached for her hand, but she withdrew.

"Not today," she whispered. They stared at each other until the scene called them back.

- - -- --- -----

With the lack of sleep and the emotionally draining crime scene, she went home to take a nap early in the afternoon. At dinnertime, Jamilla came into the bedroom to wake her.

"Ameena, habibti, dinner is ready," she softly spoke, rousing her daughter.

"Ungh," she stretched, trying to wake up.

"I'll give you a few minutes to wake up. Dinner will be on the table soon."

"Okay, Momma."

Ameena slowly began waking up. Her mind analyzed the events of the day when she suddenly remembered the evidence bag with her blouse in it. She scoured her room for the missing item and could not find it anywhere. She quickly searched everywhere in the house, including the basement and garage. When she came back up, Jamilla was setting the table.

"What's wrong, sweetheart?"

"Momma, do you remember if I brought an evidence bag in the house yesterday?"

"No, dear. I haven't found anything like that."

Eoghan and Derek came down the stairs. She asked them the same question.

"What did the bag look like?" Derek asked.

"It was a clear bag with an orange band across the top. It's sealed with one of my shirts in it."

"No, Mom, we haven't seen it. You weren't carrying anything like that yesterday."

"Huh," she thought out loud. "Then I have no idea where I put it."

With the end of that discussion, everyone sat around the table for dinner. Jamilla prepared a simple meal called *mujadarrah*, a rice and lentil dish topped with plain yogurt and pickled turnips. Ameena's mouth watered with the thought of the pickled turnips, though Derek and Jenna made ugly faces.

Everyone retired to their rooms early after dinner. She shut the door to her bedroom and settled in at her laptop. A couple of hours into writing her report on Angie's body she received a text message. She glanced at her phone: unknown caller.

> Hello, I would like to chat
> if you're available. ~nc

"Brazen, I'll give him that," she said under her breath.

> Hi, I'm on my
> laptop at the moment

> Familiar stomping

grounds, then? ~nc

Sure. 5 min.

She finished saving all her documents and then exited out of her applications. She went into the old chatroom window and waited. With a flicker, the room was cloned, and he was there. She did not expect the flush of emotion from seeing his name.

```
NCPoland1543: Good evening, Ameena
Roar317811: Hello, Copernicus
NCPoland1543: I'm sorry to learn of
Angie's death
Roar317811: What do you know about
it?
NCPoland1543: Not enough to help you
NCPoland1543: Yet
Roar317811: The condition of her body
was unsettling. I didn't expect to
see her brutalized in such a manner
NCPoland1543: If I could be your
shield, I'd protect you from those
wounds and war
Roar317811: There would be many
shields needed
NCPoland1543: Then let me be your
armor, wrapped and forged around you
Roar317811: If only you knew...
```

She saw a slight flicker on her computer screen and her mouse moved a couple of centimeters.

"What the fuck?" She watched the movement continue. A D.O.S. window appeared, and code scrolled through.

What the hell is he doing? Should I stop him? No no no. Let's see how this plays out.

A matrix of what appeared to be random characters rambled across the window. Then she recognized a couple of words—the names of files she recently saved. The window disappeared, and a new message popped up in the chatroom.

NCPoland1543: I have downloaded the data you have processed, including the photos
Roar317811: You hacked my laptop!
NCPoland1543: And your phone
NCPoland1543: You know I've been monitoring them for some time now. There's no use getting another laptop or phone. Each can—and would—eventually be linked to me. I can see anyone's cyber activity, with enough time.
Roar317811: …
NCPoland1543: ?
Roar317811: It's frustrating to me. HOW are you doing it?
Roar317811: And more importantly, WHY???
NCPoland1543: The process is complex
Roar317811: Then explain in layman's terms
NCPoland1543: As you wish (more)
NCPoland1543: Let's start with your phone. The device is nothing more than a miniature computer, full of hardware and software. You have the basic operating system running in the background, and various apps either pre-programmed or downloaded. I can piggy-back onto any app installed on your phone. You could go to the App Store and download ANYTHING you wanted, and I can STILL clone the app you purchase and sabotage your device with malware, code, or anything else I want. By all outward appearances,

your app would still appear and function rather properly, send/receive information the way it was first designed. (more)

NCPoland1543: Now think of this: any laptop, smart TV, or voice-recognition software can easily be tapped into in a similar manner. Your electronics are monitoring you. They listen. And wait. (Think of what the N.S.A. does at this moment.) Some words are pre-programmed, and once spoken, signal the Voice to communicate with you. Now, imagine, if you will, the ability to re-program a few vital words. You could mention—verbally or written—a word like "Fasciata" or "Angie" or any critical word related to your case, and your devices would trigger a set of sub-commands and then relay the data to an external location, such as my servers or cloud service (more)

Roar317811: And this is why the Orders use keywords such as "Merchants" or "Craftsmen"? They're trying to avoid words which could get flagged?

NCPoland1543: Precisely!

NCPoland1543: This is what modern warfare looks like: not missiles flying across vast stretches of land to drop bombs, but the right algorithms and series of numbers. Just the correct number of Ones. And Zeros.

Roar317811: You make it sound terrifying…

NCPoland1543: IT IS! It's chilling, and I've seen the devastation done.

I've witnessed the effects of
calculated attacks. Characters you
press with the tips of your fingers
are keys to vast spaces which unlock
horror and wonder. It's almost
incomprehensible to fathom. (more)
NCPoland1543: Why am I doing this?
Everything you do on your tablet and
phone is within, and will always be
within, my ability to monitor,
because I must keep you safe. You're
in danger of finding that which does
not want to be found. This goes
deeper than you are aware. I will
keep you as safe as you allow me. I
have not—and will never—betray your
trust, however minute it may be at
the moment.
*Roar317811: Do you hack other
government laptops?*
NCPoland1543: If I want, but there's
no need. I've learned that the higher
the rank in the office, the less
digital footprint there is.

*Hmmm. It makes a lot of sense. Conrad's always writing
things down on a pad. I think he even has a Polaroid camera in his
car. But why does Copernicus want MY devices? Why me?
Wouldn't he find what he wants with someone else?*

*Roar317811: So basically, you've
taken away my freedom to choose to
have you in my life? I am forced—
against my will—to be connected to
you?*
NCPoland1543: That is not what this
is meant to be, Ameena
*Roar317811: And what if I asked you
to permanently go away? What if I
ignore you?*

NCPoland1543: My heart could not bear
the thought
Roar317811: And what of my heart? I
cannot bare my heart to you. Or
anyone.
NCPoland1543: Our losses are
unbearable
Roar317811: Our losses?
NCPoland1543: Yours is Michael. Mine
is someone else.

She watched the cursor blink and felt the tears build at
the sight of her husband's name.

Roar317811: Did you know him? Did you
work with him???
NCPoland1543: I knew OF him
NCPoland1543: I knew what he meant to
many others, besides yourself.
NCPoland1543: I knew he was deep
undercover. And I know it was his
work which got him killed, in more
ways than one.
Roar317811: I don't understand. What
do you mean "more ways than one"?
NCPoland1543: The same organisation
which employs you, is the one
responsible for his murder.
Roar317811: I'm working with my
husband's killers?????
NCPoland1543: Not directly
NCPoland1543: However, they did
nothing to prevent the hits from
being carried out. They knew the
dangers, but they ignored the
evidence I brought them.
Roar317811: I think I'm going to be
sick

Ameena swallowed the bile and emotions back into her

stomach. She stared at the computer for several moments, lost in thought until she heard the muffled ping of another reply.

> NCPoland1543: Are you still there?
> *Roar317811: Yes*
> *Roar317811: I don't know what to think right now*
> NCPoland1543: Neither did I, at first.
> NCPoland1543: You want to know if you can trust me. Then let me give you proof. I'll crack the door for you to see in.
> NCPoland1543: Ask Mr. McMillan about the Newtonian Collaborative
> *Roar317811: The Newtonian Collaborative?*
> NCPoland1543: NC is darker than you know
> NCPoland1543: Words of advice: DO NOT DO A DIGITAL SEARCH FOR IT! Do NOT ask around the office. The name itself is so secretive, most detectives don't know what it is or have never heard of it. ONLY ask your Deputy Director as securely and secretive as you can.
> *Roar317811: ok*
> NCPoland1543: Find out about the NC, and then contact me, here, and we'll chat more.
> NCPoland1543: I promise, now and always

The screen flickered.

> *Roar317811: Wait! I wanted to talk to you some more!*

She waited several minutes, but he was gone. She grabbed her phone and stared at the front-facing camera.

"Copernicus?"

No response.

She looked up at her laptop, but there was still no reply.

"Copernicus? I—" She sighed. "I hope you truly are trying to protect me. I hope you're telling me the truth. And, if you can hear me, thank you. I wish you knew how much this means to me."

For the first time in years, she finally had a lead into her husband's unsolved murder. When Michael died, the F.B.I. investigated the death and arrested a potential suspect. However, with the lack of concrete evidence linking the suspect to his murder, the government let the person go. She put her faith in the organization, but over time, there was less and less communication with the agency. Slowly, the case became buried under taller stacks of paperwork. It was eventually put in a stack of other cold case files, then filed in a storage box, then placed in a large warehouse in a remote building somewhere in the country.

By the time she finished overanalyzing everything in her brain, sleep beckoned. Her mind rambled through a near infinite amount of possibilities and imaginative ideas of what the Newtonian Collaborative could be.

Her mind had much to process.

- - -- --- -----

Tuesday, February 16, 2021

Conrad pushed their weekly meeting back another week. He participated in a two-week conference in various cities across the U.S., and she knew he would ignore correspondence. She could not email or call him and ask about the Newtonian Collaborative; it was a conversation to be done in person, at the right opportunity.

Instead, she set a meeting with Cassie to go over Angie's autopsy results. The medical examiner greeter her with her usual chipper demeanor, but the best friend immediately knew something was wrong.

"Alright, missy. Tell me what's wrong."

"Do I have a choice?"

"Can you sneeze with your eyes open?"

"Uh…"

"Sweetie, the answer is no, you can't." Cassie printed the report copies for her.

AJ spilled the story about the interviews, the lost evidence bag, and then the passionate kiss with Tony.

She could not bring herself to reveal the conversations with Copernicus; those were of an intimate nature she did not want to share with anyone, and only Conrad knew the pertinent information.

"Wwoooww. Just. WOW." There was a long pause as Cassie, still stunned, stared at AJ. "Holy shit, girl."

"I know, right? I've been swimming with all these things jumbled in my brain."

"I mean. Tony. WOW."

"Yeah, I know." AJ took a deep sigh.

"But Tony? WOW!"

"You've already said that."

"I know, but WOW!"

"Cassie?"

"WOW!"

"Cassie!" AJ blushed. She had not seen her friend so flustered since she and Tony dated the previous year.

Cassie started giggling like a little girl and sang, "You

and Tony, sittin' in a tree. F-U-C—"

"CASSIE!"

AJ laughed at her and stopped her from continuing, though the thought brought a deep crimson out in her cheeks. The medical examiner made sexual motions and gyrated against the detective before AJ pushed her away.

"Come on, AJ, tell me again about how *hot* and *heavy* you guys have gotten before. I know you guys have made *looove* before."

"Cassie!" AJ laughed some more, "We haven't had sex — well, besides—"

"Oh my, look at the eight-nine flavors of flustered on you!"

"We've been good, I swear!" AJ took the reports and started fanning her face.

"You know I love you, right?" Cassie batted her eyes.

"I know, I know."

"I have to bust your chops from time to time. If Tony was my type, I would've jumped his bones a looong time ago. Just sayin'."

AJ sighed. "I *am* attracted to him, Cass. A big part of me wants him and wants the intimacy, but I—I can't right now. You know that." Her mood changed as she thought of Michael.

"I know, sweetie. I know." Cassie changed the subject. "Hey, when do you want to come to dinner with me and Nadine? We need to discuss the wedding plans."

"What about this weekend?"

"I'll check Nadine's schedule and make sure we can still meet up. By the way, how's your dad doing? Is he improving from the physical therapy?"

"Yeah, it's definitely helping. He still gets quite winded from time to time, though. I thought he'd be better by now."

"Honey, you know sometimes it takes longer to heal when the wounds go deep."

"You're right. I know."

"Okay. Ready to talk shop now?" Cassie's demeanor

changed as she took a more serious tone. AJ nodded. "Are you sure? I know you said the scene disturbed you. This is NOT going to be better."

"I'm sure. I can do this."

"Okay, but if you need to stop, let me know."

With that signal, Cassie went into the cold room and wheeled out Angie's body. She slowly unzipped the body bag and pulled the plastic back for the detective to take a good look. The body appeared much different since being cleaned and processed. Cassie carefully brushed and smoothed Angie's hair. All wounds were sutured, though there was nothing she could do for the damage to the woman's face. AJ never noticed all the tattoos before.

"Oh. She looks more peaceful now."

"I cleaned her up best I could. The victim's mother wants to come see her before the body is transported to the funeral home."

"Is that a good idea?"

"No. Not in the least bit. But I respect the family's wishes. They'll be here later this morning. I know they wanted to bury her last week, but I wanted the extra time to be thorough."

"What did you find out?"

"Let's start with the tox panel. Page three of the report."

AJ scanned the toxicology section. "Everything here's clean. I don't understand. I thought she'd have coke or heroin in her blood."

"No, she didn't have any drugs in her system. Not even aspirin. Considering the viciousness of her wounds on her breasts and inner thighs, I did a rape kit." Cassie went into details about the damage, then said, "I found semen and ran DNA. AJ, there were three donors."

"*Three*? She was raped by *three* guys?"

"Yes. And tortured, repeatedly. She was strapped down, probably in a chair of some sort. Look at her ankles and wrists. See how there are deeper striations across the front and they fade away towards the back? That's because she was struggling to break free. Based on the pattern left on her skin, I'd say probably zip ties were used. She also has several circular burns on her body caused by cigarettes or cigars being extinguished on her.

"She'd been punched several times in the stomach and chest, the discoloration you see was caused from that. I noticed one of her ribs had a hairline fracture, assuming that's from the beating she took. Of course, it's obvious from her face the assailants did not stop at her tor — Are you okay?"

AJ stared at the wounds, her face ashen. Her eyes teared. "Yeah, I'm fine. Please, keep going."

"Sure, sweetie. They managed to knock out two of her teeth. I swabbed the inside of her mouth and her gums. Believe it or not, I found DNA. It matched one of the semen donors."

"What can you tell me about the DNA?"

"Male, obviously. European descent, mostly Italian with some Portuguese. Irish. All Caucasian."

"What about the cuts?"

"The cuts were ragged. A serrated blade was used — most likely to inflict as much pain as possible. She had deep cuts on both sides of each breast, almost as if the assailants were carving them off. But, the wounds were not necessarily deep. So, I don't think they were trying to remove the breasts or genitalia. I think they were only humiliating her as part of the assault. There were more cuts through her hip area, lower abdomen, and inner thighs."

"Anything under her fingernails?"

"Traces of polyurethane and wood. My guess? The chair she was strapped to. She dug her nails in, probably from the pain being inflicted."

"What about her tattoos? Did she have a tentacle anywhere?"

"No, nowhere. There's no evidence of even a cover-up under any of her other tattoos. C.O.D. was a gunshot. It was a through-and-through. I made a cast from the entry wound. I would guess a medium caliber weapon, but to know for sure, we would need to find the bullet. Any ideas on her last location?"

"Not yet. Peter is looking through the phone data. The cell towers pinged in Manchester for a bit but disappeared. She could've been anywhere."

AJ could not take her eyes off Angie's corpse.

"I've sent all my collection over to Peter for analysis," Cassie said. "Love, are you okay?"

"Not really. It's—it's still shocking to me. I mean, I'm looking at this woman on the slab and the sexual violence she endured." She felt a tear fall and wiped it away quickly. "Cass, I feel sick for joking around about sex with Tony. I wanna throw up right now, I feel so disgusted."

"With what was done to her? Or with yourself for wanting to get laid?"

AJ stared at her and thought about it. "Maybe both."

"Look, Ameena. Us joking earlier is nothing to feel guilty about. Wanting and having a biological urge—an instinct which goes back to the beginning of all life—is perfectly normal. So, have your fun with Tony. Enjoy yourself!"

"And what about her? Angie didn't deserve this!"

"You're right. She didn't. No one does. But what happened to her FAR exceeded any biological urge. It was cold, calculated, cruel. Vicious! Those are *mental* urges. The men who violated Angie are *not* normal. Do you understand the difference?" She nodded. "I know, love. This was a brutal, disturbing crime, which is why I wanted more time with the body. I wanted to triple check every detail, every microscopic piece of evidence I could find. I want justice for Angie. And if this cartel Order is behind it, *please* be careful. Don't go anywhere without backup. Promise me!"

"I promise."

The phone rang. Cassie went over to the counter and answered it. "Yeah. Sure. Give me two minutes and then send them. Thanks." She hung up the phone. "That was the front desk. Angie's family is here."

"Oh." AJ grabbed the reports and stuck them in her binder. "I should get going then."

"Okay, sweetie. We'll talk more soon."

Cassie closed her eyes and AJ watched her begin her meditation—a ritual the medical examiner said helped her focus her energy on comforting victims' families. As the detective walked down the hall, she heard the elevator ding and saw three people walk towards her.

"Excuse me, are you the Medical Examiner?" the older woman asked. Her eyes appeared tired, sunken in, and swollen from crying. "Wait. You look familiar."

AJ recognized the woman.

"Mrs. Carmicle, I'm Detective Jardine. I was with Agent Aserbbo the other evening when we came to visit. I came to get the reports I needed on your daughter. Cassie, the medical examiner, is down the hallway through the last door on the right. I want you to know the M.E. was extremely respectful of your daughter."

Angie's mother covered her mouth and nodded. Tears formed again. AJ gently touched the woman's shoulder, and the woman broke into sobs. The other two individuals with her started crying; one, a man, walked off, shaking his head.

Mrs. Carmicle fixed her gaze on AJ, her eyes pleading. "Please find my baby's killer. Please find the person responsible for this. I need to know!"

"Yes, ma'am. Honoring Angie and finding her killer is my only priority right now. I *will* find out who did this. I promise you. No matter how long it takes."

"Thank you."

"Would you like another business card? In case you lose the first one? You're welcome to call me at any time."

"Yes, that's kind of you."

AJ fumbled through her pockets until she found a couple of cards. She handed it to the mother.

"Detective, how—bad—does she look?"

AJ's heart sank, and a large lump surfaced in her throat. She swallowed it back in place. She did not want to break the news of a child's condition to a mother, no matter the age of the child.

"Mrs. Carmicle, there is no gentle way to say this. Your daughter was the victim of an incredibly brutal attack. You won't be able to have an open casket."

The woman sobbed hysterically and fell into the detective's arms. "My baby, my baby…" she repeated multiple times.

"May I give you some advice?"

She nodded as she wiped her eyes on her sleeves.

AJ held her gaze. "*Don't* go in there. Let one of your companions go, if you must. You *don't* want to remember Angie this way. If you go in there, that image will forever follow you and will be the *only* thing you will focus on for the rest of your life. Please remember how beautiful she was. Please."

"Mrs. Carmicle," came a voice from behind AJ. "I'm the medical examiner, Dr. Cassandra Owen. I can take you in there if you like, but I do want to add something to what Detective Jardine just said.

"I've been doing this specific job for many, many years now. I've seen *so* many aspects of death that movies and books can't and don't properly describe. I've had so many mothers — such as yourself — walk through my door behind me. I've seen their reactions. I've witnessed and felt their pain. In Angie's case, Detective Jardine is right."

"But I wanted to see my daughter one last time." The mother choked through her tears.

"I know, Mrs. Carmicle. I know. And every mother who has walked through my door has told me the same thing. And every mother who's had a daughter in Angie's condition has never. Been. The same.

"Remember the beauty and love and charisma your daughter had. Don't go in there, please. Not this time. Let the detectives and those working her case remember the ugliness and brutality of what was done to her. Let Detective Jardine's eyes relive that agony. Let *her* carry the burden, while *you* remember your baby's peaceful and beautiful face."

There was a long moment of crying and sobs. AJ saw tears in Cassie's eyes and struggling turmoil in the mom's. The mother finally wiped her tears.

"Okay…" Mrs. Carmicle nodded. "Thank you — both, for all you're doing."

Angie's mother left with her two companions. AJ and Cassie watched them in silence. They heard the elevator chime and then the group disappeared.

"And that's why I became a medical examiner," Cassie whispered.

"Why exactly?"

"To spare families the unnecessary grief of it all. To give them clarity in the foggy fuckery death creates. To help the dead speak up one final time."

- - -- --- -----

CHAPTER SEVENTEEN: 21

Tuesday, March 2, 2021

AJ watched Conrad sit quietly and listen to her findings. He appeared more solemn than normal. "Sir? Is something wrong?"

"Paperwork, Jardine."

"From your meetings?"

"Among other things."

He tapped his fingers on the desk, lost in thought. She knew he had a lot on his mind, but she also needed to ask him about the Newtonian Collaborative. She wanted to know if it had anything to do with Michael's murder.

"Sir, there's something else I need to tell you. I haven't told anyone else yet, nor documented it."

"Yes, Jardine?" He continued to tap his fingers as he stared at her.

"May I have a piece of paper? I don't want to say this out loud."

He stared at her for a moment, then slid his notepad and pen over to her. She wrote two words down, then tore the piece of paper off.

"Sir, while you were away, I received another message from Copernicus." She told Conrad the relevant information and then recalled the information about Michael. "Copernicus gave me a name and asked me to ask you about it. He said not to do any digital searches, nor discuss it with anyone else except you. From what he told me, I think he knows you or at least knows *of* you. This is the name he gave me."

She slid the paper over to him and watched him pick it up. His eyebrows dropped, and his expression immediately changed. He quickly glared at her. His eyes pierced hers and she became unsettled in her chair. She did not know what to expect him to say or do.

He folded the piece of paper once and then reached into his desk to pull out a lighter. He removed the plastic liner bag from the metal trashcan next to him, lit the paper on fire, and burned it while he continued to watch her. When he was done, he poured his drink over the fire and extinguished it. Then he stared at her again.

"What you wrote on this paper, Jardine, you are never to say out loud or mention to anyone. Ever. Do I make myself clear, detective?" He carefully and slowly worded his sentences.

She stared back at him and nodded slightly, apprehensive of his reaction. "I'm sorry, sir. I didn't mean to upset you."

"I cannot emphasize this enough: Do. NOT. EVER. Mention this to anyone."

"Y-yes, sir."

"Go home, Jardine." His tone changed, became softer and more reassuring. "Tomorrow's a fresh start."

She nodded again and left, not wanting to upset her mentor anymore.

- - -- --- -----

She stewed and pondered over Conrad's reaction all evening, and she shut herself in her bedroom to avoid everyone. Her laptop streamed a TV show in the background as a distraction, but it did not help to quieten her mind. Finally, and fed up, she shut the browser down. She stared at her screen and double-clicked the chatroom icon.

> *Roar317811: Hi, are you there?*

She waited for several minutes.

No response.

Shit. I really wanted to talk to him.

Her phone buzzed with a text message from Tony checking on her after the day's events.

Tony, dear, not today. You're not the one I want to chat with right now.

She ignored the text and stared at her monitor. After several more minutes of silence, she exited out and shut down her computer.

She laid on the bed and stared at the ceiling. Her brain churned, disappointed by the man she needed answers from and conflicted with the man she wanted most.

- - -- --- -----

<u>Tuesday, May 18, 2021</u>

She had not been in the field for nearly two months and itched to get out of her cubicle and away from the shackles of her computer.

Additional leads on the Fasciata and Angie's murder dried up, and Conrad took advantage of the downtime to put AJ on several New Hampshire cold cases again. She also processed the backlog of dozens of rape cases.

Since the mention of the Newtonian Collaborative, Conrad kept a distance from her; or rather, she felt like he did. She drifted into a slight depression for several weeks. The feelings of failure and self-doubt with her abilities to do the job crept in and took hold. She imagined never being in her boss's good graces again, and that scared her more than anything.

She tried several times to reach out to Copernicus, but he appeared to have vanished. Her only means of communication were the chatroom; it was too risky to attempt emails or old phone numbers in her call list.

From time to time she laid in her bed and spoke to her phone, hoping Copernicus would be listening. Sometimes she confessed her emotions, sometimes she updated the hacker with the latest of what she knew, sometimes she poured her burdens into the mouthpiece if only to take the weight from her shoulders and place it on someone else.

As she keyed data on the latest case file, her phone buzzed.

"Jardine."

"Yes, sir?"

"My office."

"Yes, sir."

When she opened Conrad's door, Tony and Taylor Rion sat across from her boss. Her heart skipped a beat when she saw Tony smiling at her.

"You wanted to see me, sir?"

"Come in and shut the door."

Taylor stood up and extended his hand out, smiling

down at her. "Good to see you, AJ."

She blushed, slightly. "Likewise." She glanced at Tony; he, still smiling. "Hey, you." It was all she could muster.

"Hey, AJ." Tony inflected her name in the same manner as Taylor.

"Here, you can have my chair." Taylor motioned for her to sit down.

She settled in next to Tony, then looked at her boss, nervous for what to expect. "Sir, is everything okay?"

"Jardine, Mr. Rion contacted me this morning and has some information for us on Frierson. I called Agent Aserbbo and you into my office to hear what he has to say." He nodded for Taylor to continue.

"AJ, do you remember back in February when you came to see Carl, and I told you he had a three-week vacation coming up that following week?"

"Yeah, he was eager to finish some reports and get out of the interview."

"Exactly. So, he took the vacation and was back at work on the eighth of March. When he came back, he seemed more focused, less anxious. Like I told you, your questioning lit a fire under his ass."

"That's a good thing, right?" she asked.

"Yeah, it definitely is. For the last couple of months, his performance, reports, timeliness—everything, has been exemplary. On par for a promotion, in fact. Anytime he needed to go anywhere, he let me know, documented everything, gave me an E.T.A. on when he'd be back. I mean, this guy's been at the top of his game and has really put others to shame.

"So, this morning when Carl didn't show up for work, everyone on the team got worried. We tried calling, texting—no response. We had I.T. ping and track his cell phone, but it appeared to be at his apartment. I went over there with one of my agents, and his roommate said Carl never came home the night before."

"Why didn't his roommate call it in?"

"He didn't think anything of it. He said it wasn't unusual for Carl to take off from time to time."

"So, Frierson's disappeared?" Tony sounded shocked.

"Yeah. Took his keys and wallet but left his phone. His car's gone, and the vehicle's G.P.S. tracking system has been disengaged. So, we put out a B.O.L.O. on the car, but no hits yet. It's only been a few hours, though."

"Do you think he took off for a few days to clear his head, for whatever reason?" AJ asked.

Taylor shook his head. "And leave his phone behind? No, not like him. We think something happened to him."

Tony's phone rang, and he looked apologetically at everyone. "It's Larsson, I need to take this." He got up and stepped out of the office.

"Taylor, you said he had a roommate?"

"Yeah, Trooper Sotelo. He runs the Interstate 89 state patrol between here and Lebanon."

She turned to Conrad. "Sir, I think we should go interview Sotelo and see if he can provide us more information on Carl. Maybe we can determine where he went and track him down."

"Not alone, Jardine. Take Aserbbo with you."

"Yes, sir."

Tony stepped back in and looked directly at Conrad. "Sir, they just found a body."

- - -- --- -----

Darkened, cloudy swarms of black flies, freshly emerged with the year's Bug Season, prevented them from reaching the body. It was discovered north of the Town of Claremont, and only meters from Mill Brook, a long meandering waterway still full from recent snow melts and percolating soils.

"Goddamn fucking bugs!" she fumed, swatting at the tiny flies. "We can't get back there to the body."

"Look on the bright side, AJ. At least they only last a few

weeks." He grinned at her frustration.

She flipped him off as they walked back to his car and waited inside. They sent an officer to purchase netted masks and rain gear to protect against the biting menaces. The other officers and county medical examiner waited in their vehicles.

"What did you say you found out from the homeowner?" she asked.

"He said he heard coyotes last night and early this morning. Then saw buzzards circling around. He and his son went to check it out and could smell the decomp before they saw the body. He continued to approach until he saw torn clothing everywhere, then decided to head back to his house and call the police."

"Anything else?"

"Nope, that's all he said."

"Oh." She stared out the window, annoyed at the bugs bumping into the glass to get in.

"Sooo. What's up with you and Taylor?"

"What do you mean?"

"I saw the way you blushed when he shook your hand. See! You're doing it right now!" He teased her and playfully tickled her cheek.

"Tony!" She smacked his arm and smiled. "Nothing's going on. We went to lunch last week to go over some evidence for one of my cold cases."

"Mmm hmmm."

She squinted her eyes at him. "You're jealous, aren't you?"

"I'm not saying a damn thing!"

She leaned closer to him and gave him a mischievous grin. "And if I *am* dating him, what would you say then?"

He leaned closer to her. "I'd say 'The devil's knocking on your castle door, princess, and doesn't want your knight in shining armor to get in the way.'"

She inched nearer. "And I'd say, 'Not today, Satan.'"

He mimicked her movement. "And *I'd* say, 'One of these

days you'll let me in.'"

"And *I'd* say, 'Only if you let me in first.'"

She studied his smile and watched his reaction. His eyes fell heavy with thought. And though he continued to smile, she knew his mood changed.

He whispered, "And I'd say, 'I did. When I said I loved you.'"

She pulled back and stared at him. He was right. She knew it. And she felt guilty.

"Tony…" It was barely an audible response.

They both looked out opposite windows again and waited in silence.

- - -- --- -----

The sun already peaked in the sky and was beginning its downward journey towards the tree line when they finally managed to hike down to the decomposing body. The humid and warm air contributed to the potent smell of decomp well before they saw the corpse.

She saw one of the officers pack vapor rub ointment into his nostrils. She told him, "That might help you a bit, but the ointment actually opens up your nasal passages and odor receptors more. The best thing to do is just breathe in slow and steady until you get used to it."

"Is that why you practice Lamaze breathing?"

"Yep. Helps you stay calm and focused better."

When the group finally reached the body, she gasped. The torso and legs were ripped open with chunks of flesh and clothing scattered nearby. Animal tracks confirmed large carnivores made part of it their meal.

She crouched down to study the remains. The body, nothing more than a dirty, emaciated skeleton, had blackened extremities; the fingers, pointy and boney. She saw a driver's license on the ground and picked it up.

"It's Perales." She shooed the flies from her face.

Tony crouched down. "Shit. At least we finally know

what happened to him." He examined the remains with her. "I'm not Cassie, but if the gangrene's this severe, there's no way Perales walked here on his own, even if he was high off any drugs." He pointed to the rubber tourniquet sticking out from the left side of the body.

She finished documenting the surroundings close to the body. She watched as the medical examiner flipped the body over. The skin appeared a darkish purple where the blood pooled from lividity, and it appeared he died there, most likely in the exact fetal position he was found. His left arm was curled up at the elbow, and he held an object in the hand.

"Can we see what's in his hand, please?" she asked the M.E.

The man pried Perales's hand open. The sound of bone cracking made one of the other officers walk away to throw up nearby.

"It's a pine cone." He held up the item.

"A pinecone? Hmm. It's also evidence, so let's bag and tag it."

"Ma'am," the sick officer called from a few meters away, "you should come see this."

They walked over to the officer. He pointed to the ground not far from where he vomited.

"Bingo! We have some prints!" Her voice held excitement with the sight of shoe impressions. "Tony, can you follow those and see where they go? We also need to get a casting done."

"Sure, be back soon." He motioned for another officer to join him.

She continued to document and tag the evidence as the medical examiner left with the body. She collected the tattered clothing between bug swats. The tiny gnat-sized flies remained relentless and pestered her as she tried to take photos. She managed to collect some in the bottles and delightfully drowned the insects in isopropyl alcohol. She collected other bugs, brush, and debris—anything she deemed important.

Tony and the other officer finally walked back up. "We lost the tracks in the brook several meters upstream. They just disappeared. Smells like a skunk sprayed the area, so we didn't stay long."

She wiped her forehead and stood up. The men looked away. Tony snickered.

"What?" The men annoyed her.

"Your face is covered in bug guts and dirt."

She rolled her eyes. "It's these fucking flies. I got bit on the face and smacked the bastard." Before he could say anything else, she asked, "Did you make molds?"

"Yep. Grabbed a few, if it helps."

"Good. I think I'm done here. Let's get this stuff back to the car and head out."

- - -- --- -----

Abbott and Costello demanded pats on the heads before they allowed Ameena in the house. She sighed and obeyed.

Normalcy was slowly returning to the Andrewson home. Ernest had finished physical therapy in April. Months after the car accident, he could finally walk up the stairs again and insisted all the furniture returned to where it belonged. With the help of Eoghan, Derek, Peter — and to Jamilla's joy, Tony — beds, dressers, and all form of furniture were restored to their original locations.

Eoghan and Derek continued to share the large bedroom adjacent to Jenna's smaller one. Derek started a job in the evenings and saved enough money to buy two twin-size bed frames: one for him, one for Eoghan. Ernest mentored the boy and taught him several woodworking techniques.

Derek designed and built two desks to fit underneath and elevate the bed frames. With the vertical design, space was opened within the room. The boys rearranged the area with the newly designed furniture on opposite sides of the bedroom, thus providing a large open space in the middle.

Jamilla came down the stairs to greet her daughter. "How was your day, habibti?" She smiled as she carried a TV tray to the kitchen.

"It was pretty good. Another crime scene, another shower needed soon. Where're the kids? It's not bedtime yet."

"The boys went to a friend's house to study for an exam tomorrow. Jenna should be in her room."

"Jenna," Ameena yelled, "come here, please."

A few seconds later, both women saw Jenna come down the stairs and stand near the base of the steps. Tears streamed down her face.

"Habibti, what's wrong?"

"What happened?" Ameena asked.

Jenna ran to her mom, gripped her tightly, and cried into her belly. She finally looked up at Ameena.

"It's the Van Gogh lights, Mommy. I don't want you to go see them. They want to take you away from me." The little girl buried her head again and sobbed.

Both women glanced at each other. Ameena mouthed 'what the fuck', and Jamilla mouthed 'I don't know'.

"Look at me, Jenna. I'm not going anywhere. I'm staying right here. What do you mean by Van Gogh lights, dear?"

Jenna wiped her nose. "They come from that way." She pointed north.

"Do you mean the Northern Lights? The Aurora Borealis? Is that what you mean?" Jenna nodded. "Look, I'm not going anywhere. I don't want you to worry. Okay?"

She nodded again and wiped away her tears.

"Jennie-Pennie, why don't you see if Papa needs another drink?"

"Okay, Tayta." Jenna slowly let go of her mother and walked back up the stairs.

"What the hell was that about?" Ameena whispered to her mom.

"I don't know, habibti! I've never seen her like that!"

"Did she get bullied at school? Did something happen?"

"*Lah*, sweetheart. No. She's been doing good and the teachers love her. I have no idea what happened. Maybe she had a nightmare again?"

"Possibly."

They heard Jenna come back down the stairs.

"Papa said he would like another ginger ale."

"Okay, habibti. Go get him one and then get ready for bed."

"Did you tell Mommy about her present?"

"What present?"

"No, Jenna, not yet." The grandmother turned to her own daughter. "It's on your dresser, dear. Beautiful! Go look!"

Ameena walked into the bedroom and the smell hit her before she even saw the gift. When she saw the vase, she stopped and gasped.

A lead crystal vase and gorgeously arranged flowers sat on her dresser waiting for her. The vase whimsically spiraled like a polished strand of DNA. Each spiraling edge beveled around, and the light caught every reflection, causing it to shimmer rainbows of color everywhere. There appeared to be nearly two dozen lavender-mauve flowers bursting like fireworks from the vase. The arrangement was centered; the symmetry, near perfection.

Sitting in front of the vase was a wrapped gift the size of a C.D. with a card propped on top, leaning against the vase. She opened the card and it read:

> "*We are all astronauts on spaceship earth.*"
> ~*Wubbo Ockels*
> *May these asters be your guiding stars; the vase, the traveling vessel.*
> *0100010171844001001110481377O*

She reread the card a couple of times, flipped it over, and then set it down. She unwrapped the gift: a C.D. with a printed label.

Symphony No. 3 in D-minor & Symphony No. 8 in
E-Flat Major, by Gustav Mahler

She walked out the bedroom and back to the kitchen, in
time to see Jenna take a can of ginger ale out of the
refrigerator. Ameena went over to the little girl and hugged
her, holding her for several seconds.

"Are you feeling better?" Jenna nodded in silence.
"That's good, baby. That's good. I love you."

"I love you, too, Mommy."

"Go give Papa a hug for me, please. Good night, dear."

Jenna carried the drink upstairs and disappeared.

"Momma?"

"Yes, habibti?"

"When did the flowers arrive?"

"Oh, I think sometime early this afternoon."

"There's no company name on the card. Do you
remember the name of the florist?"

Jamilla thought for a second. "No, habibti, I didn't bother
to look at the vehicle."

"Hmm."

"Are you sure you're okay?"

"Yeah, I promise." And before her mother could
interrogate her, she added, "I think I have a secret admirer.
I don't think it's Tony, but I have no clue who it could be."

"Ahh. Secret admirer!" Jamilla grinned. "My daughter
has suitors!"

"Momma." Ameena rolled her eyes.

"What? You don't think you're worth it? You are prized
cedar from the mountains! Enjoy the attention!" She gave
Ameena a kiss, and then added, "I need to check on your
father and Jenna. Go, enjoy your gifts and I will see you in
the morning."

She watched her mom disappear up the stairs.

- - -- --- -----

She flipped over on the bed, restless. She could not fall asleep. Her brain held her body for ransom, demanding she process the day's events. From Tony's flirtation, to the condition of the body, to Jenna's cryptic Van Gogh lights comment, her mind wanted to think.

Finally, she got up, turned the light back on, then sat up against the headboard. She stared for several long minutes at the vase and flowers.

She opened her laptop up, grabbed the C.D., and played the music. With the orchestral songs in the background, she researched and analyzed every aspect of the gift.

Asters. Popular garden plant, bright and vivid flowers. From the ancient Greek word meaning "star".

She examined the vase again and counted the flowers.

Twenty-one asters. I wonder why it wasn't an even two dozen flowers? Then again, I'm glad it wasn't two dozen roses.

She searched for the quote online.

Wubbo Ockels. Oh wow! He was an astronaut of the European Space Agency and a Dutch physicist. He had an amazing career, it seems. Then she saw he died a few years prior. *On May 18th, the same date as today.*

What about Gustav Mahler? Okay, he's another European. A late-Romantic composer. An extensive career in music, yada yada. Composed several symphonies, yada yada.

"Ohhh, wow!" she gasped out loud.

She stared at his date of death. It was the same date as Wubbo Ockels' death, save the years were different.

She focused on the symphonies. The music, not something she typically listened to, sent goose bumps down her arms. She could feel the emotion rise and fall as the orchestra progressed.

Are the goosebumps from the music? Or the gift giver? There's no name on these, but I know, have a gut feeling, Copernicus sent them.

She hoped the mysterious man was listening and watching through whichever device he hacked.

"Did you send me these? I love the flowers. And the vase is like nothing I've ever seen before." She spoke into her phone, taking the chance he listened. "It reminds me of DNA strands. And tornadoes! I don't know why I just thought of tornadoes.

"The asters are beautiful. They're a pinkish and lavender mauve color. The person who delivered them arranged them in a beautiful geometric shape, too. I wondered if it was you, but you wouldn't have been so bold to show up at my house. Or would you?" She paused to think about that possibility.

"I love the quote and see how it goes with the flowers. How did you know I love the stars so much? The night sky intrigues me. Did you know that, too? I love everything up there. It's so magical, in a sense. So much imagination and wonder. And the music. Heh. This wasn't something I expected. I don't typically listen to classical music, and I've never heard of Mahler. I really like Symphony No. 3."

She finally shut off her computer. The more she talked, the more relaxed and sleepy she became. She laid back down in bed, under the covers and listened to the frogs croaking through the open window.

"Copernicus? Thank you for the gifts, if that *was* you. And thank you for listening, if you *are* there."

Only the frogs replied.

- - -- --- -----

<u>Tuesday, June 1, 2021</u>
"Hey, beautiful! How are you doing?" Cassie's voice sounded too happy for AJ that early in the sleep-deprived morning.

"Ugh, I need coffee."

"Trouble sleeping, again?"

"Yeah." AJ yawned. "Sometimes it's not too bad, but last night was rough. I remember every damn detail of this one, Cass."

She referred to the new nightmare that crept into her subconscious. In her dream, she went on a date with Tony. They held hands and laughed as they walked down a long asphalt path through an old wooded park. The trees around her grew denser and closer to the path, giving a haunting and claustrophobic feel close to the ground; she peered skyward to see the thinning branches open in stark contrast. The stars vividly flashed in place.

When she looked back to her date, the image of Tony morphed into the decomposing body of Jose Perales. The eye sockets were void of the soft tissue; instead, hundreds of maggots crawling and squirmed out of the dark holes. She gasped and let go of the rotting hand.

She stepped backward, away from the skeleton, as the maggots continued to pour from the eye sockets and wiggle on the ground around the standing body. She watched as thousands and thousands of larvae poured out and stacked up from the ankles, to the hips, to the chest, and finally consumed the skull in one massive writhing and oozing heap.

In curious fashion, she took a step forward to investigate the blob. She watched as the maggots merged and morphed into elongated wiggling worms. The writhing masses continued to flail about and grow in length and girth into what appeared to be dozens of slimy snakes combining. But the snakes oozed and bubbled until fluctuating bumps formed in symmetrical pairs down each snake. She realized the maggots transformed into slimy black tentacles.

A singular mass slowly expanded from the middle of the wriggling mess, spiraling upward and outward, as if a large and slick black balloon filled with air and pushed the tentacles outward. The skull-shaped mass spiraled, then slowed to a crawl. It finally stopped. Two dark, sunken football-shaped crevices moved in unison and glared at her. The darkness took on color, and slits of menacing green glowed from the depths. Horror, malice, and anger pointed at her body as panic, dread, and apprehension took her mind.

In continued horror, she stepped backward again. But this time, she tripped over another body—a living person. She fell to the ground on her back and turned to see the person next to her. She saw no physical form of a body, only a shadow in the shape of a man. She could not recall any specific detail about the shape, other than who she <u>felt</u> it could be. She <u>knew</u> it was a man, and she <u>knew</u> it was Michael.

And then, still within her dream, the knowing of Michael disappeared and the empty shadow took on a new spirit, a new persona. The shadow man now felt like and <u>was</u> Copernicus. The fluid shape moved towards her, ensnaring her.

Always, at this point in the dream, she would wake up. Sometimes the mixed emotions were so strong she would run into the bathroom and throw up anything left in her stomach. She searched dream book definitions and tried to interpret the explanations, but she could not figure out the meaning of the men appearing in the visions. Each intricate detail stayed in her mind throughout the day. What disturbed her the most was the sheer amount of detail, almost as much as the final thought of the last man in her dream.

When she told Cassie about her nightmare, she excluded any mention of Copernicus.

He was her singular secret she kept from everyone.

"It felt like the last shadow wasn't Michael anymore. It

was someone else, but I have no idea who he is."

"Awww. I'm so sorry, hon. I wish I could help you and take away the nightmares." She rubbed AJ's arm.

"I know, Cass. I've had the same dream three times now."

"Maybe it's the stress of finding Perales's body. I mean, if you think about it, you guys searched for him for months. Maybe finally finding him has given you less closure and more questions. It's possible the morphing in your dream — ya know, the octopus — symbolizes the Fasciata, and they're the ones responsible for his death?"

AJ thought for a minute. "Yeah, it's possible I guess."

"I do have some good news for you, if you'd like to hear it." Cassie smiled as she changed the subject. "After months of debating and planning, we FINALLY have a wedding date!"

"That's good. Are you guys having a fall wedding, then?"

"Nah, I thought it would be fun to have an October wedding. Ya know, going with her proposal, Halloween, ghoulish stuff like that. But Nadine has finally come around and wants a more traditional setting."

"That's what you wanted anyway, right?"

"Yeah, so she and I have decided we'll do a Spring wedding. We both agreed on May and have set the date for Saturday, May 21st!"

AJ hugged the bride in excitement. "Congrats! We officially have a date set now!"

"I know! So, we have a little less than a year right now, but it gives us enough time to save up more money and plan our European adventure. It's all starting to fall into place." She took a deep breath and focused. "Okay. Now that's been said, are you ready to change the subject again?"

AJ yawned as she nodded. "So sorry, didn't mean to yawn."

"No worries, sweetie."

She watched Cassie go to the storage and bring out the

body. She slowly unzipped the bag and AJ could feel her heart pounding in her throat. Images of her dream flooded her mind and she started to feel sick. When she saw the body, she relaxed some. She still saw the carnage and tears in the skin, but it paled to her imaginative nightmare.

"It's not as scary as my dream," she whispered.

"That's a good start." Cassie cleared her throat. "As you can see there was carnivorous activity to the torso and right side. You'd said the homeowner heard coyotes, and the puncture wounds and rips are consistent with that. There's no petechiae anywhere on the body. Let's talk about his extremities. Are you ready?" AJ nodded. "Because this is extreme. Fair warning."

Cassie pulled the plastic back, completely exposing the uncurled and flat body. Perales appeared to be a frail bag of bones almost devoid of any fat anywhere. His skin — what was left — was loose, making him appear years older than his record indicated. His long hair curled away from his skull, and his bushy beard had months of growth. He looked like an emaciated beggar AJ would sometimes see on the streets.

The hands and feet made her gasp, especially the feet. The skin appeared dry, blackened, and peeled from the bone.

"Oh, my gawd," AJ whispered, barely able to talk. "What did this to him?"

"This is what dry gangrene looks like. Only this is the worst case I've seen in my thirteen years of doing this."

"What's *dry* gangrene? I thought gangrene was just the rotting away of skin."

"It's much more than that, sweetie. Gangrene can be caused by any number of things: weakened immune system, diabetes, smoking, obesity, a severe injury. In laymen's terms, it's basically when the blood can't freely flow through the body and feed your cells. Over time, those cells begin to die because they're being starved.

"Dry gangrene's more common in the hands and feet.

The soft tissue surrounding the bone dries up and can start to decay, turning this purplish-blackish color you see here. The skin's so dry and flaky, it falls off. That's why you see the bone protruding through. It's not because coyotes ate the skin off. Now whe—"

Suddenly, AJ made a run for the trash can, fell to her knees and emptied her stomach contents into the container. Her hands shook, and she kept heaving into the bag.

Cassie stopped. The M.E. calmly grabbed a cold compress from the small refrigerator and placed it on the back of the detective's neck. While AJ sat on the floor, Cassie grabbed a cup and filled it with water from the sink.

"Take a deep breath, sweetie."

AJ tried but gasped again. There was nothing left in her stomach to offer the trash can.

In a stronger command, Cassie ordered, "Detective, deep breath NOW."

AJ took half a breath in.

"Good. Good. Now another one." Cassie's voice remained calm and gentle. "Aaand another one."

AJ obeyed her friend. The detective's hands still shook, and the terror of her nightmare still gripped her stomach.

"Ameena, rinse your mouth out and spit the bile in the trash can."

She obliged.

"Now take a slow sip to calm your stomach. Good. Breathe deep." Cassie continued her nurturing for several long minutes.

"I-I'm so sorry. I didn't think I would throw up."

"It's okay. That's why I'm prepared," Cassie replied nonchalantly. "I've seen men twice your size pass out before I've even touched the zipper. I'll put Perales's body back inside. We'll continue in a few minutes and go over the tox report, okay?"

"Sure."

She took several more breaths and stared at her hands. The shaking subsided. AJ watched Cassie carefully wheel the body away and come back. The nausea declined, and she could feel the warmth return in her hands.

"You ready to continue?"

AJ nodded.

"Okay, sweetie." She straightened her papers. "The tox panel came back negative from everything except one drug. There were massive, and I mean MASSIVE levels of heroin. Specifically, the Prussian Black."

"Prussian Black with TTX?"

"Yes. He'd been using—heavily—for months. His organs were shutting down. Also, based on the advanced gangrene, there's no way he could walk for a while. I believe it was a body dump in the woods."

"Did you find any trace evidence on him?"

"That didn't get washed away or eaten? Yes and no. I found some fibers, but those could've been from his clothing getting ripped. Same with the strange hairs; it could be the coyotes. I sent those over to Peter to verify. Perales did have the same tentacle tattoo."

"Where was the tattoo?"

"Upper left leg and thigh."

"Anything else?"

"Not really. I sent everything—which wasn't much—to Peter."

"I'm meeting with him later today or tomorrow."

"My official cause of death is long-term heroin use coupled with advanced stages of the gangrene. His body finally shut down. It was too damaged. Considering no family have come to claim him, and considering how unkempt his body has been, I'd guess he was dumped in the woods."

"So, it's not a murder?"

"My professional opinion? No. Accessory, yes. But murder, no." Cassie gathered up her papers, handing a small stack to AJ. "You feeling better now?"

"Yeah," she sighed, "enough I can drive now."

"Good! Go take a breather and talk to Peter. Call me this

weekend so we can catch up."

"Will do, my friend."

- - -- --- -----

"Nothing? Seriously?"

"Nope. Only what was native to the landscape."

"And did you analyze the pine cone?"

"Yeah, of course I did."

"I didn't mean it in a bad way, Peter. My frustration is definitely not with you. It's with the lack of evidence."

"I know. Try having a comparison microscope not function or calibrate properly." He rolled his eyes at the machine. "Any-*who*, the pine cone was from the Eastern White Pine, pretty common here in New England. Honestly, no surprise there. But, there was one thing, though. Let me show you something under the scope. It's one of the pine cone scales. I almost missed it."

He led AJ over to the microscope set up. She could almost make out the markings. She peered into the eyepiece and studied the pine scale. "'Twenty-one'?"

"Probably carved with an Exact-o blade."

"That's it? That's the only thing you found?"

Peter raised his eyebrows and shrugged.

"What the hell..." her voice trailed off.

"I know, right? And I double-checked all the stuff Cass sent over, swabbed the insides of ALL the evidence bags, and even did a vac test on the air particles of the pine cone. Other than the carved number, there's nothing here."

"Interesting. Anyway, I'm meeting with Conrad in a few minutes, so I'll let him know. Thanks, Peter."

"Anytime, AJ. Anytime."

- - -- --- -----

"A pine cone scale?"

"Yes, sir."

"With a number carved on it?"

"Yes, sir."

"And the same tattoo as the other victims?"

"Yes, sir."

"Did his DNA match Ms. Carmicle's rapists?"

"No, sir. He wasn't one of the contributors. We still don't know who killed or raped Angie."

"No leads on that either?"

"No, sir." She paused, then added, "I'm sorry, sir."

"Why's that, detective?"

"Because I feel," she paused again to find the right words. "I feel I'm bringing you more questions than answers, and I know you don't like that. Sometimes it makes me feel like a failure and like I'm letting you down."

"Jardine, that's the nature of this business. We don't always have the answers we need. Or want. It takes patience and time to solve some of these cases if we even solve them at all. We don't always get the bad guys. Sometimes the good ones die for the wrong reasons. But we keep doing what we do, so those odds diminish. Do you understand?"

She nodded.

"The cases coming through our doors are like heartbeats on a medical monitor. You'll see ups. You'll see downs. You'll *feel* those ups and downs multiple times. You'll have gains. You'll have losses. And you'll repeat those gains and losses multiple times.

"But the *minute* you don't feel those ups and downs anymore—the *minute* you flatline into the monotony of the job, you cease to be a good detective. *That's* when you fail the victims. *That's* when you fail me. And *that's* when you fail yourself."

- - -- --- -----

CHAPTER EIGHTEEN: SNIPPETS

Tuesday, June 8, 2021

AJ and Tony went over the details of Carl Frierson's missing person's report in their weekly meeting with Conrad.

"Sir, we never had a chance to interview his roommate, the state trooper. Taylor mentioned the name a few weeks ago, but I don't see his name written down in my notes."

"*Taylor?* Calling him by his first name," Tony teased.

"We went out for lunch again, so yes. I am," she replied, smiling. "Just like you did with Tiff—"

"Okay, okay!" He threw his arms up in defeat and laughed.

"I'll call *Taylor* and get the roommate's name again. Wanna check it out with me?"

Tony nodded with a smirk. "Sure. I'll go get your chariot, my princess."

He stood up, took a knightly bow, and walked out of the office. She grinned at the silliness until she saw the look on Conrad's face. His stoic nature made her blush with embarrassment. She collected her folders and walked to the door when Conrad stopped her.

"Have you had any more contact with Copernicus?"

"No, sir. Not in a few months. It's like he dropped off the

face of the planet. Do you want me to reach out to him?"

"No, Jardine. Wait for him to come to you."

"Yes, sir," she replied.

"That's all." He returned his gaze back to his monitor. "Now get out. Princess." She noted the amusement in his voice.

- - -- --- -----

"So, this is the address your boyfriend gave you?"

"Tony," she laughed, "he's not my boyfriend!"

"Sure," he continued to tease her.

"I think you're jealous!"

"And I think I'm not going to tell you if you're right or not."

She watched his mannerisms and enjoyed the fact his puckish and playful personality was returning to normal. It was the humor and bantering she enjoyed almost as much as his blue eyes.

They got out of the car and walked up to the front door of the apartment where Frierson lived. Tony knocked on the door as she scanned the area around her. She saw the shadow of a man walk up. The door opened and remained blocked by the body of a muscular and tall bald man.

AJ looked at Tony. His expression changed, the blood drained from his face. She knew he recognized the man. She looked at the towering roommate to see the man's reaction; the expression was not reciprocated.

"Can I help you?" The man's voice was as deep as the shadow he cast.

"Are you Giovani Sotelo?" she asked.

"Yeah. Friends call me Gigi, though. Who are you?"

"I'm Detective Jardine with I.S.B. This is Agent Aserbbo with D.T.F. We're looking for Carl Frierson."

"Haven't seen him in weeks."

"Is there anything you can tell us about his disappearance?"

"Nah, I told Carl's supervisor everything I knew. All I know is he was here that night before. When I woke up the following morning, he was gone. No word, nothing missing except the car and him."

"Did he have a girlfriend or maybe family he needed to see unexpectedly?"

"No, ma'am. He's pretty straightforward with everyone. Something happened a few months before he disappeared causing him to get his shit together. He stopped partying and going out, then disappeared."

"And there weren't any signs of a struggle or anything which would cause you to suspect he'd been kidnapped?" Tony asked.

"Nah. When I left in the morning, everything was in its place. He's pretty O.C.D., and he'd recently reorganized and relabeled everything. If there was something out of place, I would've noticed it."

"Have you thought of any other details you think could help us?"

"No, ma'am. I've stayed in contact with his boss and family, but no one's heard a single word from him. Wish I could help you."

"Okay, thank you. If you think of anything else, please let us know."

"Yes, ma'am."

She watched Gigi watch them as they left.

- - -- --- -----

"I don't get the impression Sotelo's hiding anything, do you?"

"No, I don't think he is." Tony appeared distracted again as he drove back to the office.

"Do you know him?" Her curiosity got the best of her.

"Who? Gigi?"

"Yeah, because the look on your face changed after you saw him."

"Oh, that." He cleared his throat. "That's probably because he looked like the same officer who pulled me over for speeding a few weeks ago. Hard to tell without him being in uniform, though."

She watched him. He focused on the road again, his eyes distance in thought. She wanted to believe he was telling the truth.

- - -- --- -----

Tuesday, June 15, 2021

"Hey, AJ!"

She jumped out of her office chair.

"Shit, Peter! Wear a bell or something already!"

He chuckled and handed her a gift bag. "I heard about your sister-in-law. Congratulations! Oh, and that's Eoghan's and Derek's gifts for their graduation. Sorry about not making it."

"Hey, don't worry about it. I'll give this to Eoghan tonight."

"So, you're a new aunt again? Cool cool!"

"Thank you! Eight pounds, thirteen ounces and a whopping twenty-one inches long. He's a big boy!"

"So, her water broke at the ceremony?"

"Yeah, we couldn't believe it! Poor Ghada, her belly was so swollen. She kept saying she was fine, but when we all stood up to clap, that's when her water broke. Right there in the stands."

"Oh, damn, I can't imagine!"

"She was so cute about it. She tapped Faruq on the shoulder and said, 'It's time.' He was like, 'I know, Eoghan's walking the stage.' Then she looked at me and I *knew* what had happened. So, I slapped Faruq on the arm and said, 'No, dumbass, it's *time*.'" She started laughing. "Oh, Peter, you should've seen the look on all the guys' faces. It was freakin' hilarious!"

"So, what happened after that?"

"When Faruq realized her water broke, he started yelling louder and louder, 'We're having a baby! We're having a baby! Everyone get out of the way!' Everyone in the seats around us started getting up and talking and there was a *huge* commotion, so much so that the principal had to stop the procession and ask everyone to calm down.

"Of course, Faruq was too excited and yelled to the principal, 'We're having a baby! We're having a baby!' Well, the old man on stage couldn't hear what my brother was saying, so Faruq ran up and grabbed the microphone and said, 'We're having a baby! We're having a baby!'

"Everyone started cheering and clapping. Faruq was about to run off the stage, when he turned around, ran back, and said, 'Eoghan, I'm sorry. We have to go! We're having a baby! We're having a baby!' Then he ran off again. Everyone started laughing and cheering as they left the building. Kat and Mom went with them while the rest of us stayed with the boys."

"Oh, man! It would've been awesome to see Faruq so nervous!"

"I know, right? He's typically the calmest and most level-headed out of the bunch of us."

"And Ghada and the baby are doing fine now?"

"Oh, yeah. As soon as Eoghan and Derek were done, we left for the hospital. By the time we got there, the baby had been born. Faruq came out to tell us and we all yelled 'We're having a baby! We're having a baby!'" She started laughing again. "You would've gotten a kick out of it."

"That's awesome. Please tell Eoghan and Derek I'm sorry for not making it. I hope the gifts make up for it."

"Peter, don't worry about that. They know you had other obligations after your dad was in the hospital. They understand. Besides, their heads were somewhere else. They spent some time with the family before heading to their graduation parties."

"That's good."

"Yeah, everything's great. Ghada didn't have any complications. Everything went smoothly. They named the baby Hani. So now they have Hakim, Houda, and Hani. The family is growing."

"And your dad?"

"Dad's doing great, too. Couldn't ask for a better year."

- - -- --- -----

<u>Tuesday, June 22, 2021</u>

She finally crawled into her bed and stared at the ceiling. She was drained, exhausted from the long day's tasks and emotions. Other caseloads and reports piled up on her desk. Conrad took off on another cross-country expedition again. Tiffany took another stab at getting under her skin.

This day, of all days.

After several minutes, she sat up and stretched, glad all her family left shortly after Jenna's birthday party. She wanted to be alone and distract herself with a movie online.

She powered on her laptop and clicked on the movie app when her screen flickered.

Her heart leapt as she saw a window appear with a blinking cursor.

Anger followed her joy.

> NCPoland1543: Hello, Ameena
> *Roar317811: Where have you been?*
> NCPoland1543: Working on projects which have kept me away.
> *Roar317811: What do you want?*
> NCPoland1543: Rough day?
> *Roar317811: What the hell do you think…*
> NCPoland1543: I'm sorry, Ameena
> NCPoland1543: It's been eventful for you lately
> *Roar317811: To say the least…*
> NCPoland1543: I know what having so much family around you does
> NCPoland1543: I know what today is
> *Roar317811: Today is my daughter's birthday. That's what day it is.*
> NCPoland1543: I understand
> *Roar317811: Do you? Do you really understand? Why contact me today of all days when I haven't heard from you in MONTHS??? Do you know how many times I've reached out to you? How*

many times I've needed answers to so many fucking questions?
NCPoland1543: Are you upset at the loss of Michael's company all these years, or my company all these months?
Roar317811: That's not fair!
NCPoland1543: I did not abandon you. My previous location was compromised and I had to move. I needed to re-secure my servers, twice. I could not reach out to you, or I would have been caught. And I won't allow that to happen. I still have much work to do.
NCPoland1543: I've listened to you talking to me, even if I never responded.
Roar317811: Is that supposed to make me feel better?
NCPoland1543: How can I make you feel at this moment?
Roar317811: I don't know. I need to get past today. I'll feel better in a few days. I always do
NCPoland1543: I'm here for you if you need to ever talk about it
Roar317811: Thank you
Roar317811: I asked Conrad about the Newtonian Collaborative like you asked me to. He refused to tell me anything and told me to never, ever mention it again. He won't tell me anything about it.
NCPoland1543: That's unfortunate, then
Roar317811: Will you tell me?
NCPoland1543: It's not my place, and not tonight, dear
Roar317811: You call me 'dear'?

NCPoland1543: Would you prefer 'dear' or love?

Roar317811: No quotes around the latter, I notice

NCPoland1543: You did not answer the question

Roar317811: You ask me if I want your 'love'?

NCPoland1543: You already have that, and my heart

Roar317811: I can't give you that, or mine

NCPoland1543: No need to explain. I know your heart still belongs to Michael, as mine does to my wife

Roar317811: You're married???

NCPoland1543: Was. But it's a story for another day, not this one

Roar317811: So still I have fewer answers and more questions for you. You infuriate me

NCPoland1543: If it means I give you stirrings and fire, I will gladly burn for you

Roar317811: And if I scorch your heart?

NCPoland1543: I carry your heart with me in its place then

Roar317811: Your play with words could carry their own acts

NCPoland1543: And your wordplay sets the stage for our next encounters

Roar317811: And when do I have the honor of meeting you in person?

NCPoland1543: Perhaps in a few months, if you want me

Roar317811: I would want you now if you would allow me and trust me

NCPoland1543: The trust is increasing; the allowance, growing.

But tell me where your heart rests
with me, at this moment
Roar317811: Honestly?
NCPoland1543: Yes
*Roar317811: My heart is a fractured
mess. It aches for Michael. It enjoys
Tony. It grows fond of yours. I have
found myself missing the chance to
chat with you. This is a yearning
which hasn't gone away. I feel—I feel
I can trust you, even though I don't
know you. And this feeling scares the
shit out of me.*
NCPoland1543: You want knowing, then?
*Roar317811: A part of me wants to
know all of you. The knowing,
perhaps, is what I yearn.*
NCPoland1543: Then know this: we'll
know each other in person in a few
months. Right now, I'm still doing my
research, and can't see you. My work
comes first, as yours does for you.
But there will be a point in the near
future where my research crosses
yours, and that's when we'll meet.
Fair?
Roar317811: Fair enough
NCPoland1543: Please forgive my past
absence and understand my future
absences will be shorter. I promise,
now and always.
Roar317811: Copernicus, thank you
NCPoland1543: For what exactly?
*Roar317811: For the support today, of
all days*
NCPoland1543: I will always be here
for you today, of all days, and then
for all the rest of my days. May you
sleep better tonight, now. I will
keep watch over you. Good night,

Ameena.

The flicker of both the screen and her heart left both feeling empty, though the latter felt less heavy and more confused.

- - -- --- -----

<u>Tuesday, June 29, 2021</u>

AJ walked past the moving van in the driveway and up to the apartment. The front door was propped open. It appeared Gigi was in the middle of moving.

"Hello," she called out, as she knocked on the door.

"Come in. I'm in the kitchen."

She walked through the apartment and noticed dozens of moving boxes stacked in the front room, waiting to be carried out. She heard the voices of two other men. When she walked in the kitchen, three men stood there, Sotelo one of them. When they saw her, they went silent, their expressions changed. She felt the energy in the room quickly go dark.

"Detective Jardine!" Gigi's voice pitched high from the shock to see her.

"Officer Sotelo, may I speak to you in private?"

"Sure. I guess."

He motioned for the other two to leave.

One of the men, more muscular and massive than Sotelo, gave off a sinister and evil vibe. The other man, smaller in stature to the massive one, mirrored Gigi's height and weight. Both slowly walked past her, each on opposite sides, sizing her up.

"Ballsy of you to be here without your partner, *detective*." The sinister one brushed against her.

The hairs on her neck stood up. She desperately wanted to leave. She regretted showing up to the apartment without Tony or any form of backup, but she did not want her partner there as a distraction. The two men exited the room.

"How can I help you?" Gigi asked.

"I had a couple of follow-up questions I needed to ask you. I see you're busy, so I won't stay long."

"Yeah, sure. I can try to help you."

"First, do you recognize this person?"

She pulled out a photo from her folder and gave it to the trooper. It was a photo of Martín Delarosa.

"When my partner and I were here a few weeks ago, you

told us everyone calls you Gigi. This man mentioned knowing an individual named Gigi."

"Uh, no. I don't know him." He quickly handed her the photo back. She saw a slight tightening in his lower lids and his eyes darted in a couple of directions. He lied.

"Mr. Sotelo, do you know if Carl knew him perhaps? Maybe you saw him at a party or somewhere like that?"

"No, I don't. He might have. I mean, I'm a workout junky. You saw my two friends there. Carl, he's a workaholic. We didn't hang out a lot together. Different schedules."

"That makes sense." She did not believe him. She pulled out another photo, this one of Angie. "Do you recognize this woman?"

He stared at it for several seconds. She could see the expressions morphing from unsettledness and anger to casual denial. He shook his head and handed the picture back to her.

"Sorry, I can't help you." Before she could get any words out, he yelled, "Yo, Aggie! Frankie! Let's get going!"

Gigi looked down at her, his stare dead and emotionless. The other two men walked in and stood slightly behind her on each side as the trifecta threat made her skin crawl off her body. She did not feel safe, at all.

For fuck's sake, stay calm! He's a cop. He won't do anything, she told herself several times.

She cleared her throat. "Officer Sotelo, thank you for your time. May I get your forwarding address, in case I have any additional questions?"

"I'll have my profile updated in the state database and can forward it to you after I'm settled in my new place," Gigi continued to glare at her.

"Thank you. Good luck with your move."

She took a step back, then turned around and smacked right into the large sinister man. He purposely stood in her way, blocking her path. He appeared to enjoy the intimidation game.

"Excuse me." She moved out of his way and left the house.

She could not get to her car quick enough.

What the fuck are you doing, Jardine? You should've brought backup or Tony – SOMEone!

She rubbed the chills from her arm and pulled out of the driveway as quick as she could.

- - -- --- -----

Tuesday, July 6, 2021

Ameena saw her boss walk into the hospital waiting room and she immediately stood up.

She choked back the tears. "Sir, I wasn't expecting you."

"I came over as soon as I got out of my afternoon meeting. How's he doing, Jardine?"

They walked out of the waiting area, leaving the rest of her family there.

"I don't know, sir. We're waiting on the doctors."

"Ellie couldn't give me any details. Do you know exactly what happened?"

She wiped away the tears and took a deep breath. "Dad had a follow-up appointment today with one of his doctors. He's been three months post-P.T., so the doctor wanted to see how he was doing, if he was healing properly.

"Dad wanted to take the stairs—he was so proud he could climb stairs again. He and Mom were heading up to the second floor when she said some guy came running down towards them. He shoved both my parents and they fell back. Mom caught herself by grabbing the railing, but Dad fell the full flight of stairs backward. He was knocked unconscious. Mom flipped out and started screaming.

"A couple of nurses stopped to help Dad and they immediately admitted him. He's in I.C.U. right now. They're running tests to see how bad it is, but the doctor on call pulled me aside and told me not to get my hopes up. He said to call the family and get them down here. He doesn't know how much longer Dad has. I haven't told Mom yet. She won't leave his side. I don't have the heart to tell her."

Conrad grabbed her, pulling her closer to him and gave her a fatherly hug. "I'm so sorry, Ameena."

She let him hold her tightly and sobbed into his suit. She just let him hold her.

- - -- --- -----

Tuesday, July 13, 2021

The welcomed warmth of the sun contrasted the coldness she felt within. Eoghan sat in the folding chair next to her. Jenna would not take her arms from Jamilla's waist. Everyone else either stood or sat as they listened.

"We have gathered here at the final resting place for Ernest James Andrewson, a loving husband, caring father, and doting grandfather…" The man's voice trailed off.

Ameena stared at a rock near the coffin. Her vision tunneled as she focused on the stone and she lost herself in her mind again. The last time she had been to a funeral was—

—*Michael's memorial.* Her mind raced with a raging headache of turmoil and grief. *How can this be happening this was a tragic accident didn't need to happen what will Momma do poor Jenna never left Dad's side she's not going to recover from this…*

"…and I would like to honor the *love* Jamilla and Ernest shared. Though they came from *diverse* cultures and religions, they did not let those *minor* differences stop them from the *joy* and *good* they shared with everyone. Let them be an example of how two *incredible* faiths—Christianity and Islam—can live, learn, and love from each other. Let their beautiful example show you the *best* of what God can do.

"For those who would like to attend," the priest continued, "I have offered my church this evening for the *Salat al-Janazah*, the Islamic funeral prayer, for Mrs. Andrewson and her family. All are welcome. Mrs. Andrewson," he turned to her, "it is my honor to be there with you.

"We will conclude this eulogy as Ernest's body is lowered into the ground with Ecclesiastes 3:1-8:

> *"To everything, there is a season,*
> *And a time to every purpose under the heaven:*
> *A time to be born, and a time to die;*

A time to plant, and a time to pluck up that which is planted;
A time to kill, and a time to heal;
A time to tear down, and a time to build;
A time to weep, and a time to laugh;
A time to mourn, and a time dance;
A time to scatter stones, and a time to gather them;
A time to embrace, and a time to refrain from embracing;
A time to search, and a time to give up;
A time to keep, and a time to cast away;
A time to rend, and a time to sew;
A time to keep silence, and a time to speak;
A time to love, and a time to hate;
A time of war, and a time of peace.

"In the name of the Father, Son, and Holy Spirit. In the name of Mohammed, His last Messenger, and Christ, His only Son. In the name of God, praise be to Allah. Ameen, Amen."

- - -- --- -----

She stayed after the prayer service to help clean up and load the plants into the car. Kat, Tony, and Derek volunteered to stay behind while the rest of the family went home; the latter two moved tables and chairs back where they belonged.

"Ameena," Kat, softly said, "these were addressed to you. Thought you'd want to see them."

She took the arrangement — a peace lily plant with deep green limbs bursting from the center of a woven basket — from her sister-in-law and walked it out to her car. A singular lily bloomed, standing tall in the middle. With the light from the church parking lot, she read the card:

Ameena: I cannot comfort you, but know you are

comforted. If I could shield you, I'd wrap you in my
armor. Psalms 89: 13
~nc

"Who's that from?" Tony's voice startled her.

Ameena watched him lean against her car. She folded the note and quickly stuck it in her pocket.

"A friend of mine sent it. I didn't expect to hear from them. They left a Bible verse."

He stared at her and she could see the sorrow in his eyes. The darkness softened his features.

"How're you holding up?"

"I'm not, Tony. I'm just not. More so than Mom and Jenna, but still."

"Come here."

He gently pulled her body into his and wrapped his arms around her. He cupped the back of her head and caressed her. His warmth relaxed her.

"I'm so sorry, Ameena."

She dug her face into his neck and chest, breathing in his aftershave. She did not want the moment to end.

- - -- --- -----

She sunk into her bed with Ernest's Bible and flipped through the Psalms to find the one Copernicus left for her. It read:

> *You have a strong arm;*
> *Your hand is mighty,*
> *Your right hand is exalted.*

She opened her laptop and double-clicked on the chatroom window.

`Roar317811: I don't know if you're`

*here but thank you for the peace lily
and the verse. I could use the
encouragement right now. It's been a
rough week for all of us. I'm sure
you've been listening, but I feel I
need to write this to you. I just
want to see my thoughts written in
front of me, even if they disappear
after I close the window. The
concussion caused a cerebral edema.
He never woke up. Three days after
the accident, Dad passed away. I hope
he could hear us say goodbye. And
that we loved him. My God, I miss
him. I know how my mom feels and I
ache for her. The police are still
looking for the person who shoved
him. They've examined the security
footage. They can't tell who it was.
Some guy, tall, medium build. Wore
scrubs. That's all anyone remembers.
I don't know why I'm pouring all this
out here. Maybe through the
anonymity, you've gained my trust. I
hope you know how special your
condolence is to me. Now and always.
Roar317811: Good night, Copernicus.*

- - -- --- -----

Tuesday, July 20, 2021

She exited the elevator. She heard and saw a group of coworkers standing around Tiffany's cubicle.

" —he had a heart attack. That's what I heard," Tiffany told everyone.

AJ caught the tail end of the conversation. "You heard wrong, Tiffany."

"I'm just saying what someone told me."

"They're wrong! He was pushed down the stairs, cracked his head and his brain swelled. He never woke up. He died three days later. THAT'S what happened." AJ stared at everyone. "And if ANY of you want to know EXACTLY what happened, you can ask ME, not her."

She walked off and overhead Tiffany huff, "What a rude bitch coming over here."

Then to her surprise: "Tiff, give it a rest." "Her father just died." "You're the bitch."

When AJ sat down in her cubicle, she wiped the tears from her eyes and started her computer. She saw someone approach.

"Hey," Greg said. "I'm sorry about your dad."

"Thanks. I guess."

"I'd also like to apologize for the way Tiffany treats you."

"Thank you, Greg, but she's the only one responsible for what she does. Not you."

"Then let me apologize for any hurt I might've caused you."

"There's no hurt, other than losing my dad."

He nodded. Before he walked away, he gave her a hug. "If you need anything, let us know. You do have friends here, whether or not you believe it."

- - -- --- -----

Tuesday, July 27, 2021

"Eoghan, that's NOT acceptable!"

"Mom," he protested. "It's MY decision, not yours! I'm staying here and going to L.R.C."

"You don't have a scholarship to Lakes Region College like you do for U.N.H. How are you going to afford it? Do you want to be trapped in student loan debt like me, YEARS after graduating?!"

"Habibti, we have the money. Eoghan doesn't have to spend anything. Your dad made sure to set up funds for both the kids."

"Mom, what about Faruq's children? Or Ari's children? What about THEIR colleges and THEIR education? It's not right!"

"Sweetheart, I already talked to your brothers. Ari's biomechanical job makes enough for everyone. He refused any help from us. And Faruq is trying to GIVE me money now. His children are covered, I promise you!"

"And what about Nabih when he and Dana get married next year and start having children? I don't feel right about it."

"Ameena, listen to me. I discussed this with all your brothers, and they are fine. They want you to take the money for Eoghan and Jenna."

"Mommy." Jenna walked up and Ameena could tell she had been crying. The sight of the little girl's tears made her heart sink.

"Jenna, why are you crying? Come here." She hugged her daughter.

"Mommy, I don't want Eoghan to go away. I want him to stay *here* with us. *Pleeeeease!*" Jenna dug her head into her mom's chest and wailed. Then her words pierced Ameena's heart. "I lost Papa, and-and, I don't want to lose my big brother, tooooo!"

Ameena was torn by what she thought was logical for her son and his future, and what was needed for the family at the present time.

"Fine." Her voice was quiet in defeat as she was outnumbered three-to-one. "It's fine. If that's what you all really want, then that's what we'll do. We'll stay together."

- - -- --- -----

Tuesday, August 3, 2021
"Ameena! You need to get home now."

The urgency in Jamilla's voice made her panic. Worst-case scenarios raced through her mind as her car sped home. When she pulled into the driveway, her mother stood outside with a man she did not immediately recognize. She was unsure of what the problem was until she walked up and finally recognized him.

Her anger took over.

"What the fuck are you doing here, Paden?"

"Habibti, that's no way to talk to your father."

"My DAD was buried less than a month ago."

"Ameena." Paden took off his Irish flat cap and clutched it in both hands.

"Just—" She was unable to materialize a sentence. "Just. Leave." She walked into the house and slammed the door to her bedroom, locking it. Turmoil, sheer anger, shock, hurt— she wanted to punch the wall.

Several minutes later, she heard a knock on her door. "Habibti, please come out."

"Is he gone?"

"Yes, sweetheart. He came by to pay his respects and apologize. Please come out so I can talk to you."

Ameena stared up at the ceiling and tried to ignore the request.

After more silence, the tone of her mother's voice changed. "Ameena! Get OUT here. *NOW!*"

The strength in her mother's words startled her. She opened the door and glanced at her mom. She immediately felt ashamed of her behavior.

"Habibti, Paden sent me a message a few days ago. He found out about your dad and offered his condolences. He then apologized for everything from the past. He begged for forgiveness, and you know for him that is something he never did before. And you know how I feel about forgiveness. You know I can't hold the past against him."

Ameena remained angry. "Do you remember the

swollen lip he left you? And the lashes across my back? What about those?"

Jamilla sighed. "I don't expect you to want him in your life. But I could not live with myself if I did not see him again and accept his apology."

"Momma, I'm not ready to talk to him. I don't want him in my life right now. If ever."

"That's fine, dear. All I ask is you talk to him before it's too late. Please, do this for me."

"I will, but not now."

"Okay. Take small steps. Keep an open mind and an open heart. Hear what he has to say. He said he has lived in the Boston area for some time now and he spends parts of his summers in northern New England. He will be back next month if you want to talk to him then."

"I'll think about it, Momma. I'll think about it."

- - -- --- -----

<u>Tuesday, August 10, 2021</u>
"Hello, Blues, did ya miss me?"

The voice startled her. AJ spun around and dropped the box in the office parking lot. Her back was pressed against the trunk of her car as she stared at the ex-convict.

"Martín! What're you doing here?"

He smirked. With a swaggered step, he came towards her. "Don't worry, Blues, I got out last week. Good behavior and shit." He licked his lips and looked her up and down. "Wanted to say I missed my favorite detective. Like the fresh suit? Cut and styled!" He still had the appearance of a cocky banker.

She tried to regain her composure. "Martín, is there something I can help you with?"

He shook his head. "Nah, I'm square. Wanted to let you know I'm out now." He took another step closer in her personal space. He was not as tall as Tony. "I'm lookin' to have some fun now."

"Martín, please go. I need to unload my car and clock in for a meeting."

He nodded his head and smiled at her, then stared into her eyes. His brown eyes almost shone in the sunlight. He leaned in closer to her, inches from her face. She was pinned against her trunk.

"I'll see you around, Blues. Maybe we can have fun. *Soon.*" Then he backed away in all his cockiness, made a gun motion with his hand as if to shoot her, and swaggered off.

She took a deep breath and checked her fear back in its place.

- - -- --- -----

Tuesday, August 17, 2021

"How was your vacation, sir?"

"It was good, Jardine. How's your mom doing?"

"She has good and bad days, sir. She's happy Eoghan decided to stay at home and attend college nearby."

"That's good. And how are the kids going?"

"Jenna's still heartbroken, but she's feeling a little better. She's excited to go back to school soon. She's also had more time to spend with her cousins. My brothers and their families have been around all summer helping out with what they can."

He nodded. "That's good. I wanted to let you know I received a phone call from Agent Aserbbo this morning. Delarosa's gone missing."

"What? How does—"

"—Tony know?" Conrad completed the question. "As I've mentioned before, Aserbbo has dozens of C.I.s everywhere. He's one of the few agents who has an excellent rapport with informants. They know they can trust him, and they know he'll take care of them if something happens."

"And one of his C.I.s knew Martín and knows he's missing?"

"Correct."

"So now we have a missing agent *and* a missing ex-convict?"

"Also correct."

"Humph. At least *one* of them will be missed, sir."

"I hope you're referring to the law enforcement one, Jardine."

- - -- --- -----

<u>Tuesday, August 24, 2021</u>

After another meeting with no new leads on either Frierson or Delarosa, she stared at her monitor, feeling defeated.

"Hey, AJ."

"Hey, Peter. What brings you out of the lab over here?"

"I found something and wanted to share it with you and Conrad. Wanna come down to the conference room?"

"Sure."

They walked downstairs and entered the conference room to see Conrad, Taylor, and Tony waiting for them. Peter shut the door and took a seat between her and Tony.

"Mr. Yates, what did you want to share with all of us?"

"I knew you guys were running into dead ends left and right with the cases and Ms. Carmicle's murder. I wondered if her death was connected with the disappearance of Martín Delarosa and Carl Frierson. So, I retrieved the evidence from Angie's case and pulled up the DNA reports on the semen contributors."

"You got a match?" Tony asked.

"Yeah, but not the first time I ran the check."

"What happened?" AJ asked.

"When I ran the DNA through C.O.D.I.S. months ago, I only tried matching the samples to convicted offenders and arrestee profiles we had in the database. My thought process back then was that we were looking for previously convicted men. Then I figured maybe those involved in the rape and murder disappeared because they didn't want to get caught."

"Shit." Taylor broke his silence. "Carl."

Peter nodded. "Yes, sir. One of the three samples matched Frierson's DNA. He was one of the rapists."

"Mother fucker." AJ looked at Conrad. "I think Sotelo and his friends may also be involved."

"What makes you say that, Jardine?"

"Because when I went to re-interview Gigi, he—"

"Wait." Tony interrupted her and immediately sat up. "You did WHAT?"

"I went back to interview Sotelo."

"You went by YOURSELF?"

Everyone in the room remained quiet. AJ stared back at him, confused at his reaction. Peter slid his chair away from the line of fire.

"Tony, I was fine. His friends intimidated—"

"His FRIENDS were there too?" A new tone—that of panic—resonated in his voice.

"Yes. Giovani called one of them Aggie. I remember because of the Aggies at Texas A&M University."

"Goddammit, Ameena! What the fuck were you thinking?" He slammed his hand down on the desk, got up, and stormed out of the room. She stared in sheer disbelief at her partner's reaction. She stood up to follow him when Conrad stopped her.

"Jardine, not today." Then Conrad looked at Taylor. "Put out an A.P.B. on Frierson. He's no longer Missing Persons. He's now our murder suspect."

- - -- --- -----

Tuesday, August 31, 2021

Schools started for Eoghan and Jenna, and both were happy to be back in a normal routine. The community college was only a few minutes from the house, between the downtowns of Belmont and Laconia. Ameena was happy Eoghan stayed home.

Derek still lived with the family. He decided to skip a year from college and save up as much money as he could to put himself through school with no student loans. Jamilla was happy to have her adopted grandson there, though at times Derek felt guilty from her generosity.

Jenna continued to be plagued with nightmares all summer after Ernest's death. She would wake up in the middle of the night screaming and crying or would sometimes talk in her sleep about the Van Gogh lights and a black balloon with arms.

Jamilla moved her into her bedroom. Both grandmother and granddaughter would fall asleep in each other's arms. With the small bedroom now empty, it was offered to Ameena, but she declined. Then, it was offered to Derek in the hopes he would feel more like a family member and less like a roommate; he made sure she did not want the room before moving his things in.

Ameena heard the doorbell ring. This excited Abbott and Costello. She heard her mother open the front door.

"Ameena! It's Tony!"

Her heart skipped a beat. She moved Alyx out of her lap, then went into the dining room to see Tony and her mom standing there.

"It's good to see you, Tony!" Jamilla kissed him on the cheek and smiled at Ameena. "We were just heading upstairs, habibti. I'll let you two alone. Goodnight!"

They stood in silence staring at each other until everyone was upstairs and bedroom doors were shut. Ameena's cheeks flushed with anger.

"Can we talk somewhere privately?" he asked.

She nodded and walked to her bedroom. Once inside she

shut the door. He sat down on the edge of her bed; she stood by the door, her back against the wall with her arms crossed.

"I'm listening."

"Look, I'm sorry. I shouldn't've flipped out on you."

"Ya think?"

"I messed up again, I know."

"Tony, you flipped out on me in front of everyone! Then you stormed out and disappeared for days. What the fuckety fuck???" She flared her arms up in the sky in sheer frustration.

He caught her hand and pulled her close to him. She did not resist his touch as she stood over him. He peered up at her. His blue eyes were soft and made her heart melt again.

"Ameena, please." His voice pleaded for forgiveness.

"Tony, I-I don't understand. WHAT is going on?"

"You mentioned Aggie in the meeting. He's an extremely violent member of the Fasciata. He killed one of my C.I.s a few years ago, but we couldn't make it stick. I've had him on my radar for a while now. I wouldn't doubt it if he was one of the other men who raped Angie. He does terrible things to women, AJ."

She sat down on the bed next to him. "Why didn't you say something then?"

"Because I can't let anyone know. It's too dangerous. *He's* too dangerous. *They're* too dangerous. I needed to leave and track down another informant after that, make sure they were okay. We had to put them in protective custody immediately."

"Tony, I—You want to know why I went there by myself? Because of the reaction you had when you saw Giovani. You know him, and you lied to me about that. Why?"

He looked at her with a longing like he wanted to tell her everything, but then she knew the answer.

"He's Fasciata, isn't he?"

"Yes."

The reality of her error in judgment began to set in.

"Oh my gawd," she whispered. "But, why not arrest him?"

"We can't, Ameena. It's not that easy. And the only reason they didn't hurt you is because they were ordered by the Fasciata Lord not to harm you or any law enforcement. How long this order stands, I don't know."

"Oh my gawd..."

He interlocked his fingers with hers and kissed her hand. She saw the tenderness in his eyes. "Don't. *Ever.* Go. Without me. Again."

He leaned over with his free hand and tucked her hair behind her ear, then caressed the side of her face. She nodded softly and leaned into the warmth of his hand. Then, gently, he kissed her. He pulled her closer into a protective embrace and they both laid down on the bed.

They fell asleep, together on top of the sheets, in the same embrace the grandmother and granddaughter did in the bedroom above them.

- - -- --- -----

CHAPTER NINETEEN: 13

<u>Tuesday, October 12, 2021</u>

AJ smiled as Tony drove. She enjoyed the beauty outside the passenger window this time of year. The sun was high above them.

She smiled as their car curved along Route 3A, meandering with the Pemigewasset River and passing the Franklin Falls Dam. She enjoyed the view of the massive engineering structure.

She smiled because they were heading to the Town of Hill in Merrimack County where Delarosa's body was discovered in a house off Addison Road. She grinned ear to ear knowing the cocky sonofabitch would no longer intimidate her.

They were warned the crime scene was extensive, so Conrad sent the C.S.I. bus first. They would meet the newly hired crime scene investigator there. The last time AJ remembered seeing a C.S.I. bus was at the Rune Killer's burial site when all the extra equipment was needed to process the scene.

Tony parked the car. She gazed out the window at the two-story colonial. The driveway was freshly asphalted and split in two: one path led to the new house, the other led to a large barn nearby. A new model—and rather expensive—vehicle was parked in the driveway along with a few other unmarked cars.

They saw a group of individuals deep in discussion hunched over the hood of one of the vehicles. The group stopped, and a petite woman walked over to Tony's car.

She was fully donned with P.P.E.s, but AJ could still make out her Indian features. Her bright dark eyes were young; her hair, peppered with grays poking out from under the hairnet. Her age was impossible to guess. The woman carried herself with confidence and authority, a force beyond measure. The detective liked that.

They exited the car and introduced themselves.

"Dr. Tarakini Amin. A pleasure to meet you both. I'm the lead C.S.I. here at this scene." She extended her hand for a firm shake. Though she spoke perfect English, Dr. Amin still had a slight Asian accent.

"What can you tell us about the crime?" Tony asked.

"I'm not through with my processing yet. It could take three more days to collect and document everything, but I can show you what I know so far and let you in later this afternoon to take a look."

Tarakini picked up her notepad to show them a sketch of the house interior. Using a pen, she pointed at various rooms one by one.

"We came in through the front door and it appears there'd been a recent struggle. There is broken glass and furniture everywhere. We saw blood spatter in some areas and are documenting that right now.

"The kitchen and dining room here," she pointed to one end of the house, "had more blood. Not a lot, but it initially appeared someone cut themselves and cleaned their wound in the sink. Upstairs is where the carnage is."

"There's more blood?" AJ asked.

"Oh, yes. Definitely more. There are three bedrooms and two bathrooms upstairs. Two of the bedrooms appear to be lived in, and I believe the house was occupied by at least two individuals. Now this third bedroom," she pointed to a corner room on the drawing, "that's the shocker. It's lined from ceiling to floor in thick polymer."

"It's a kill room."

The doctor nodded. "Yes, Agent Aserbbo. Without a doubt. Each layer of the polymer has been taped together to provide a sealed and controlled area. There is blood — both fresh and quite old — everywhere. There is also smeared blood streaks on the floor, as if someone sloppily tried to wipe up after a spill. I cannot yet confirm how many people may have been murdered in this room, but preliminary signs point to multiple individuals."

"Holy shit."

"There's more, detective. When we checked out the other two rooms, there was a body in the master bedroom. Your M.E., Dr. Owen, will be here soon to get the body. We did find a driver's license. Martín Delarosa.

"Delarosa's body has several cuts and abrasions on his person, and I believe his is some of the blood from downstairs and in the bathroom, but again, we won't know until we process all the evidence back at the lab.

"By preliminary evaluation, it appears he did not die of the stab wounds, but possibly of an overdose. You can see the body later after Dr. Owen arrives. You will need to don the proper P.P.E.s and I need a chance to finish doing my collections in the bedroom."

"Thank you, Dr. Amin."

"There's more, which you may find interesting."

"More?" Tony asked.

"Yes, sir. The other live-in bedroom and bath appeared quite odd to me. The door was shut. We could smell bleach everywhere. When I opened the door, we were overcome by the smell. We needed to open windows and ventilate the area before we could proceed. We'll try to process the room, but I highly doubt we'll find anything. It was devoid of all furniture, save a single twin-size mattress and small table. There was nothing in the closet or bathroom other than toilet paper and one towel.

"The bathroom was wiped down and cleaned extensively. There was not even hair or dirt in the corners behind the toilet. The bedroom itself appears to be a lost cause. Every surface has been sprayed and wiped down with oxygenated bleach, hydrogen peroxide, and possibly other professional chemicals. The table and mattress are ruined and still damp from the cleanup."

The pair studied the layout. Tarakini excused herself to finish processing the scene where Delarosa's body was located. They went back to Tony's car and sat inside waiting.

"Professional cleanup and hit room?" AJ watched Tony's demeanor.

"It's called a Wheel House."

"What do you mean by 'Wheel House'?"

"There's a medieval form of torture called The Wheel. I won't go into details, but it's a brutal way to die. This house, here, it's one of the Octave's torture locations. They have houses like this one scattered throughout various states. Nice remote locations, or sometimes in plain sight, where you can't hear the screams. And if you heard gunshots, it wouldn't be out of the ordinary considering all of the hunters in the woods everywhere."

"Geez. Do you think Angie was tortured here?"

Tony nodded slightly. She noticed the darkened skin around his eyes and the lines around his mouth.

"AJ, whatever we find in there, it won't be pretty. This is why I'm trying to protect you. I—I don't want to think of seeing you in a place like this."

She watched Tony's mannerisms. She wanted to believe he was trying to protect her. She wanted to believe she could trust him again.

- - -- --- -----

The pair were finally granted permission to go into the house well after three o'clock. Dr. Amin said she would provide them with all her findings and documentation, but AJ still wanted to take her own photos and analyze them.

Cassie agreed to not move the body until they could see it.

Broken and splintered pieces of furniture, plastic and glass littered the living room. The large flat-screen TV had been knocked down and shards of glass crunched under their cloth-covered shoes. Large blood drops—mostly gravitational—polka dotted the floor as if someone paced back and forth with a weapon in their hand. The air felt salty and heavy with unusual humidity.

She was eager to see the upstairs area. As they climbed the stairs, she could smell the iron from the blood and the bleach from the bedroom; the latter had an unmistakable and unforgettable odor. Her hands felt clammy, and she realized her anxiety heightened.

She stopped midway up the stairs and took a few chlorine-laden breaths. Even with the upstairs windows open and a mask covering her face, her eyes and lungs burned. Tony did not appear to be exempt from the effects either. She focused on reaching Martín's body.

The master bedroom was impressive with the king-sized, spiraling bedpost furniture and marble-topped dressers. The equally thick-wooded nightstands held expensive sculptures and jewelry. Framed art decorated the walls. Everything appeared polished and cleaned, and nothing appeared out of place, except the body.

"Hey, you," Cassie said. She stood by the bed, waiting for the two to get there.

Martín rested on his left side in a fetal position, shirtless, sockless, and in his jeans. He appeared to be sleeping, both hands resting under his head. She did not see a tattoo anywhere on his upper body. However, when she approached the bed, she realized his left hand was curled up and around, clutching something.

Just like our last overdoses. Surely, this cannot be coincidental. I wonder what Pinick would think about this one? He was eager to look at Perales's police and autopsy reports months ago. I'll talk it over with Tony later and see what he thinks.

She continued to study the body. Numerous scrapes and

cuts checkered his torso. She noticed bruising across his face and nose. His knuckles were raw like he wrangled with a sander. When she knelt to examine his left hand, she got a whiff of a familiar chemical.

"Hey, Cass, what's this smell like to you?"

She leaned in and whiffed. "Smells like bleach. I'll be sure to swab his hands thoroughly."

Tony leaned in and sniffed. "Maybe he's the one who cleaned up the bathroom and bedroom?"

AJ nodded. "Possibly. Or maybe someone got into a fight with him, didn't want their DNA found, and soaked Martín's hands in bleach?"

"Anything's possible," Cassie added. "You'll have to wait until after I perform the autopsy and get you the preliminary findings."

AJ continued to study the positioning. "Hey, there's something in his hand."

"Knew you'd want to see it, so that's why I waited." Cassie carefully grabbed Delarosa's hand and pried it open, exposing the item. She picked it up and held it to the light. "Well, this is a new one."

AJ gasped and smiled at both. "It's a Jack Storms piece! Holy shit, I never thought I'd see one in person!" Cassie handed it to her. "This—this is more beautiful than the videos lead on. And heavier!" She bounced the object in her hand a couple of times.

"Huh?"

"Jack Storms. He's a cold-glass sculptor and creates some of the most beautiful pieces of glass art out there. I've been following his work for years. Here, let me show you."

She gave the sculpture back to Cassie, took off her gloves, and pulled out her phone. She tapped on the artist's website and pulled up his gallery images. After scrolling for a few seconds, she found the collector's piece. A tap on the image brought up the video of the sculpture on display.

"See! He uses dichroic glass, geometric shapes and precise mathematical cuts to create his pieces. This one's *The*

Resinova, in honor of the Red Pines here in New Hampshire, where he grew up. He hand-carved and polished each of the spiraling rows of scales. It's perfection if you ask me!"

AJ glanced at Tony. She saw him return the smile. She put her phone away and grabbed a fresh set of gloves to put on.

"Hey, check this out." Cassie flipped the sculpture upside-down.

"What is it?"

"It's a number carved on the base. 'Thirteen'. Maybe it's the thirteenth of a limited edition?"

"Maybe. Still, though, that's pretty amazing."

"You almost ready?" Tony asked AJ.

"Yeah. Let's check out the other rooms and then head out."

- - -- --- -----

"Aren't they beautiful! They almost look like daisies. I had to google them. They are called cineraria."

"They're stunning." Ameena stared at the flowers sitting on the kitchen counter.

Each flower was fully opened and appeared almost flat like a saucer. Vibrant purples and deep navy blues exploded from each stem. The colors wrapped around an inner white band which haloed the darker stamen. The bouquet rested in a smoothly polished, egg-shaped lead-crystal vase.

Ameena picked up the card and opened it.

> *All life is a pattern… but we cannot always see the pattern when we are part of it.*
> *~Belva Plain*
> *01000101280125010011104823205*

"Who's it from, habibti?"

"It doesn't say. There's no signature."

"I think they're from Tony, and he doesn't want to tell you."

"I asked him about it before, and he said he hasn't sent me anything."

"Ah. Okay." Jamilla opened her mouth to say something else but then changed her mind. Ameena caught the change in her demeanor.

"Momma, is everything okay?"

"It-it's nothing, habibti. We can talk about it another time."

"Mom. What is it?"

Her mom paused as she tried to formulate the right words. Ameena knew it had to be something big when her mom was speechless.

"Sweetheart, your father, Paden, and I have been in contact for a while now." She opened her mouth to protest, but Jamilla quickly cut her off. "Lah! Let me finish before you interrupt me. He has only been respectful and has kept his distance until you and your brothers want to see him."

"That's never gonna happen."

"Ameena, don't say that."

"Mom, it hasn't even been three months since Dad died! How many years has it been since you fled from Paden?"

"That doesn't matter."

"Mom. How. Many. Years?"

"I don't know, dear. It was a lo—"

"Thirty-four, Mom. Thirty-four years since you fled from him. I was almost thirteen. I haven't forgotten. I haven't WANTED him in my life since then, and I don't NEED him in my life now."

"The thorn of a rose can still make an experienced gardener weep."

Ameena rolled her eyes at her mom's euphemism. "Mom, I don't understand."

Jamilla sighed. "It means when a man has been hurt by the thing he cherishes the most, it can change how he feels. The pain humbled him. I'm asking you to give him a chance to explain himself. Talk to him."

"No." She stormed off.

From behind, her mother blurted out, "You have two brothers."

Ameena stopped. "What did you say?"

"Your father, he remarried. You have two other brothers. Habibti, I'm not asking you to love him or have a relationship with him, though I'd like you to think about that. All I'm asking is that you not punish his family for his mistakes."

Jamilla walked off and went upstairs; her daughter stood there, stunned at the words.

- - -- --- -----

Tuesday, October 26, 2021

"Holy shit, girl! Your real dad is back?"

"Father," AJ corrected. "Paden's only a sperm donor for all I care. My real dad died three months ago."

Cassie rubbed her friend's arms. "Sweetie, give it time and take it slow."

She glared at her friend. "I can't believe you're siding with my mom!"

"All I'm saying is give it time. Your mom's right about not punishing his family. Think about it. Now, tell me about those flowers!"

"They're called cineraria. They're part of the sunflower family. I took several pictures." She pulled them up on her phone for Cassie to see.

"WOW! Those are some vivid colors. And you don't know who sent them?"

"No. They're not the first anonymous bouquet of flowers I've received."

"Oooo, mystery," Cassie teased.

AJ rolled her eyes. "Let's go over the case now before we get any more distracted."

"Whatever you say, precious."

"Please tell me you have some good news."

"Maybe. Martín's body was covered in abrasions and cuts. Some of the cuts across his torso and the condition of his knuckles were caused from fighting. However, other wounds appeared to be consistent and even in depth and size. They looked deliberate."

"Wait." AJ looked around. "Where's his body?"

"Funeral home collected it immediately. The family even brought in their lawyers if I didn't hand him over right after the autopsy. I documented all I could. There's a folder on the server with all the photos for you to look at."

"Shit."

"Yeah. I had to work fast. Now, I did swab the abrasions and cleaned his fingernails and cuticles, but his nails were already chemically sterilized. Any epithelia were useless.

The bleach and peroxide destroyed everything."

"Was this a professional cleanup?"

"Yeah, my opinion, I'd say so. His lacerations weren't too deep, just enough to have him bleed everywhere. There were no other signs of foul play. My guess? Either he got into an altercation with someone and when Delarosa overdosed, they panicked and cleaned up the scene to cover their identities. OR, he was kidnapped, brought to the house, tortured, and then given a lethal dose of Prussian Black. Either hypothesis is plausible."

"Anything else about the body? What was the actual C.O.D. then?"

"C.O.D. was an overdose. Plain and simple. His tox screen only showed the heroin."

"Prussian Black?"

"Yep."

"And did he have the octopus tattoo?"

"Yes, again. Located on his upper and right thigh. Even glowed under the black light. That's all I have on this one, sweetie."

"Hmm. That's a start I guess." AJ sounded disappointed. "I hope Dr. Amin's findings give us more answers."

- - -- --- -----

Tony and Conrad listened as AJ reiterated Cassie's findings on Delarosa's body. She had the opportunity to review Dr. Amin's reports, pictures, and other paperwork before the meeting and briefed the men on the findings.

"Dr. Amin was extremely thorough with the scene. I'll start with the second floor of the house and work my way room by room.

"The master bedroom is where Martín was found. They processed for prints and came up with Martín's, Frierson's, and a couple of other unknowns. We assume those belong to other Fasciata members or the person Delarosa fought, but we aren't sure. The sheets were clean of any seminal or vaginal contributions. All the furniture and everything else was wiped clean.

"The master bath had traces of blood everywhere. Gravitational droplets were found on the floor and around the toilet. Blood was found in the drain pipe. All of it was Martín's. No other fingerprints or trace were found. The other bedroom with the twin mattress—there's nothing there."

"What do you mean there's nothing there?" Conrad asked.

"The chemicals destroyed everything. The carpet was thoroughly vacuumed and cleaned, the walls *and* ceiling were wiped down. All the oxygen bleach and peroxide destroyed any possible trace evidence. Not even luminol detected anything unusual.

"The bathroom joining the bedroom? Exact same M.O. Cleaned from top to bottom, corner to meticulous corner. There was no blood in the drains, no hair caught in the tub. No fingerprints, no urine, nada."

"Is there any good news, Jardine?"

"Yes, sir, there actually is. The kill room. There were several layers of dried blood on the polymers. Peter's the one who helped process the evidence from the room. He found fingerprints on the plastic which belonged to Martín, two other unknowns, *and* Frierson. Peter ran the unknowns in C.O.D.I.S., and no hits popped up.

"He's still working on the DNA from all the blood spatter in the room, but it may take a few more weeks to sort out. Once we have the analyses, we'll check cold cases, missing persons, and whatever other databases out there to see if we can match samples.

"He did find some brain matter. He said it was several months old, and when he ran it in the system, we got a match." She took a deep breath. "We can now confirm Angie was killed there."

"Shit," Conrad muttered.

Tony remained quiet, listening to AJ.

"Downstairs was also promising. Obviously, there was a struggle. No other trace evidence except Martín's and Frierson's. Dining room, same way. However, there was blood in the laundry room which Dr. Amin noted in her report. She'd processed the washer and dryer and found a partial fingerprint and blood swipe on the lint catcher in the dryer.

"Both the blood and the fingerprint are still a mystery; they don't match any of the samples upstairs or even in the kill room. It's possible that, if Martín was struggling and fighting his murderer, the unknown person was also bleeding. This may be our first big lead."

"That's assuming he was murdered, AJ. We still don't have concrete proof," Tony said.

"True. But the evidence is more than what we had when the last overdose happened."

"Did C.S.I. find anything in the barn and car?" Conrad asked.

"Nothing spectacular in the barn. Expensive winter toys and a super nice mini-yacht were stored there. Martín must have had access to quite a bit of money. The car, same thing. Only Martín's prints were found. Everything else was clean."

"Any updates on finding Frierson?" Conrad looked at Tony for an answer.

"Not yet. My C.I.s haven't seen or heard anything. He vanished like Perales did."

"Let's hope he doesn't turn up like Perales."

"Sir?"

"Yes, Jardine?"

"I'd like to take all of this to the professor and see what his thoughts are."

"AJ, that's a bad idea." Tony's voice held an edge.

"Why?"

"Because he's a crazy old man obsessed with his son's death. That's why."

"Tony, I disagree. I think he can provide us some

valuable insight on this new overdose."

"Don't waste your time, detective. He's not worth it." Tony's voice became increasingly agitated. She did not understand why.

"I think he *is* worth it, *agent*. He was extremely thorough with his research and can give us an unbiased opinion."

"Jardine, Agent Aserbbo's correct. We don't need a civilian involved in this."

"But, sir —" She tried to protest.

"Do not contact Dr. Pinick, detective."

"But, why?" She stared at her boss and could not believe he sided with her partner.

"Jardine, this investigate has deep waters. Bringing in a civilian is too dangerous."

"Yes, sir." She refused to believe him, though.

"Was there anything else we should know about?"

"No, sir. Two steps forward and one step back."

"As it goes, Jardine. As it goes."

- - -- --- -----

She stared at her bedroom ceiling with Delarosa's and Perales's case files spread all around her. She revisited the information but was no closer to finding a solution, other than the one she proposed earlier in the day.

Finally, her logic decided to defy her boss's order. She needed answers and wanted to catch Angie's killers. She promised Angie's mother she would. And she needed another set of unbiased eyes.

The phone rang on the other end.

"Hello?"

"Dr. Pinick, this is Detective Jardine."

"Hi, Detective! It's good to hear from you!"

"Sir, do you have time to meet with me next week? We have a new case and I'd like your input on it, if you don't mind."

"It's another drug overdose, isn't it?"

"Yes."

"And — and they had something in their hand, didn't they?"

"Yes."

"And they have the tattoo?" She could hear the excitement escalating in his voice.

"Again, yes."

"I knew it! Yes, please! Come over when you can!"

"I'm still waiting for some reports to come in at the end of this week and then I'll meet with you. How about next Tuesday perhaps?"

"Absolutely! I'll have the coffee ready for you!"

"Okay, see you then."

She hung up the phone. She felt guilty defying Conrad, but smug with her defiance against Tony. His response earlier felt unusual, like he wanted to hide something. She was not having it.

Not today, dammit. Not today.

- - -- --- -----

<u>Tuesday, November 2, 2021</u>

"Welcome! So good to see you again!" Raymond ushered her in. "Did Agent Aserbbo not join you this time?"

"No, sir."

"Please, have a seat and I'll get the coffee. You like it regular, cream and sugar, correct?"

"Yes, sir."

"Please. Call me Raymond."

"Only if you call me AJ."

After they both had their drinks and settled in the living room, AJ pulled out her binders from her backpack, removed several clipped stacks of papers and handed them to Raymond.

"These are for you."

His eyes went wide. "Seriously? You're entrusting me with all of this?"

"Yes. I really think you can help us break into this investigation."

He sat back. "Wow. I'm honored you'd give these to me."

She took a sip of her coffee. "I haven't convinced my supervisor we have a serial killer on our hands, so please do not share this information with anyone. After this last death, I'm starting to see a connection and believe you."

Raymond skimmed the reports, then put the papers down on the table. "I have to be honest, AJ. I was beginning to doubt myself. Everything in my being is telling me these are all connected to the same person. What does your partner think?"

"Tony and I got into a heated argument over this, Doc — I mean, Raymond. He doesn't believe you or trust you." She saw the professor's face drop. "I'm sorry to tell you that. I don't want to mince words."

"No, that's fine. I understand. I can appear unleveled, at times."

"Raymond," AJ's voice was as gentle as possible, "yes, you can. It's because you've been through traumatic events in the last few years. And I'd guess you haven't had anyone to talk to in a long time. I know the feeling all too well. I was the same way. It took me years before I felt any type of normalcy. And sometimes I still don't. Michael's death still haunts me."

"You still don't know who killed him?"

"No. He—the police reports said there were multiple assailants who drove off in a vehicle. But that's as far as it went. No one knows who killed him. The guns were never found. It's remained an unsolved case for nearly a decade now."

They sat in silence and sipped their coffees. After a respectable pause, Raymond put his cup down and stared at the papers again.

"Why?"

"Why what?" AJ did not understand his question.

"Why give these to me if your partner doesn't trust me?"

"Because *he* may not, but *I* do. You and I, we're kindred spirits. We're both looking for answers."

He nodded. "Thank you, again, for this." He gestured with the papers in his hand.

"You're welcome. I wanted to go over these with you and get your feedback."

"Yeah, anything I can do to help."

"First, I want to give you some background information. I had the unfortunate opportunity to interview Martín Delarosa in jail several months ago. Let's say he's an asshole, womanizer, and deserved whatever treatment he received."

"I understand."

"Martín's body was found in a nice—and expensive— house northwest of the Town of Hill. Do you know where that is?"

"Hill? No, not right off hand."

"It's between here and Bristol off Route 3A."

"Oh! So not far from here?"

"Correct. When we arrived on scene, we saw there'd

been a struggle. We found some blood and trace evidence. When our lab technician ran it against Delarosa's, they were not a match."

Raymond gasped and sat up in the chair quickly. The sudden movement alarmed her.

"I knew it! I was right!"

"Let's be cautious. *I* believe you're correct, but we still have circumstantial evidence here." His smile faded slightly. "Here, let's go over the autopsy report together. Open the report to the tox page. Do you see the findings?"

His eyes scanned the document until he found the magic word: "Tetrodotoxin!"

"Yes, he had—"

"Prussian Black!"

"Yes, again."

"This is amazing!"

"Raymond, do you remember Jose Perales's autopsy?"

"The last victim?"

"Yes, he was the person who went missing at the time of Mary Fay's death. His and all the others—your son's, Damian Winters's, Nathan Hull's, Mary's—all had the same EXACT chemical makeup as Mr. Delarosa's. They all—supposedly—overdosed on Prussian Black."

Raymond mumbled under his breath and counted on his fingers. "Wow, we have a good body count now. I was right about a serial killer."

"Possibly. Quite possibly."

"You doubt we have a serial killer, AJ?"

"No, sir. I've been staring at these case files every day for weeks now. I've studied the ones I gave you. And everything is telling me they're related. This many people with this many quote-unquote coincidences? Highly improbable and illogical." She took another sip of her coffee and then set it down. "I want you to look at this."

She thumbed through the stack of her papers and showed him some scanned photos. "Every single one of these victims, ALL with the same tentacle tattoo found on different locations of their bodies, overdosed in the same way: a drug—Prussian Black specifically—was injected with a hypodermic needle in the left inner elbow. The arms were curled up, and they were all holding something in their hand."

"That's right! Chris had a bag of sunflower seeds. One hundred forty-four to be exact. I can't forget that. Ever." His eyes turned light pink.

"Raymond, I know. You won't ever forget. And that's okay. I promise." She changed the subject before his mind drifted off on a dark tangent. "You showed me photos of the paper snowflake from Damian's hand. And Nathan Hull had a shell. His wife had daisies. Both Perales and Delarosa were holding pine cones. Perales's pine cone was natural. Martín's was manmade. He had a cold-glass sculpture, something made with lead crystal and dichroic glass. Do you know what dichroic is?"

"Dichroic? Two colors?"

"Yes, something close. Dichroic glass produces a variety of colors depending on the angle of reflection. So basically, it appears one color from one angle, but when you turn it, it appears a different color from another angle. It can make glass look like diamonds."

"Ah, I see."

"This particular sculpture was a rather remarkable and unique pinecone."

AJ pulled out the photo for Raymond to examine.

"And you said Perales was found with a pinecone?"

"Yes, he was actually found with a *real* pinecone with the number twenty-one carved on one of the scales. But *this* pinecone was made by artist Jack Storms. Have you ever heard of him?"

"No. Who is he?"

"He's a phenomenal artist. Here, let me show you his website."

She pulled out her phone and keyed in the website: www.jackstorms.com. She clicked on the Gallery tab and showed Raymond the artwork.

"He's one of the few cold-glass sculptors in the world. He glues, cuts, polishes, and repeats the process over and over to create these mesmerizing pieces of art you can stare at for hours. I've always wanted to see one in person, and last week I finally did. Delarosa was holding this one."

She clicked on one of the images and pulled up the same pinecone.

"It's called *The Resinova*, based on the Red Pine, *Pinus resinosa*, here in New Hampshire. It took weeks to hand carve and polish each pine cone scale after the dichroic pattern was created."

She smiled and clicked on the video clip of the creation on display.

"See this spiraling of the interior? There are thirteen of them wrapping around the base. It mirrors the Golden Spiral. In fact, all Storms' sculptures are based on the Fibonacci Sequence. Isn't it incredible?"

Without warning, Raymond grabbed her hand, causing the phone to drop to the table. He stared at her, his face ashen. He did not hurt her, but the action made her put her free hand inside her jacket on her gun. He was oblivious to the motion.

Slowly and quietly he said, "Repeat that. Please."

Equally as slow and quiet, she repeated, "All of Jack Storms' sculptures are based on the Fibonacci Sequence."

He remained quiet, lost in his own thoughts. She wondered if she wore the same expression on her face when it happened to her.

He slowly stood up and walked out of the room, oblivious to her confusion. She stood up and followed him, keeping her hand on the cold metal under her jacket. He stood at the end of the hallway, in the door to the computer room. She walked up next to him and studied the expressions on his face.

Finally, she broke the silence. "Did I say something wrong?"

"Huh?" He glanced down at her. "No. I think you actually said something right."

"What are you thinking?"

"AJ, I may have figured it out—the murders, the connection. But I need to spend some time thinking about all of this. Can—can we meet next week or after that?" He looked back at the photo wall and maps. "I need some time. Just a little time."

"Sure." She mimicked the soft tone of his voice. "Take all the time you need."

He put his hands on her shoulders. The wrinkles in his eyes and forehead appeared relaxed as if a weight lifted from his body. He uncovered something he did not want to share. Yet.

"AJ, you've taught me to be cautiously optimistic when it comes to the evidence and drawing conclusions. I-I don't want to get my hopes up again, especially if it's nothing. But, *if* this is what I think it is, then you may have cracked the case without knowing it."

He gave her a paternal kiss on the forehead, then he turned his attention back to his computer room.

He stared through the doorway at all the photos on the walls. "Would you let me be alone? Just for a while. Please."

"Sure. Whatever you need." She was still stunned by the turn of events, including the fatherly role he just assumed. "Call me if you need anything, Raymond."

She left him, there: a shadow man standing in the doorway of his office, the only light on at the end of a dark hallway.

- - -- --- -----

CHAPTER TWENTY: CODE

Tuesday, November 9, 2021

"Mmm, hello?" her tired voice answered.

"AJ!" the ecstatic voice yelled.

"Mmmm, yes? Who is this?" She shoved her messy hair out of the way and blinked several times in a futile attempt to wake up quicker.

"It's Raymond. I did it! I cracked the code! I was RIGHT! We have a serial killer!"

The words caused her to sit up quickly in bed and lose her phone in the sheets. She scrambled to find it and put it back to her ear.

"Hello? You there? What did you say?"

"I cracked the code! It IS a serial killer! You have to come over to the house so I can show you. It's all here, all the clues were there the whole time!"

"Raymond, hold on. You said you cracked the code?"

"Yes! It was right under our noses the whole time!"

"Go on, I'm listening."

"No, I have to SHOW you! I have everything hanging up on my walls and organized and on display and it's MASSIVE! You HAVE come here to see it all to understand everything. When can we meet?"

"What time is it now?"

"Two o'clock in the morning."

"Ughhh."

She flopped back down with her head face-planted in the sheets, the phone still to her ear.

Why does everyone call me at this time of the morning?

"Do you want to wait until later? Maybe eight o'clock?"

"Yeah, I need more sleep first."

"Not a problem! I'll have some coffee ready for you when you get here!"

"Okay, see you around eight then."

She hung up the phone. The home screen illuminated part of the bed and she stared at it. She wanted to leave then and there and visit the professor to find out what the code was, but exhaustion weighed her down.

She rolled back over and fell asleep.

- - -- --- -----

It was a little past eight o'clock when she pulled into the professor's driveway. Pinick came out, excited to see her.

"Come in, come in, come in!"

He quickly motioned for her to enter the house. Then he shut the door, handed her a cup of coffee — exactly how she liked it — and escorted her to the computer room. When she walked in, she gasped.

"Holy fucking shit!"

Every wall was covered, from floor to ceiling, with images, mark-ups, and the case files. She assumed he must have replaced cartridge toners in his printer multiple times.

She spun around to see the entirety of the room. "Shit! You weren't kidding when you said this was massive. How long did it take you to do all this?"

"All week," he boasted proudly. "What'd'ya think?"

"It's — I don't know where to start."

"We can start at the beginning! With the first murder!"

AJ took a step back from the professor and studied his demeanor. "Raymond, how much coffee have you had this morning?"

"Five cups. Why?"

"Just wondering."

He put his hand on her shoulder and ushered her to one side of the room. "Here! Let's start here with Chris!"

He pointed to one corner of the room and began:

"Last week you mentioned all the similarities of each of the murders. I'm calling them *murders* now, by the way. Each body was staged. None were random. And neither were the items in their hands.

"Chris had sunflowers, *one hundred forty-four* to be exact, the *SAME* number carved on the exterior of one of the seed shells."

He pointed to the pictures of his son's body and the sunflower seeds. Then he pointed to the next body and item.

"Damian Winters had a paper snowflake with fractal elements on each branch of the cutout. Each *octagonal* member has *five* branches and each of those *five* branches have *three* sub-branches. And what number was written in the corner of the paper? *Eighty-nine*."

He moved over to the section of wall with Nathan Hull's data.

"Nathan Hull was found holding a seashell—a banded tulip spiral shell. It was sectioned in half so you could see the proportions inside. And what was carved on this one? *Fifty-five*."

He pointed to another set of photos.

"Now, Mary Fay's body had daisies. She was holding *thirty-four* daisies in her hand. They were Oxeye daisies, and each flower had a total of *thirty-four* petals on them. I know, I counted! And—*and*, I found this!"

He pointed to one of the images on the wall. It was a closeup of a dried daisy petal. There were darkened marks on it.

"It's the number *thirty-four*!"

"Wait, our lab technician didn't find anything on the flowers. How is that possible?"

"I took the photo images and adjusted the contrasts and brightness on the daisies until it appeared. It's incredibly faint, but someone wrote the number *thirty-four* on one of the petals."

AJ stood there staring at the image. She could see the outline of the number. "I can't believe Peter missed that. He's so thorough."

"It's possible he missed it because of the rain. Most of the ink washed off. It was barely even noticeable."

"That's possible. The rain started pouring down and the petals did get wet. I almost thought we'd lose some of the evidence."

He nodded. "Now look at this." Raymond moved to another location on one of the walls and pointed to Jose Perales's information.

"Perales was found with a natural pine cone. It had *twenty-one* seeds in it. And there was a number carved on one of the scales: *twenty-one*."

He moved to the next set of images on the wall.

"I went through all of the data you provided me last week on Delarosa. He was found with a different pine cone. You told me it had *thirteen* spiraling sets of scales on it. AND it had the number *thirteen* engraved on the bottom!"

Raymond grinned. He shook his fingers and pointed around the room again:

"One hundred forty-four.

"Eighty-nine.

"Fifty-five.

"Thirty-four.

"Twenty-one.

"And thirteen!"

AJ stared at him, slightly confused.

Then it hit her.

She repeated each of the numbers back to him and then stared at Raymond with wide eyes.

"It's Fibonacci!"

"YES! It's the Fibonacci Sequence!"

He grinned ear-to-ear, proud of solving part of the mystery.

"I'm not done," he continued.

"There's more?"

"Oh, AJ, there's *so* much more!"

He escorted her over to another wall with a column of calendars taped together.

"Check this out! Chris died on March 17, 2015. It was a Tuesday. I looked at each of the murders that have occurred so far. They ALL have occurred on *Tuesdays*! AND they have been getting closer and closer together."

"Oh my gawd," she whispered, as she stared at each of the circled Tuesdays on the piecemeal calendar.

"It gets better. What was the number found on Chris?" he quizzed the detective.

"One hundred forty-four."

"If you count the same number of Tuesdays, you get the date Damian Winters was found. And what number was found on Damian?"

"Eighty-nine."

"Count eighty-nine Tuesdays, and guess what you get? The date Nathan Hull's body was found. And his number was fifty-five. Care to guess what date happened fifty-five weeks after Nathan's murder?"

"Mary's," she whispered. The reveal of the Code began to overwhelm her.

"Yes, and so forth, and so forth. Each body is providing the clue to the next murder. And I don't think the Fibonacci connection stops there either."

"What do you mean? There's *more*?"

He smiled down at her. "Look at each of the hands of the bodies." He went around the room pointing at each photo. Then he curled his left hand up in the same position. "Our hands are created with mathematical exactness. We're not random shapes, but precise proportions. If you take the top two joints of each finger and add them together, you get the distance of the third joint, near the palm. Add *them* together, and you have the palm of your hand.

"Look at the distance from the tip of your middle finger

to the bony protrusion of the ulnar styloid process in your wrist. It's the length of your forearm to the inside of your elbow. The total of the two before becomes the next part of the sequence. So, each hand curled was done as a Fibonacci gesture."

She stared at her fingers and curled them in the same position. She made mental measures of each.

"Oh my gawd. I never knew it was this extensive."

"Even our faces are proportional to the Golden Spiral. In fact, the most beautiful people — and this is according to science — are the ones with the eye, nose and chin ratios lining up to Fibonacci squares.

"There is *so much more*, AJ!

"Now, look at each of the items left with the bodies: sunflower seeds, a fractal snowflake, a spiral shell, oxeye daisies, a pine cone — both natural and manmade. Each has the Fibonacci embedded in its natural design.

"Look at this picture of the sunflowers."

He pointed to an image he printed from the internet.

"The centers of sunflowers spiral outward. Each seed spiral produces a set of thirty-four or fifty-five clusters, depending on whether you spin clockwise or counter-clockwise. Each flower has one hundred forty-four or eighty-nine petals.

"The sunflower is one of the best representations of large Fibonacci sequences found in nature. Many fractals — such as the one seen in the paper snowflake — are Fibonacci based. Fractals have a recursive definition to them, a repeating pattern. While not all fractals follow Fibonacci, their geometric shapes can be quantified into a mathematical proportion.

"This snowflake has *five* and *three* iterations on it, and *those* numbers are Fibonacci. And if the paper could be cut in more the same pattern, you would see more of the iterations in smaller numbers."

She stared at the image. She was awestruck.

So detailed!

"Now look at the shell. Do you see how it's sectioned?" She nodded.

"It was done in such a manner to expose the mathematical proportions of the columns and spirals within. If you take a ruler to each part and divide it by the smaller one next to it, you will get approximately 1.61803, which is *phi*. *That* is the quantifiable number assigned to the sequence—the Golden Ratio.

"The ox-eye daisies are *another* flower with petals averaging in Fibonacci. I would guess that's why they were chosen for Ms. Fay. And the pine cones? Those spiraling scales are Fibonacci in design. Even the *shape* can be overlaid on a Fibonacci spiral and lined up."

"Geez. I didn't think it was THIS extensive."

"Neither did I until I began doing the research. Fibonacci in and of itself is a powerfully sacred ratio and design. When you go home today, pay attention to how water is stirred in a pot or the way it flows down the drain.

"Go take a walk in the woods and study the structures of trees, the gravitational pull and curvature of fern leaves, the number of petals on flowers, the way a gecko or salamander twists itself. Look at acorn caps and the designs spiraling on them. Watch how your cat curls up next to you, or the way your daughter swings her wet hair back. It's all connected!

"Fibonacci is the structure of every life in the universe. You can find the spiral or the number or a phi relationship in everything from plant cross-sections under the microscope to the farthest galaxies you can see with the strongest telescope.

"And speaking of space, have you heard of the Rose of Venus?"

"No," AJ replied. "What's that?"

"It has to do with planetary rotations around the sun. In the time it takes Earth to rotate *eight* turns around the sun, Venus creates *thirteen* revolutions. When the rotations are plotted on a graph, it forms a mandala-style rose pattern:

"And mandalas! I found an example where male Japanese puffer fish create artistic mandalas in the sand to attract females. The branching designs are loosely Fibonacci numbers!

"Our faces, our hands, our feet, even our ears — *all* Fibonacci. The way a rose blooms, the shape of a hurricane — all Fibonacci. Art, computer coding, music — those *also* can be embedded with the Golden Ratio. Here, check this out!"

He grabbed her arm and led her to the family room. He went over to the piano and lifted the keyboard cover. "What do you see?"

She looked down, a bit confused.

"Black and white keys?"

"What else?"

She stared at the keys for a few seconds and then understood what he knew. She saw him grin ear to ear and nodded.

"I see a set of two black keys and then a set of three black keys, for a total of five keys."

"Yes! And how many white keys are between octaves?"

She counted the keys from Middle C including the next C, then looked at the professor again.

"There are eight keys. And together that makes a total of thirteen keys between each octave."

"YES!" he yelled excitedly. "Two, three, five, eight, and thirteen! Isn't this incredible!"

They stood in silence as she absorbed all the information and details. She knew a little about the Golden Ratio and design, but everything Raymond listed amazed her. She remembered Michael's gift to her — the one she lost on the night of his murder.

It was a Fibonacci pendant.

Then the blood drained from her face.

Her mind flew back to the last few years. She needed to do something as soon as she got home, and she did not want Raymond or anyone to know.

"Raymond, this is incredible research. I'm blown away by the extent of this. Is there any way we can determine WHO the next victims will be?"

"I tried researching that also. All I know is each person has the tentacle tattoo and they appear to be connected with the Fasciata. My guess? The next murder will be a member of the Order, but which one? I couldn't say."

"So, we have part of the WHO, which is the Fasciata. WHAT is killing them is our serial killer. And the HOW they are dying is the Prussian Black overdose. We now have the WHEN, based on the research you've done. What about WHERE the murders are taking place? Any luck on that yet?"

"No, not yet. Other than Chris' death, all the deaths have been here in New Hampshire. I still need to do more research and figure it out. I was so focused on the WHEN, I didn't bother to consider the WHERE. I'll see what I can dig up."

"Speaking of, when do you think the next murder will happen?"

"Now *if* I'm right and this truly is the Code and we DO have a killer out there, we have to wait thirteen weeks before the next body appears."

"That long?"

"Not actually. It's been a few weeks since the last murder. We have to be patient and wait until January 11, 2022, to arrive."

"Good grief, that's a long time away."

"I know, I know. But the good news is the murders are happening closer and closer. We don't have to wait as long between each. And that means the killer will more likely make mistakes and get caught."

"That's *if* he makes any mistakes."

"True. That's true."

"I wonder what will happen when he reaches the final one," she thought out loud.

They paused again. She analyzed everything the professor told her.

"Raymond, please do me a favor."

"Sure! Anything!"

"Let's keep this to ourselves. For now. I won't tell my boss until we know for sure what's going on."

"What about Agent Aserbbo?"

She thought about her response and worded her answer carefully. "Tony has been supportive until recently. He's been working several other cases and hasn't been able to focus solely on this one like I have. I'll be honest. He doesn't believe this is a murder investigation and we've gotten into numerous arguments about it. If a body does show up in January — on the exact date you gave — then he can't dispute it anymore."

Raymond let out a deep sigh and picked up his coffee cup. "Would you like to sit down in the living room for a little bit? I'd like to make myself another cup."

"Sure, but are you positive you need more caffeine right now?"

"I'll be fine." They made their way to the living room. "Have you profiled the killer yet?"

"No, sir. But you're correct, he must be highly intelligent. He hasn't made a single mistake until the Delarosa case. Remember I told you we found blood at the scene which didn't match Delarosa's?"

He walked into the kitchen. "Yes. I skimmed through the report. The blood wasn't the victim's. It was an unknown male of Anglo-Saxon descent. You said there was a struggle?"

"Um hmm, it appears so. When the autopsy came back on Delarosa, he had ligature marks around his neck. I'm guessing the killer got more than he bargained for and tried to strangle Delarosa, at least to make him pass out before drugging him with the Prussian Black. Only the lethal dose of heroin killed him."

Raymond walked into the living room and sat down across from her. He leaned back in the chair and took a sip of his coffee.

"Another low-life off the streets. Ya know, I'm glad there's a serial killer getting rid of these people. I wish," he started to say, then stopped and sighed. "I wish Chris wasn't a part of this. He was such a good kid. We never saw this coming."

"Raymond, I think Chris was killed because he was a part of this organization. I know you want to believe he was a good kid, and I think he *was* at one point until he got involved with heroin. I've seen drugs ruin *so* many people's lives. And this was no different."

She tried to be as kind as possible with the truth she gave him. The sadness returned to his eyes and the weight of his son's death aged the professor.

"My son was a good kid, AJ." Tears welled, and he wiped them away. "But my brain tells me you're right. The Fasciata killed him. *They* did this to him. *They* are responsible for his death, not this serial killer. I—I know that now."

"I'm so sorry. I really am."

His gaze went distant as he stared at his coffee cup. He seemed lost in his memories again.

"AJ, may I ask you a personal question?"

"Yes. Go ahead."

"How? I—I don't know how to ask this without prying too much."

"That's fine, Raymond. Please feel free to ask me anything."

When she locked eyes with him, she knew the question.

"How did you handle it? How did you get over your husband's death?"

She sat back slightly. She could feel her own emotions building inside at the thought of her husband and the events surrounding his death and unsolved murder.

"The truth?"

He nodded.

"The truth is, I haven't. The loss, the memory of everything—it never goes away. It's always there. But it *has* lessened, some, over the years."

"But how were you able to move on? You appear so calm and collective all the time."

She chuckled at his comment as they both sipped their coffees. She stared at the rim of the cup.

"For the first several months after Michael's death—and Jenna's birth—I was constantly going and going. I was in physical therapy for several weeks. Actually, several months. I went back to work as soon as I could. My mom helped out as much as possible and my family came over to the house several times a week. The truth was, I was so incredibly busy, it didn't really begin to set in and hit me until much later."

She unfocused her eyes and squinted, attempting to dive deep into her memories.

"I can't pinpoint when the flashbacks started. I think it was some point when Eoghan was in school and active in football. Michael enjoyed hearing about our son's games. Work deadlines picked up and I was studying for the P.E. exam that October."

"What is the P.E. exam?"

"It's the Professional Engineering exam to get my civil engineering license. After engineers-in-training spend several years under the supervision of a professional engineer, we can become licensed ourselves. The exam is an eight-hour exam, split into two sections. It's pretty intense. I'd already taken it three times before. Twice I failed by one point."

"That's like a lawyer taking the bar exam?"

"Exactly. It's stressful beyond belief and highly

demanding. And I think it was the stress, combined with the stress of everything else happening, which caused the flashbacks to begin.

"I remember one flashback happened when I was in the middle of a study session. The fluorescent lights above us flickered from a brownout. The sudden darkness and the bright flash of light triggered the memory of seeing the flash from the gun barrel. I ran out of the room and threw up in the bathroom."

She took another sip before continuing.

"There was another time, I was walking to my car from work, and I heard a woman walking closer towards me. Her heels clicked on the pavement in such a rhythm, it triggered the memory of me walking down the sidewalk, hand in hand with Michael. And then, slowly, more memories and visions would randomly pop into my head at odd and inconvenient times.

"I even freaked out on my physical therapist one day when she popped and released an adhesion in my abdominal scarring. I—I thought I'd been shot again because the pain was so intense."

"AJ, I honestly can't imagine."

"Raymond, I tried my best to fight off the memories, but the more I resisted, the more they occurred. And the more I began losing my wits. I was angry all the time. I snapped at the people closest to me. I was a bitch and awful to everyone around me: family, coworkers, even my kids."

"It's hard for me to imagine you being a bitch to anyone."

"Oh, I was, trust me. Finally, my boss had enough. I snapped at him one day. He pulled me into his office and flat out told me I was a bitch. Didn't even mince the words. Just said, 'Ameena, you've turned into such a bitch.' He was ready to fire me because my attitude spiraled out of control. That's when I broke down crying hysterically. I curled up on his floor against the door. He asked me what was wrong. So, I told him everything."

She paused again, sipping her coffee and savoring the

smell.

"What did he say?"

"He told me, 'Ameena, you may have P.T.S.D. You need professional help. Go see a grief counselor.' I sat there, dumbfounded."

"You had P.T.S.D.?"

She nodded.

"I still do. It's funny, because the stress and cases of the job, the trauma from solving the Rune murders—it never triggered my P.T.S.D. I could handle that. I could handle seeing dead bodies and taking a shot from the Rune Killer. But this was SO different.

"I told my boss I didn't want to see a shrink. He said it wasn't the case here. *He* saw a grief counselor after his young daughter passed away. It was counseling—*guidance* of sorts, to get back to some sense of normalcy. I resisted, but he said he would suspend my contract and pull my projects if I didn't."

She paused, and again, stared at her cup.

"Did you finally see a counselor?"

She nodded again. "Yes. I had no choice. I didn't want to lose my job."

"Did it help?"

"Yes. And no. It helped me get my focus back. It helped me face the cold reality nothing was bringing Michael back. It helped me focus on what was best for my kids, and that wasn't in San Antonio anymore."

She set the cup down on the coffee table and stared at the professor.

"I had to finally admit to myself I couldn't handle my physical limitations alone, I couldn't handle raising two kids by myself. And I had to finally admit to myself I wasn't going to find closure anytime soon. I had to come to terms with my own sense of failure and humility. I was forced to check my pride at the door."

"Would you like another cup of coffee? I need another one myself." He stood up.

"A little more, please." She handed him the cup.

He walked into the kitchen and called out to her. "Everything you described sounds identical to what I've been going through."

She looked around again at the hanging photos surrounded her. So many memories and stories stood still in time. She closed her eyes, and for a brief moment in the silence, she thought she could hear a young boy's laughter. Raymond walked back into the living room, startling her.

He handed her the fresh cup. "Is everything okay?"

"Thank you. Yes. I closed my eyes for a minute."

She glanced up at the photos again and he looked around.

"Sometimes. Sometimes the photos are too much for me. I find myself missing them too much."

His slim frame sunk into the chair as he sat back and leaned his head against the wall. The conversation continued to pause at what felt like just the right moments. She did not mind. It was the familiar and respectful quiet she knew.

Finally, she sighed. "I took all my photos down."

He rolled his head over to her direction.

"Did it help as well?"

"Yeah. That and the medication."

"Medication?"

She nodded. "The counselor recommended I go on an anti-anxiety medication, temporarily." She huffed. "Oh, I resisted. I didn't want to. I felt like it was another failure. Again. I didn't want to have a mental illness. I didn't want to feel like I had mental problems."

"But you were grieving? That's not a mental illness?" Raymond's questions sounded more like statements.

"At the time, it felt like he suggested I needed psychiatric help at a mental hospital. But that was nowhere near the case. The grief counselor explained the anti-anxiety medication was a low dose, enough to stay calm in stressful conditions, such as studying or handling work deadlines. It also helped me sleep a little better. He said it was only temporary until I felt I didn't need them anymore. He reassured me I didn't have a mental disease."

"Are you still on the medication?" He quickly added, "If that's not too bold to ask."

"Oh, no, Raymond, it's fine to ask. I don't mind at all. I haven't needed the medication since I switched careers. The counselor was right, it was temporary. But it was also necessary. I had to stop being so proud and so independent. I was so stubborn for so long, it ate at me. I finally came to terms with myself. I needed the advice. I needed to listen. I needed to take the help being offered by others."

"I don't know if I'm ready to see a counselor."

"You'll never be ready."

There was another long silence.

"AJ, what do you think I should do?"

They both stared at each other across the coffee table. She could see the pain in his eyes and almost feel the anguish he had.

"Honestly?" She glanced back at the walls. "Take the photos down. Clean them. Wrap them up carefully. And then box them away until you're ready again."

"Take the photos down?"

"Yes. Take the memories down. Not forever. Definitely not forever. But long enough so that you can heal. Long enough so that you don't have the constant pain every time you walk into this neglected room."

"How do you know I don't—"

"Because I've done the same thing, not wanting to go into a certain room ever again. After Michael was murdered, I couldn't sleep in our bed anymore. I couldn't even walk into the bedroom. I moved my stuff in the dining room and slept on the couch. I couldn't stomach being in a bed for a long time after that."

"How did you get over that?"

She laughed a little.

"After I moved up to live with my parents, my mom

made me do it. She told me I needed to start sleeping in the guest bedroom or she would take the wooden spoon to my noggin." She tapped the side of her head.

He smiled and let out a chuckle. She set her cup back down on the table and leaned towards him.

"It takes *time*, Raymond. It takes *time* and *patience* and *understanding* to heal.

"You may never completely get over the loss.

"You never forget about them.

"But, that's okay.

"You keep.

"Moving.

"On.

"And sometimes you don't do it for yourself. Sometimes it's only done for them."

Her eyes motioned to the two others in the photos. She reached out and held his hand. He squeezed slightly, and she could feel his fingers shaking. Tears fell down his cheeks from under his glasses.

"Put the pictures away today. See the counselor tomorrow. Baby steps. It takes baby steps. But each step forward—no matter how small—is still a step in the right direction."

She stood up, and he followed suit.

"You should also continue the work you're doing. I do appreciate the energy you put into this. I'll keep you posted if we have another body on the date you provided."

"Thank you, AJ. I do appreciate that."

They walked to the front door. "Raymond, if you ever need anything or need to talk to someone, please don't hesitate to call me." She looked up at him and added, "Not many people truly understand loss. And fewer understand P.T.S.D. It doesn't make you weak. It doesn't make you a bad person. It just becomes another part of you. Don't let it break you. Let it make you stronger."

"Thank you, AJ. I—just, thank you."

"You're welcome. You may not be okay now. But you

will be someday."

She took a step out the door and extended her hand out formally. Instead of shaking her hand, he leaned down and gave her a strong hug. She hugged him equally. She could tell he needed it. He finally made a connection with someone.

She would let him go when he was ready.

- - -- --- -----

"Habibti? What are you looking for?"

"Do you know where the microscope is?"

"Yes, dear. It's in the office cabinet at the bottom. Eoghan put it back after he finished his biology class."

"Thanks, Momma." Ameena unpacked the equipment and set the microscope up. She was so focused on the task in front of her and studying each of the prepared slides, she did not hear her mother call her name.

"Ameena!" Jamilla yelled.

She jumped. "Sorry."

"What are you doing?"

"Oh, nothing. I wanted to look at these slides and see the patterns in the plant stems."

Jamilla stared at her, unsure if she should continue the conversation. "Oh. Okay."

Ameena set up another prepared slide in position under the microscope. She adjusted the focus when Jenna walked over.

"Mommy, can I see?"

"Sure! Look through the eyepiece here."

Jenna stood on her tiptoes and peered into the eyepiece at the cross-section of a bamboo stem. "It looks like one of Tayta's doilies. It's so pretty!"

"It is, isn't it?"

"It reminds me of playing in the woods."

"What makes you say that, sweetheart?"

She looked at her mom, smiling. "Because it spirals.

Peacock feathers spiral, too."

She stared at her daughter in disbelief. "It *spirals*?"

Fibonacci in nature. Raymond did say everything was connected.

"Yes, it spirals. So do peacock feathers. They're like your sunflowers. Feathers and flowers are a lot alike."

"That's a good observation."

"You told me if I wanted to be a detective, I should start paying attention to my surroundings."

"That's right, I did, didn't I?"

"Jenna," Jamilla said, "it's starting to get late. You need to go brush your teeth and get ready for bed."

"Yes, Tayta." The little girl gave her mother a big hug and received a kiss on the forehead. "Good night, Mommy!"

"Good night, baby. I love you."

She watched her little girl run up the stairs.

"Give me a hug, habibti. I'm going to tuck her in."

More hugs and kisses later, Ameena was finally alone downstairs. She stared at the microscope, then decided to put it away.

She needed to do something else, now that it was safe.

As soon as she closed and locked her bedroom door, she opened the lower left drawer of her dresser and piled its contents on her bed. She dug through the memorabilia until she found the items she wanted, then put everything else back in the drawer where it belonged. She spread the remaining items across the comforter.

December 19, 2017, the date Damian's body was found.

She stared at the card with the specific date on it. She remembered receiving flowers but could not remember the exact kind.

Maybe they were sunflowers? I know I received sunflowers at one point. Dammit, think! What were they?

She tried to recall her graduation but could not recall the gift she received. She reread the quote on the card:

In any racing engine, the nearer you are to it

disintegrating, the better its performance will be.
~Keith Duckworth
0100010133669501001110495871 8

Such an odd quote. Why this one? Am I approaching disintegration? This card also has those strange numbers on the bottom. What the HELL do those mean?

She took out her phone and researched the name, Keith Duckworth. He was a mechanical engineer who died on the same day the card was given.

Another death quote on another significant day…

She flipped through the other cards.

Here's the one from Nathan Hull's death: September 3, 2019. The day I was given the bonsai gardenia. Still have the tree in the office.

She looked at the card and poem left with the gift.

"I carry your heart" from e.e. cummings. But why a gardenia? Unless…

She researched the gardenia again.

The leaves and flower clusters vary. Wait!

She pulled out her external drive and searched through her photos. When she finally found the picture she wanted, she zoomed in.

One, two, three, she counted the petals. *Damn, I can't see how many petals are in each. Wait! It spirals!*

She looked at the shape closely. It was a Golden Spiral. Then she searched for the next gift.

Mary's death is this one.

She glanced at the card's date: September 22, 2020. She reread the quote:

Do not the most moving moments of our lives find
us all without words?
~Marcel Marceau

The mime. Another death quote. Do I find myself without

words? Perhaps I'm beginning to. What was the gift I received here? Crap, I need to look through my photos again.

She searched her external drive for the new date.

Daisies! That's right! It was like what we found on Fay's body. Daisies in a crystal lead vase.

She got up and dug through the cabinet next to her bed. When she found the vase, she pulled it out and stared at it, twisting it in her hands for the light to catch the cut glass.

Spiraling pineapple designs. Like Fibonacci!

She glanced at the C.D. and card she received the day Perales's body was found, and she remembered the significance of the date. She remembered the flowers and knew they had a specific number of petals to them. She knew the flowers, the glass sculpture, and the strange poem were also significant.

Wait…

She again searched through all the memorabilia and dug through the drawer one more time.

There's not one for Chris's death. It was March 17, 2015, the date of the aurora. Think, Ameena, think! Did you receive anything that day?

She kept thinking about each detail of the memory: the fight with Eoghan, seeing the Northern Lights, the kiss with the stranger on the mountain, the thought-seed of a new career change. Then she remembered Marcus Aurelius. She took out her phone and searched for the Roman emperor.

That's right, he died on March 17th! That means…

Her unsettling thought chilled her to her core.

She opened her laptop and went into the chatroom.

> Roar317811: Copernicus? Are you here?
> Please! I need to talk to you!

She waited a few minutes, saw a quick flicker of her monitor, and then her heart skipped a beat with the ping on her screen.

NCPoland1543: Good evening, Ameena
Roar317811: I have questions for you
NCPoland1543: I may have your answers
Roar317811: You gave me all these
gifts? The flowers and the cards on
the days of all the overdoses?
NCPoland1543: Yes
Roar317811: Why?
NCPoland1543: Are you not deserving?
Roar317811: Nick?????

The screen flickered.
He was gone.
She was left in cold silence.

- - -- --- -----

CHAPTER TWENTY-ONE: 8

Tuesday, January 11, 2022

She stared at her reflection in the bathroom mirror and splashed water on her face. Another nightmare, another sleepless night. She did not know if it was from the anxiety that January 11th finally arrived, or from the depression of upsetting Conrad when she told him about her visit with Raymond.

She managed to keep her meeting with the professor a secret for a total of three weeks. By then, the guilt forced her to confess to her boss.

And he was not happy. The reprimand stung, and the forced desk duty resulted in more than a couple of confrontations with Tiffany and some of her clique.

She studied her hands. The tip of her thumb spasmed and she clenched her fists to stop it. The demons in her mind tried to push through again from the lack of sleep; they wanted to attack her self-esteem and give her even more self-doubt.

"Not today, demons," she whispered to the reflection. "I'm right about today. Raymond's right about today. I'm right about the Code."

- - -- --- -----

"Did you look through the case files, Jardine?"

"Yes, sir. Anonymous calls were placed in the mornings of all the previous overdoses."

"It's three o'clock in the afternoon, detective."

"I know, sir."

"Anything?"

"No, sir. Not yet."

"What are your thoughts?"

"The day's not over, sir. I know Raymond's right about this. *I'm* right about this."

"Hmm." Conrad studied her from across his desk. "Has Dr. Pinick been able to predict who the next victim is?"

"No, sir. All we know is it'll most likely be a member of the Fasciata, and they'll have the octopus tattoo on them."

"How many others know about your meeting with the professor and this Code?"

"Just you, sir. I still haven't told Tony anything."

"Keep it that way. We can't risk him telling the Boston Octave anything. If the Fasciata find out, there could be repercussions we aren't prepared for."

She nodded and then thought for a moment before asking, "Sir?"

"Yes, Jardine?"

"Are you still upset at me?"

His stoic behavior unnerved her.

"Jardine, your reckless and defiant stunt has been noted in your personal file and you were reprimanded for it. What's done is done. But you broke my trust. And we're not done with that."

"Sir, I didn't mean to—"

"I know. You thought you'd take the initiative on this. You thought you'd find more answers and catch Ms. Carmicle's killers, or even a possible vigilante killer out there. And you thought you'd do it alone, without Tony, without any backup whatsoever."

"That was part of it, sir."

"Do you remember what you told me after the Rune Killer shot you?"

"That I wouldn't do something so reckless as trying to apprehend a dangerous suspect on my own." She argued, "I see where you're coming from, but I—"

"Stop," he interrupted her. "I know you haven't tried to arrest anyone yet, but look at the position you put yourself in when you went back to interview Mr. Sotelo. You hadn't expected to be caught off guard with *two* other men there with him. And Fasciata members at that. And now, you—again—went out on your own to talk to Dr. Pinick, potentially giving him classified and sensitive information. You're making mistakes, detective. And one day, you may make a fatal one."

The receptionist buzzed Conrad's phone.

"Yes, Ellie?"

"Sir, you have an urgent phone call on line five."

"Who is it?"

"It's someone from the Concord Police Department, sir."

"Patch it through. Thank you, Ellie."

He pressed the blinking light and then the phone's speaker button.

"This is McMillan," he addressed the caller.

"Afternoon, sir. This is Officer Reeves with the Concord Police Department. We received an anonymous phone call this morning that a body could be found on one of our ponds."

Conrad and AJ stared at each other. Her excitement rose, and her thumb twitched again.

YES! I knew it! We're right!

The officer continued, "It took us the better part of the day, but we finally found the right pond. There was a license next to the body. When we ran it, we saw the flag-and-tags on it and called you immediately."

"Who is it, Officer Reeves?" Conrad continued to stare at AJ.

"Carl Frierson."

Conrad wiped his forehead, then pinched the top of his nose between his eyes. "Secure the scene and don't touch anything. I'll send someone to your location. Detective Jardine will call you shortly for the address to meet you."

He hung up the phone and looked at AJ, then tapped his fingers on the desk.

"*Felix culpa.*"

"Sir?"

"It means 'happy fault,' Jardine. It appears your mistake with Dr. Pinick may provide positive results after all. Call Agent Aserbbo and have him go with you to the crime scene. Process what you can."

"Yes, sir." She quickly stood up to leave, eager to see the body.

As she grabbed the doorknob, Conrad stopped her. "Detective, do *not* tell Tony about Dr. Pinick's Code or that you shared information with the professor. It remains as secretive as the information we know about Copernicus. For now. This is our advantage we don't want to lose for the moment."

"Yes, sir."

"Now, get out of my office."

She may have seen the corner of his mouth raise in slight approval.

_ _ __ --- -----

Long after sunset — and well below freezing — Tony and AJ pulled up to the abandoned field on Horse Hill Road, northwest of downtown Concord. They met with Officer Reeves who briefed them:

"A little after eight o'clock this morning, we received an anonymous call stating there was a body on one of the lakes north of Horse Hill. It took us several hours before we found him, but that's only because there were several ponds in the area to check, and we didn't know which one it was. We found him on Little Pond."

"Did you notice any tracks or prints on the ice?" Tony asked.

"No, sir."

"Has the M.E. come by yet?" AJ asked. She pulled her coat tighter around her head.

"Dr. Owen sent another medical examiner to get the body. He's there right now."

"How did Frierson look? Does the scene seem unusual to you?"

"Ma'am, that's for you to determine, not me to speculate," Officer Reeves replied. "No disrespect."

"None taken. How far is the body from here?"

"One of the residents in the area has allowed us to park at their house. They're off Blackwater Road, not far from here. Once we park, we'll need to walk after that. I recommend you put thermal gear and ice cleats on first. If the wind picks up, it'll be brutal."

- - -- --- -----

Another hour later and everyone trekked through the woods, ice, and snow. Temperatures yoyoed all week between the single digits and teens at night and just above freezing during the day; this effect caused the top layers of snow to melt, freeze, thaw, and freeze again until a shiny thick ice coated every surface imaginable. She hoped they would be done and back home before the temperatures dropped into the single digits again.

The bitter cold walk challenged everyone in the group. Each step crunched and cracked underneath their feet. Carrying flashlights and backpacks full of equipment added to the difficulty. The ice made it impossible for A.T.V.s or snowmobiles to climb the steep hills or maneuver between the thick trees.

When they finally reached the lake, she saw portable lamps set up around the perimeter. A green, eerie glow reflected off the lake ice. The moon waxed brightly in the sky, illuminating the shadows around them. Other than the crunches of human steps and an occasional branch snapping in the woods, death-like stillness surrounded her. Every sound echoed; every breath burned from the cold. She hoped the processing would not take long.

With extra digital camera batteries in her coat pockets, she snapped several images along the trek and more at the pond. She took some photographs with the flash and some with longer exposure times; she hoped the different settings would provide clues the naked eye could not see.

As they approached the body, she saw the corpse frozen in a fetal position, much like many of the other overdoses. Frierson's body appeared gray with layers of ice sticking to the exposed skin and clumping the hairs on his head. He did not have the same emaciated appearance as Perales's body, but the empty and cloudy expression on his face stared back in pure horror.

The left arm curled up into itself, and she could not see if a needle stuck out of his arm. There was, however, something in his hand.

"Jesse," she asked the Assistant Deputy Medical Examiner, "can you look at his hand and see if he has anything in it, please?"

"Sure." The young man squatted down and pried the frozen fingers apart.

The ligaments and bone made cracking noises and echoed off the frigid lake.

She shivered from more than the cold. The sound would not easily be forgotten.

"Almost got it." He grimaced as a finger snapped open.

With a final crack, the object was released. Jesse held it up as she shined the flashlight on it.

"What the hell is that?" Tony asked.

"It looks like an urn." Jesse handed the object to the agent.

"You're kidding me? An urn?" She expected many things, but not a small urn-like object.

What could be in an urn which would match the Code?

"Is there anything in it?"

Tony shook the container. "Yeah. Sounds like ash of some sort."

Cremains of some sort? But whose? This doesn't make sense at all.

"Okay. We'll have Peter analyze the contents later this week and get us some answers. Any inscriptions or writing on it?" She covered her mouth to warm her lips.

Tony studied it some more. "No, I don't see anything."

Shit, it's not matching the M.O.! Maybe Pinick's wrong.

"Wait," he squinted. "There's a number on the bottom. It's the number eight in an octagon."

YES! Calm down, calm down. Don't say anything yet. Don't give away your emotion, Jardine!

"Let's bag it and everything else and get out of here before we get frostbite. Did anyone find a hypodermic needle?"

Officers looked around. One by one, they shook their heads.

"Tony, do you think it's *in* the lake?"

"Possibly, if this really is a drug overdose again."

"Oh, it's an overdose, I'd bet my sanity and brass bra on it." She looked around, then had an idea. "Anyone have a magnet?"

Multiple responses of "no" echoed into the woods.

"What about in the fish shack?" an officer asked. "Maybe someone's left one in there. It's not uncommon for fishermen to use them."

He went over to the shack with another officer and both came back smiling several minutes later. The officer held up a large, round, and heavy magnet attached to a thick rope.

"Let's dredge this area and see if we can find the needle. It's a long shot, but worth trying."

It only took a few minutes of searching before the hypodermic needle was found. The strong magnet quickly collected the evidence.

Jesse finished straightening the body and officers helped him carry it back to his vehicle. AJ finished examining the area and collected anything she thought important. By the time she was done, the temperatures were well into the single digits.

As they made their way back to the vehicles, she realized how cold her body was. Her lips cracked and burned from the wind. She slipped and fell a couple of times, sending her hands and knees deep through the ice and into several inches of snow underneath. As the ice melted, it soaked and seeped into her pants and coat. The chill crept into her bones.

By the time they reached Tony's car, her fingers raged, and she could not bend them. Hypothermia began to set in and she could not stop shivering. Tony quickly cranked the engine and blasted the heater.

"I-I ca-ca-can't st-stop sh-sh-shaking, T-Tony."

"That last tumble you took probably caused your body temp to start dropping. Let me hold your hands to warm them up."

She closed her eyes.

"Hey! Keep your eyes open." His voice commanded her, but she did not want to obey.

"I w-want to g-g-go to s-sleep." Her body convulsed and she kept yawning.

He pulled her closer to him and rubbed her hands profusely. She was drained, exhausted.

"Let me drive you home. It's late, and you shouldn't be driving if you're still shivering this violently. I can pick you up in the morning and take you to work."

"O-o-ok-kay." She mumbled her words and decided not to argue with him.

- - -- --- -----

When they pulled into her driveway, she no longer shook, but she could not stop yawning. Tony parked the car and walked her up the hill to the front door. She stared at him in the moonlight, and her heart melted even more at the softness in his eyes.

"Thank you for bringing me home." She stood on the step above him, almost eye level.

"You're always welcome."

He gave her a long hug and then pulled away slowly, ready to leave. She grabbed his hand and gripped it a little tighter, not letting go, then opened the front door, and guided him straight to her bedroom. No words were needed as they stripped their winter coats and boots.

They climbed in the bed together, warming under the covers. She flipped over to turn the lamp off and felt him pull her closer. Her back pressed against his chest; her head rested on his arm. His free hand wrapped around her and she held it with hers.

She missed this the most: the gentle and warm touch of a companion, the calm emotional state of her brain and body, the safety she felt.

Tony fell asleep first and quickly; she, no further behind him.

- - -- --- -----

<u>Wednesday, January 12, 2022</u>

"Ameena! Wake up, sweetheart, you'll be late for work!" she heard her mother say from the other side of the door.

"Hunh," she mumbled.

She was almost back asleep when she heard her door open.

"You need to wake u—OH MY GOD!"

She knew her mom did not expect to see a second body in the bed. She knew her mom was embarrassed and thought the worst.

"Momma! It's okay." Ameena flipped the comforter and sheets off quickly. "See? Nothing to worry about. I'm still wearing yesterday's clothes."

"We didn't do anything, I promise, Jamilla!" Tony sat up quickly. He seemed scared of what the Middle Eastern mother might do.

Her mom took a deep breath and glared at both of them. "It's fine. I was not expecting multiple bodies in here. That's all."

"We didn't get home from the crime scene until after one in the morning," Ameena said.

"We had a body to process in Penacook late last night, and Ameena started to develop hypothermia," Tony added.

"What did you say? Are you okay, habibti? Why didn't you tell me last night?" Jamilla's voice cracked with concern.

"Thanks a lot, Tony," she mumbled to her bed partner. Then louder, she said, "Mom, I'm fine. I promise. It was so late and so cold last night, Tony drove me home. And instead of making him drive all the way to his house, and then all the way back here in the morning to get me, I asked him to spend the night."

"As long as you're okay." Jamilla stared at both of them. "I'll set an extra plate for breakfast for you, Tony. You are welcome to shower here, but you are not allowed to leave until you eat something first."

"Yes, ma'am."

Jamilla walked out. The pair looked at each other and snickered like teenagers.

"Why don't you go take a shower? We also have spare toothbrushes, new in the packages. You're welcome to grab one and use it."

Tony grinned. "We're at the toothbrush stage now, are we?"

His tease caused her to blush. She gave him a pat on the cheek and then got up out of bed.

"I'll help Mom with breakfast while you shower."

She left Tony there on the bed and walked out to the kitchen where she heard the sizzling of turkey bacon and eggs on the stove.

Jamilla stirred the eggs and set the coffee maker. "Oh, habibti, that package came in for you yesterday."

"No flowers this time?"

"No, dear. Only the box. Were you expecting something else?"

She shook her head. "No, just wondering. Wasn't expecting anything at all."

Tony walked into the kitchen as Ameena was about to tear the package open. She stopped, not wanting him to see it, especially since she did not know the contents.

"Ah, Tony, breakfast will be ready in a few minutes. You have time to take a shower."

"Thank you, Jamilla. I'd like to apologize for last night. I didn't mean to startle you this morning."

"Tony, stop." She shook a utensil in her hand. "You do not need to explain anything. I would have insisted you spend the night anyway. You have done a lot for my daughter and I am grateful for that. Go. Take a quick shower, and I will see you back down here in a few minutes, understand?"

"Yes, ma'am." He smiled at both women and went upstairs.

As soon as he was out of sight, Jamilla raised an eyebrow at her daughter. "He's a good match for you. He has a heart of precious metals."

"Mom. He's my *partner*, and I can't—shouldn't get involved like that."

"Okay, okay. Have fun with your mystery suitor, then." Her eyes twinkled, and Ameena was not entirely sure how much her mother truly knew.

She took the package into her bedroom and shut the door, locking it this time. The plainly wrapped package was shaped as if it held a large book. If there were any prints, too many people had handled the package to be able to distinguish them. She saw no forwarding address, no indication it went through the postal service, and the label addressed to her was typed.

Still, I should grab some gloves and carefully open this. Maybe I can preserve evidence on the inside. Wait, should I even bother? Conrad doesn't know about the gifts. No one knows I may have an I.D. on this guy. It's not like I can tell Tony anything, and Conrad only knows the pertinent things. Besides, if this is from Copernicus, he's doing us a favor by eliminating the Fasciata one at a time. FUCK! You idiot! You can't side with a killer against the law! That's NOT why you took this job!

Her thoughts toiled with ethical ideas of what to do. If she sent the box to the lab for processing, she would have to reveal the other gifts to her boss. Since she finally made it back into Conrad's good graces, she really did not want to disappoint him again, so soon. She also wondered if Conrad would question her ability to work the Fasciata case. She sighed. She had no other choice.

Rip! She pulled the tab on the package and carefully slid its contents on the bed. A card rested on top of the photo. It read:

> *Information is power. But like all power, there are those who want to keep it for themselves.*
> *~Aaron Swartz*
> *01000101285470010011104794170*

She studied the card and then flipped it over. There was nothing else written.

Then she stared at the photo. Immediately, she knew the connection. A framed black and white photo of a spiraling staircase revealed the sacred geometry of Fibonacci. In the bottom-right corner an inscription read:

Bramante Staircase, Vatican

The knock on her door startled her. She placed the picture on her dresser and opened the door to see Tony standing there.

"Everything okay?"

"Yeah, I received a package and was looking at it."

He walked in and saw the picture. "Black and white photography?"

"Oh, it's something I ordered online," she lied. "I forgot I placed the order a while back. Took almost eight weeks to get here."

"Oh, okay. Your mom has breakfast ready for us. Then we need to get going."

"Be there in a sec. I need to change clothes."

With that, she shut her door again, put her hand on her heart, and leaned against the wall. She felt tears stirring again as her mind swam in deepening turmoil.

There was a tug-of-war battling her body: a desire between the wanting of a hacker or the companionship of an agent.

There was a tug-of-war battling in her mind: an ethical conundrum between trusting the conversations of a serial killer or accepting the secrets her partner kept from her.

There was a tug-of-war battling in her heart: a conflict between one mysterious stranger and one alluring friend.

- - -- --- -----

<u>Tuesday, January 25, 2022</u>

Peter held up a small bag.

"There wasn't much to work with, AJ. The syringe had Prussian Black in it. No prints, nothing else we could recover because of the water."

He held up another bag.

"His clothes provided no clues for the same reason: too much water damage. The only thing of interest was the little jar you thought was an urn."

"You mean, it wasn't an urn?"

"Nope. Check this out." He went over to his computer and pulled up microscopic photos of the contents of the jar. "At first, I thought it was an urn and human ash on the inside. I tried to run DNA on the sample, thinking some of the larger chunks were bone."

"I thought you can't run DNA on ashes?"

"You can, but you need bone fragments or teeth. But get this. When I tried processing the sample, the machine kept giving me an error."

"Wait, so this is not organic?"

"Nope. Care to guess what it is?" He clicked his mouse and maximized an image.

She looked at the photo he pulled up on the monitors. Tiny reflective crystals and linear striations crisscrossed with white clustery patches in the image.

"If it's not organic, then it could be rock of some sort. This looks like limestone with something else in it."

"Almost. It's limestone and dolomite which makes —"

" — Marble!"

"Exactly! White marble, to be more precise. I didn't know why marble would be in this, so I ran more extensive tests. Even tried some carbon dating. Did you know you can't use carbon-based radiometric dating on rock younger than fifty-five millennia?"

"Yeah. We learned that in one of my geology classes. Can't you use other radioisotopes to determine the age?"

"Yes, but I didn't need to do that. Once I identified this

as marble, I did a color analysis test on it. See how pure white the marble is? Only a few places in the world produce this. Took a few days to pinpoint the exact location and age of the marble, but I did it. You won't guess where it's from. Or how old."

"How old, Peter?"

"I placed the age at around Five B.C.E."

"Say that again." She stared at him in disbelief.

"Five B.C.E., AJ. It's white marble from Mount Pentelicus. It was used to make the Acropolis. See?"

He pulled up images from an internet search. She skimmed through them and one caught her eye.

"Stop! Click on that one!" She shook her finger at one of the pictures.

The image on the monitor showed the front side of the Parthenon with Fibonacci geometry overlaid on top. She studied the proportions and the images, privately noting everything about the structure.

"AJ, you okay?"

"Yeah. Out of curiosity, how far is this from the Vatican to the Acropolis?"

"That's an odd question."

"I know, but I thought there's a similar structure there around Italy," she lied.

A few clicks and searches later, Peter had an answer. "Two hours, by plane."

"Very interesting."

"Other than this, there's nothing unusual with the overdose."

She gathered her copies of the findings. "Thanks, Peter. I'll show this to Conrad."

"Hey, before you leave, have you talked to Cass about the bachelorette parties?"

"No, not yet. I'll come back here this afternoon or tomorrow and we can go over the details after I talk to her."

She left Peter and walked back to her desk, grabbed the Fasciata case files and then went to Conrad's office. She sat down, explaining everything to her boss. She started with Cassie's autopsy findings and ended with Peter's discoveries about the clues.

"It's official then. We have a serial killer, someone who's using this Fibonacci math as a calling card."

"Yes, sir."

He tapped his fingers on his desk for a few seconds.

"Sir? Now that it's official, do we lose jurisdiction? We have the one death in New York State and the rest are here. Do you think the Federal offices will take over?"

"No, Jardine. I doubt they'll want to touch this one."

"What makes you say that, sir?"

"A hunch." He did not elaborate. Before she could ask another related question, he changed the subject. "Do you think this is related to Copernicus?"

"Possibly, sir. I haven't asked him. Yet."

He raised an eyebrow at her. "You've spoken to him?"

"Yes, sir, but not in several months and I have no way of reaching him. He reaches out to me."

"Is there anything you are *not* telling me, detective?" His stare penetrated her mind. She knew he searched for a deeper truth she was not telling him.

"Sir, ever since I came to you and asked you about *that*," she referred to the Newtonian Collaborative, "he's hardly talked to me. I tried reaching him through the chatroom once. I told him you wouldn't answer me, but neither would he."

"Does Aserbbo know about Copernicus yet? Or the *other*?"

"No, sir. I'm not about to mention it to him. Or anyone. I can't. Each death of the Fasciata brings us closer to catching them, especially if they had anything to do with Loki's and Angie's deaths. And it brings us closer to catching this serial killer. There's no way I'll risk saying anything right now."

He continued to study her. "Do we have an idea when the next body will appear?"

"Yes, sir. Eight weeks from Frierson's death, which puts

the date at March 8th."

"And there's no way to know who's next?"

"Not yet, sir. Dr. Pinick believes it'll be a Fasciata member, but he hasn't been able to pinpoint precisely who yet."

"You're sure we can trust him?"

"Absolutely, sir. Maybe even more so now that his lead, Frierson, is dead. I know it sounds awful, but he doesn't have anyone to feed him his addiction: these overdose cases."

"A different type of heroin problem, it seems."

"Yes, sir. I can trust him not to say anything to Tony, so we can still keep this a secret."

"Do it, then. Go meet with him, give him all the data we have. But the moment of trouble or any distrust, you come back to me."

She nodded and stood to leave.

"And, detective?"

"Yes, sir?"

"Reach out to Copernicus. Whether or not he's the killer, we need to track him down. He knows *much* more than I ever anticipated, and it can make him more dangerous than the Fasciata."

She nodded again, though she disagreed with her boss's last statement.

- - -- --- -----

Her stomach ached from the sitting and a full day of meetings. She stretched out on her back on the bed, alleviating the pain. Her mom knocked on the door frame before she came in.

"Habibti." She closed the door, then sat down next to her daughter. "I need to talk to you for a moment."

Ameena sat up, her back against the headboard. "Is something wrong?"

"No, sweetheart, but we need to talk about your father."

"Gawd, Mom!" She grabbed a pillow and face-planted her head in it. She did not want to discuss the subject of her father.

"Stop! Listen to me. I know how you feel about him, and I know you said you don't want anything to do with him, but you need to give him a chance."

"What I *need* is to get some rest."

"Ameena." The condescending tone immediately made her feel guilty. "Ever since your Dad passed away, your children have been suffering, we all have. But Jenna, especially. Her heart aches for her Papa. I know Paden will never, and I mean never, replace her Papa, but she has the right to know she has another grandfather who wants to be in her life. The same with Eoghan and little Ghada, and all of the cousins. All I ask is that we invite him here and have a dinner. Just talk to him. Let him see his grandbabies. Please. Do this for me, habibti."

Ameena still carried anger for the abuse she suffered as a child. She was angrier at what he did to her mom. Yet, her mom forgave him and seemed at peace with her decision, something she still did not fully understand. She knew her mom would continue to press the unwanted subject until she got her way.

"Fine. I'll talk to him."

"Good, we'll have dinner here at the house sometime soon. I'll see when he can drop by." With that, she stood up and looked at her daughter. "The horse with no rider should not be punished for never winning the race."

"Mom, you and your quotes…"

"It means even if you don't have a relationship with him, don't punish his family or yours for the decisions they make." Jamilla walked out of the room.

Ameena sat on the bed and watched as all the lights disappeared in the rest of the house. Save for the creaking of the floor above her and the occasional sound of the furnace humming, the house slipped into silence.

She powered on her laptop and opened the chatroom

window, then sent a salutation to Copernicus. She waited for a response for almost an hour. Finally, she decided to shut down her computer. Then she saw several flickers.

NCPoland1543: Good evening, Ameena

She hesitated, unsure if Conrad asked her to contact Copernicus as a trap to capture him. She hesitated, unsure if her computer and phone were bugged.

Roar317811: Hello
NCPoland1543: How are you doing?
Roar317811: I'm exhausted.
NCPoland1543: Are you worried your boss has bugged your devices and is spying?
Roar317811: He wants me to reach out to you
NCPoland1543: I know. But you don't have to worry about the spying eyes of others. I have isolated any Wi-Fi transmissions to your bedroom. The only ones here are you and me. Our own private room.
Roar317811: He thinks you're more dangerous than the Order. He wants you stopped from going after the Fasciata
NCPoland1543: Do you?
Roar317811: Do I want you stopped? Or do I think you are more dangerous?
NCPoland1543: Answer both
Roar317811: Are you the serial killer?
NCPoland1543: Must you even ask?
Roar317811: You're a dangerous creature, killing.
NCPoland1543: Do you want the danger to continue?

> Roar317811: *Am I glad they are dead?*
> *Yes.*
> NCPoland1543: You circumnavigated the
> question. Do you want me stopped?

She paused, briefly, contemplating an appropriate response. Then she asked a bold question.

> Roar317811: *Did the Fasciata murder*
> *Michael?*
> NCPoland1543: As I told you in our
> last chat a few months ago, I have
> been doing research. I've been
> finding long buried answers in the
> vaults of member's minds. To answer
> your question: yes. The Fasciata
> carried out the hit on Michael.
> Perales—before the Fasciata Lord sent
> him to the Boston Octave—had driven
> the getaway car. I'm still hunting
> the others involved.

Ameena gasped, staring at the message. She covered her mouth as tears developed in her eyes.

She finally knew! She was finally closer to solving her husband's murder!

> NCPoland1543: They also carried out
> the hit on Rebecca.
> Roar317811: *Was she your wife?*
> NCPoland1543: yes
> Roar317811: *I'm so sorry. I didn't*
> *realize they killed her. When did she*
> *die?*
> NCPoland1543: A decade and a day ago.
> The memory is still as vivid and
> traumatic as the day it happened.
> NCPoland1543: So I ask you again
> NCPoland1543: Do you want me stopped?

Do you want to stop me?
Roar317811: I
Roar317811: The detective in me wants to bring you to justice. But the widow, the mother raising her two children, one of whom will never know her father, says no. THAT part of me wants you to kill every last one of them.
NCPoland1543: As you wish
Roar317811: Wait!
NCPoland1543: Yes?
Roar317811: What do I tell Conrad???
NCPoland1543: Now and always, tell him what you must, my dear. You should tell him we chatted and let him know we will arrange a meeting in person in a few weeks.
Roar317811: Before or after March 8th?
NCPoland1543: Clever, clever girl
Roar317811: I know you're using the Fibonacci and there is a countdown.
NCPoland1543: The professor has been excellent in guiding you
Roar317811: What happens at one? Does it mean the killing is over? What happens to you?
NCPoland1543: We will discuss it in person when the time is right.
Roar317811: May I ask you a personal question?
NCPoland1543: You may
Roar317811: How is Rebecca related to me and Michael? How do we know each other????? Nick, is this you?????
NCPoland1543: Ameena, it is too dangerous for me to tell you that, now, at this moment. Know I have been guided to you and we are connected

```
more than you know. After all, The
Code originated with you.
```

The screen flicked several times and a DOS window appeared. Random characters scrolled through as a program uploaded. She assumed it was either him or her boss doing what they must.

After the window closed, she shut the laptop and put it away. She stared at the ceiling, lost in repetitive thoughts and ideas until her mind finally tired.

- - -- --- -----

CHAPTER TWENTY-TWO: 5

<u>Tuesday, February 8, 2022</u>

❙❙ You said her name was Rebecca?"

"Yes, sir."

"Did he give any other details, other than she was his wife?"

"He said she died over a decade ago. It would put the death on or around January 24, 2012, sir."

"And did you research all deaths on January 24th?"

"Yes, sir." She pulled out her notepad and skimmed what she had written. "I pulled data for the day before and after as well. There were 196,418 deaths that day."

"Goddamn. That many?"

"Yes, sir. More deaths occur in January than any other month of the year. Plus, I didn't want to limit us to the United States, so I looked up death records around the world."

"Any luck finding her?"

"No, sir. There were 377 Rebeccas or similar names from this specific time period. I'm still going through the list."

"That's quite a database to scour."

"Yes, sir. But we can't make any assumptions about her or him or anything related to the Fasciata."

"Agreed, Jardine."

AJ's phone rang. "Sir, Tony's calling me."

"Put it on speaker."

"Hey, Tony."

"Where are you?"

"I'm in the office. Why?"

"I need to come get you. We have another scene to process."

AJ and Conrad stared at each other.

"What happened?" she asked.

"Remember that state trooper, Sotelo?"

"Gigi?"

"Yeah, him. He's missing, and his car was found abandoned, flipped in a ditch not far off the interstate. I can swing by and pick you up in five."

Conrad nodded his consent.

"Sure, I'll be waiting downstairs for you." She hung up the phone, then grabbed her things.

"Jardine, be safe out there."

"Yes, sir."

"Let's hope this state trooper isn't the next victim."

Her head nodded in agreement. Her mind thought something else entirely.

- - -- --- -----

She squatted near the side of the road. "Those look like drag marks."

"Can you make out any foot impressions? Signs of a struggle? Anything?"

She continued to study the slush and ice.

"No, the temps are above freezing right now. Any details have already melted away."

"Can you plaster or powder them or *something*?"

AJ stood up and studied him, examining every detail of emotion on his face. Desperation caused his voice to inflect higher. She saw new wrinkles around his eyes and temple.

"Tony, are you okay? You seem on edge right now."

"I'm fine. The department's freaking out that one of their own is missing. The nervous energy has rubbed off on me, I guess. Imagine if it were Peter or someone you knew missing. It's the same for those guys over there."

He was not telling her the complete truth.

"There's nothing I can easily see or determine, other than there's been a struggle. The getaway vehicle left, peeled out, so we can take photos of the tread marks. His cruiser might have fingerprints and evidence that could be processed. Maybe some of it'll match the unknown DNA and partial print from the Wheel House. We should also interview some of his friends and figure out his last moves."

She turned to walk back to his car, but he grabbed her arm and twirled her back to face him.

He gripped her tightly. "You are *not* going near them without me. Understand?"

She nodded, stunned, unsure of what to say.

- - -- --- -----

They drove through a middle-class neighborhood and pulled up to the townhouse address from Gigi's file. The multi-family structure was nestled on the outskirts of the Town of Nashua near the Massachusetts border.

They walked up to the door and Tony knocked. Through the glass pane, AJ saw the silhouette of a woman approaching.

A young, attractive woman opened the door. She wore yoga pants and a tank top. Her hair was pulled up into a messy ponytail. AJ thought they interrupted her workout. She also thought she saw a bright tattoo on the woman's neck.

The woman's eyes went wide when she saw the agent.

"Tony! What the hell are you doing here?"

"I should ask you the same fucking thing!"

He pushed his way inside, and before AJ could walk in, he slammed the door. She heard the locking mechanism fasten. Surprised by what happened, she pounded on the door.

"Tony!"

She heard a bunch of yelling on the other side. After several minutes, he emerged, grabbed AJ by the arm, and escorted her to the car.

"Tony! Let go! You're hurting me!"

He said nothing. He opened the passenger door of his car, shoved her in, and then slammed the door. Uncharacteristic anger fueled his actions and she froze in fear. He walked to the driver's side, got in, and sped off. His eyes never left the road.

"Tony, what was that all about?"

"Just shut the fuck up right now." His hands tapped nervously on the steering wheel.

"Tony?"

"Not. Today."

The words oozed with menace and warning. She never experienced such emotion or dread from him. She had never seen such anger from him directed at her. She never thought she would fear him.

- - -- --- -----

AJ had no idea where they were, other than in a rural and remote location near the Town of Franklin, more than an hour drive from Gigi's townhouse. They pulled into the driveway and snaked up to the tree-hidden house. He parked and got out of the car. She followed him up the front steps of the porch.

"Stay in the car." He told her as he grabbed the door handle.

"No, I'm staying with you."

He turned around to face her and was about to say something when they heard the front door open. A menacing shadow stood in the doorway, blocking the interior light. It was Aggie. He appeared shocked to see

Tony.

"V—" Aggie started to say.

WHACK! Tony sucker punched him in the face, sending the burly man backward several steps inside. The front door swung open and Tony pushed his way in.

She followed.

Aggie regained his composure and took a step towards Tony. The sinister one nearly stood a head taller than him and was twice as intimidating. Tony did not budge. She watched the interaction between the two men.

"Hello, detective," came a voice behind her.

She spun around and recognized the man standing there. It was the calm one. Frankie looked at her, his face void of emotion, though he studied her movements. It unsettled her in much the same way the first time she met him.

She took a step back away from Frankie and bumped into the menacing one. She realized too late Aggie moved in behind her. Massive hands grabbed her shoulders and applied pressure.

"SHE'S NOT TO BE TOUCHED!" The ferocity in Tony's voice drained the blood from her face as hands released her. Tony's anger was even more profound than before. He pulled her closer to him and placed his body between her and Aggie.

"Aggie, you heard him. You can't have fun with this one," Frankie said.

Tony took her by the waist and escorted her to the door. He gently placed his palms on her temples and forced her gaze from Aggie to his. The light reflected vivid blueness and deep concern in his eyes. She felt his intensity.

"Go wait in the car, AJ."

"Tony?" She feared what the two men would do to him.

"Go. Now. I'll be there in a few minutes."

He shut the door on her. AJ hurried to the car and waited. Her mind raced as her brain tried to comprehend and process what was occurring. Her fear made her hands shake and her stomach hurt. She took out her gun and held it, ready in case she needed to use it.

She waited.

Several minutes later, Tony emerged from the house and got in the car. He appeared calmer as they drove off, though his fingers still nervously tapped the steering wheel.

"Is everything okay?"

"Everything's fine."

"What happened?"

"I can't tell you."

"That's not fair!"

"Ameena, please. Don't push the subject. Go home. Be with your family. At least you have a family to go home to."

She was startled by his words.

"Tony?"

He never answered.

- - -- --- -----

"*Salaam Alaikum*, habibti!"

Her mother appeared happy as she prepared several dishes in the kitchen.

"Hi, Momma. You're in a good mood."

"Just preparing for dinner with our guest."

With Tony distracting her thoughts, Ameena had completely forgotten about the dinner plans.

"Oh, fuck me." Her cheeks went hot with emotion.

"Ameena, don't say that."

"That's today, isn't it?"

"Yes, I told you about it several times, dear. I know how you feel about it, but hear him out, please. Remember, it's for me."

"Fine." She made no attempt to hide her emotions. "I'll be in my bedroom until he gets here."

- - -- --- -----

A couple of hours later, the doorbell rang. Two excited

mutts and one curious girl greeted the stranger at the door. When Ameena heard the commotion, she saved her files, closed the laptop, and put everything away.

She walked out of her bedroom and watched the frail, old man. He still had the same Irish flat cap on and wore a plaid shirt two sizes too big. His jeans sagged from his thin body. With his curly gray hair sticking out from his cap and the salt-and-pepper mustache, he reminded her of Albert Einstein.

Her stomach knotted from the nerves, and she wished she was thousands of miles away in any direction. She was not ready to face her birth father; she did not think she ever would be.

"Hi, Paden." She glared at him.

"Hello, Ameena. How have you been?" He still had the same heavy Scottish accent.

"Extremely busy."

They stood in awkward silence as she struggled to find words.

"That's good," he finally said. He appeared lost and pained in his thoughts.

The tension must have been evident because Jamilla walked in and stared at both. "Everyone, please go sit in the living room. Paden, would you like something to drink?" She ushered them into the next room.

"Water, please."

He eased himself in the recliner, grimacing with pain. Ameena watched as he tried to get comfortable. The more she saw the frail man in front of her, the more she forgot about the abusive father she remembered.

"Did you hurt your back?" Her curiosity got the better of her.

"Yes, a long time ago. The doctors never fixed the disks right."

Another awkward moment of silence passed. Jenna came running in. When Paden saw the little girl, he smiled weakly, but she saw a new pain in his eyes.

"Mommy, can I sit next to Grandpa?"

"*Grandpa*?" She raised her eyebrows, then stared at Paden and her mother, who had just walked back in the room.

"Don't worry, Mommy, he's not Papa. He's Grandpa. Tayta said he's not replacing Papa."

"Jenna, sweetheart. That's right. No one will EVER replace Papa. Grandpa Paden is here to visit and get to know all of you. He didn't want to come around with Papa here and confuse you, that's all."

The grandmother gave Ameena a stern look.

"Tayta's right, Jenna. He's not Papa, he's Grandpa."

"Can I show him my feather collection, Mommy?"

"Yeah, sure." Ameena nodded sideways.

Using his cane, Paden carefully stood up. Jenna peered up at him, happy to take his free hand and lead him to the office.

Her own heart burned with pain and her eyes watered, but she quickly swallowed those feelings away.

She watched them from a distance.

A car arrived home. She glanced out the window and saw Eoghan and Derek getting out. They walked around to the front and entered.

She watched them from a distance.

Her heart and mind were in turmoil—again—over the old man in the next room. She swore decades ago he would never see his grandchildren; and yet, there he was hugging his oldest grandson for the first time. Her mind questioned her memories. Finally, Jamilla shooed the kids upstairs and talked to Paden privately.

She watched them from a distance.

Her mother gently touched her father on the shoulder. The frail man crumbled into her mother's nurturing arms. He broke down and cried. Jamilla wiped tears from her own eyes.

She watched them from a distance, like an outsider in her own home.

- - -- --- -----

After dinner and goodbyes, Paden requested Ameena walk him to his car. She carefully helped him down the basement stairs and out the garage to the driveway. They hardly said a word.

"You've done good, Ameena." Paden finally broke the silence.

"Thanks." She did not know what else to say to him. Her emotions kept swinging to both sides of the pendulum.

"I've missed you so much. I've suffered every day since your mom left me."

She rolled her eyes. "That's hard to believe. You remarried and had two more sons. How can you sit there and say you have suffered *every* day?" When she saw the pain in his eyes, she added, "We've all done fine without you in our lives."

"I guess I deserve that," he whispered.

"You deserve more than that, to be honest," she blurted out.

"Ameena, I don't want to fight. Now that I finally found you, I want to be in your lives, that's all."

"You've been out of our lives for over THREE decades now, Paden. What do you want? WHY are you even here?"

"I—I have hurt every day you have been gone from me."

"Stop. *Every* day?" The pendulum—and her anger— began to peak. "Uh, no. You sent mom to the fucking *hos-pit-al*! And you wonder why she fled from you? You wonder why she drove THOUSANDS of miles to get away from you? You were a fucking drunk-ass, wife-beating, bipolar ASSHOLE!"

Years of pent-up anger came pouring out of her as the pendulum in her mind crested:

"You treated her like SHIT and beat her if she didn't have your dinner made after SHE came home from work. You beat me with a fucking truck antenna wrapped in electric tape after you kept breaking wood trim on my feet and hands! You're a sorry excuse for a fucking sperm donor and honestly, I do NOT think you deserve to be called GRANDPA—WHAT my mom was thinking, I have NO idea!"

He sat quietly in growing depression and listened to everything she said. And she kept going, unleashing all her fury she held from the time she was little:

"You were a violent PIECE OF SHIT. We hid the holes YOU punched in the walls behind pictures we could find that were big enough to cover the fucking damage. We cowered in FEAR from you. When you were drunk—WHICH WAS ALL THE FUCKING TIME—you couldn't stop telling me what a worthless and ugly piece of shit I was. NOW WHO'S the piece of shit? Huh?

"Do you remember THAT last night? You were on a drunken tirade again. You argued with Mom in front of the family. Then you dragged me in the living room and demanded to know who I wanted to live with. I was SO fucking SCARED of you, I said I wanted to live with Mom. Do you remember what you said? I DO, you asshole! You disowned me in front of EVERYONE! You told me I was NOTHING to you, that I deserved to burn in hell with her. All because I was TOO fucking AFRAID of YOU!"

"Ameena," came her mother's voice behind her.

"WHAT?!?" She spun around and immediately felt guilty.

"Paden has suffered enough for the pain he caused all of us. We need to forgive him."

"*You* can forgive him. *I* never will."

Her anger and rage blinded her. She never saw the hurt, sorrow, and regret in her father's eyes as she walked off.

- - -- --- -----

Jamilla walked in and sat down on the edge of her bed. She quietly watched Ameena.

"Momma, he deserved every bit of it." She defended her actions. "He conveniently shows up shortly after Dad dies? And then he has the fucking balls to say he has suffered EVERY day since you left—no, FLED from him? All the anger he gave us, especially you and me, I gave it right back to him."

Jamilla continued to sit quietly and listen.

"I'm not going to apologize to him. It needed to be said."

Her mother kept watching her.

Finally, she stopped talking.

"Ameena, he has heart disease and just found out he has blockage in his arteries. He's having open heart surgery soon. When? I'm not sure yet. But he came to me because he wants to make peace with everyone and apologize. He didn't know how to say it."

The news took her by surprise. A guilt seed was planted inside her.

"Mom, his health problems are his doing. That's not on me or my brothers."

"I know, habibti. I know." Jamilla stood up to walk out. "He wanted to make peace and feared your rejection. That's why he couldn't come to you all these years. He feared *you*, like you feared him when you were little. He just wants forgiveness."

"I don't think I can give it to him."

Jamilla walked over and kissed her on the forehead. As the wise woman walked out, she gave her daughter a few final words:

"Forgiveness is as powerful as love, as graceful as beauty, and as free as a soul can get. You should consider forgiving *all* those who've harmed you. And I'm not just talking about your father."

- - -- --- -----

Tuesday, March 8, 2022

"Jardine, where are you?" Conrad asked through the car speakers.

"I'm heading to the office right now, sir."

"No. I need you somewhere else. Trooper Sotelo's body was found in the woods. I'll text you the address."

"Yes, sir."

"Head straight over there. Tony will join you later."

"Yes, sir."

She clicked the button on her steering wheel to hang up the call, then pulled the car over and waited. A few minutes later, her phone pinged with the address, somewhere between the Towns of Henniker and Bradford off a busy route.

- - -- --- -----

"Hey, stranger." Tony's demeanor was solemn.

She smiled weakly at him. They hardly spoke to each other the last few weeks.

He moved closer to her, out of earshot of the others. "Don't say anything about his ties to the Fasciata, understand? There may be other members here."

She nodded. She gathered her things, and as they had done with the other investigations, they began trekking through the woods. "Who found the body?"

"Anonymous tip. Said we could find him south of Harriman Chandler State Forest and east of Lake Massasecum off Henniker Road."

"Anonymous?"

"Yeah, police are looking at tracking the call right now. Since it's one of our own, other officials have joined in to look for clues. I'm coordinating with a couple of them to collect the plasters, prints, and pictures. Better to have more evidence than not enough."

"True."

Mud Season was in the first stages of Spring. Much of the

snow had melted, leaving brown and dirty ice in patches across the woods. Streams flowed, and the ground was extra soft and gooey. The landscape made her think of American Painted Horses. Muddy muck eventually covered everyone's shoes as they trekked through the slippery landscape.

When they arrived at the site, they found the body in a sitting position, hunched over, with both arms curled upward and inward.

Gigi's body was placed in an almost-perfect fetal ball. Only a muscle shirt and boxer shorts covered his body. Few tattoos were visible, but she did not see the trademark tentacle. She did, however, see a rubber tube strapped around his thick left bicep.

The ground around the body, and most of the trails in and out of the location, had been trampled by all the foot traffic. There would be no way to determine if the killer's footprints were among them.

When she asked everyone around, no one had taken any photos or molds of pre-existing prints in the mud. The careless blunder frustrated her to no end.

She photographed and bagged everything she could before Sotelo's body was finally removed; it took three people to lift the bodybuilder up. AJ knew Cassie would have her work cut out for her.

With nothing else to gather or process, they all left.

Tony hardly spoke the entire time.

- - -- --- -----

When Ameena walked in the door, she saw her mother on the phone, a blank expression on her face.

Jamilla put her hand over the mouthpiece and whispered, "It's about your father." Then she focused her attention on the caller.

Ameena knew that meant nothing good. Paden was admitted to the hospital for triple-bypass surgery and was still recovering. Because of his bipolar diagnosis, doctors decided to place him on anti-depressants at the same time. The combination of the drugs, the surgery, and his diabetes—which she found out about a week prior—all caused him to suffer mental confusion and delusions. She did not know anything else beyond that.

Jamilla hung up the phone. "That was your step-mother. She said Paden is not doing good."

"What happened?"

"He hasn't been eating anything. They don't know if it's the drugs or the surgery, but he just stopped eating. And the doctors have not given him the tube in the gut."

"You mean a feeding tube?"

"Yes, that thing. The doctors want to wait a few more days to see what happens."

"Have you told the guys yet?"

"Yes, Faruq and Nabih have called their step-mom, finally. Ari has refused."

"That sounds like him. You know he's stubborn."

"So are you at times, sweetheart. You should call your step-mother and talk to her."

"I'll do it this weekend when they know more. Maybe we can make a trip to Boston Memorial and visit him?"

"That would be a good idea. You still haven't met your half-brothers yet."

She rolled her eyes. "Momma, that's because I've been working a murder investigation and have been given cold case files up to my neck to solve in between that. After we found the Wheel House and the kill room, we've had some gains in solving old crimes, but it's slow and tedious."

"Ugh," Jamilla shivered. "I don't want to talk about kill rooms and death." She started to walk off, then stopped. "Oh, I almost forgot. You have a gift waiting for you on your dresser. Your secret admirer again."

Another gift from Copernicus, I presume. I wonder if it's flowers again?

When she walked in her room, there were no flowers or

large gifts; merely a singular box and card sat propped on her dresser.

She opened the card first. It was different than the others. An illustration of a chess piece — a knight — had been inked in the top right corner.

Offset from the center, and proportionately balanced with the image, a quote:

> *In order to improve your game, you must study the Endgame before everything else.*
> *~Jose Raul Capablanca*
> *0100010126670001001110479096S*

She sighed.

More words of wisdom from an obscure dead person, I see. I wonder what game he's referring to?

She opened the gift box. When she saw the beauty of its contents, she inhaled deeply.

"It's so beautiful!" she whispered.

She pulled the snake-style silver chain out of the box and stared at the dangling pendant. It was a vivid blue and striking larimar stone wrapped in silver along the edges. Fibonacci spirals curled playfully towards the center of the stone. The larimar felt smooth, round, and cool against her fingertips. The back was flat with solid, thick, polished silver. An inscription was etched in the metal:

Now and always

Ameena put the necklace on. It rested perfectly above her cleavage in the center of her chest. She looked at it through the dresser mirror. The marbled sky-blue stone accented her skin tone.

She opened her laptop and went into the chatroom.

Roar317811: Copernicus, are you

there?
NCPoland1543: Yes
Roar317811: Thank you for the gift!
It's so beautiful!
NCPoland1543: May I see? Uncover your
webcam.

She complied and smiled in the camera for a few
seconds. Then, teasingly, she covered the camera back.

NCPoland1543: It looks beautiful on
you
Roar317811: Thank you. I was
expecting flowers again, not a
necklace.
NCPoland1543: Would you prefer
flowers, love?
Roar317811: No, I don't expect
anything from anyone.
NCPoland1543: As I told you before,
there will be more.
Roar317811: And more will give their
lives for us to receive ours back?
NCPoland1543: Yin and Yang, it's the
natural balance of things.
Roar317811: The divine proportion?
NCPoland1543: Life and love are
divine, are they not proportionate to
death and hate?
Roar317811: Perhaps. You give me much
to think about, life and love
NCPoland1543: You have given me life
and love to think about
Roar317811: I've been searching for
Rebecca's information. Conrad asked
me to do that.
NCPoland1543: I know. And I know you
have hundreds of names to scour. But
you won't find her. I knew her as
Rebecca, but that isn't the name on

her death certificate. It was changed
to protect the N.C.
Roar317811: Why didn't you tell me?
It would've saved me time.
NCPoland1543: Conrad would have told
you, but you could have asked me
Roar317811: Then let me propose this
question: when do we meet in person?
You promised me.
NCPoland1543: Yes, I did. I'm between
research projects at the moment. We
could meet in a couple of weeks. I
need to secure another location
first. Agreed?
Roar317811: You swear we will meet in
person?
NCPoland1543: On pain of death, I
swear. Two weeks from tonight. But
you must not tell anyone, including
McMillan.
Roar317811: I swear
Roar317811: But understand this. If
you back away from your promise, I
won't ever contact you again or talk
to you. Understand?
NCPoland1543: May the pain of death
never reach us. Promise me, you will
wear the necklace from now until
then? Please. I don't ask much of
you, but this I do.
Roar317811: Yes, I will. It's too
beautiful not to wear.
NCPoland1543: Good, keep your promise
you will not take off the necklace,
and I will keep mine to see you, in
person, in two weeks. Good night,
Ameena.

"Good night, Copernicus."
She looked down at the necklace, reread the inscription,

and frowned.

'Not today' or 'now and always'. Not an easy decision to make.

- - -- --- -----

<u>Tuesday, March 22, 2022</u>

Cassie's eyes went wide, and she whistled. "Oh, that is gorgeous! Where'd you get the necklace?"

"I ordered it online," AJ lied. "I've always loved this stone and thought this design was unique. Late birthday present to myself."

"Well, I approve!"

"So, what do you have for me, Cass?"

"Alotta nothin', not nearly as much as you do!"

"Ugh." AJ rubbed her temples. Her mood changed. "It's been hectic, to say the least."

"Aww, hon. What happened now?"

"The doctors finally put a feeding tube in Paden's stomach, but I think they did it too late. He's—he's a frailer bag of bones now, if that's even possible."

"And how do you feel about it?"

"Ya know, for me, I know what it's like to lose a father with Dad. Ernest wasn't just my step-father, he was my *dad*. This man, Paden's a stranger to me. But I empathize so strongly with my half-brothers and step-mom. I don't want them to go through what I went through. And if I can't be there for him, maybe I can be there for them. Does that make any sense?"

"Yes. It'll all work out, sweetie."

"I don't want this to affect your wedding or bachelorette parties."

"Ya know, Nadine and I talked about that, and she decided she doesn't want one. Honestly? I'm okay with not having a party."

"Are you sure?"

"I'd rather spend the money on the honeymoon and get all my friends nice gifts from Europe. So, don't worry about bridesmaid obligations you may think you have. It'll all work out, I promise."

"Okay, but if you change your mind, you'll tell me, right?"

"Absolutely! Now. You ready to talk about your

overdose victim?"

"Let me guess: tetrodotoxin in the heroin?"

"Yep. Now when I straightened his body back out and uncurled his left hand, he was holding a small vile of an unknown substance. I sent it to Peter for his analysis."

"And did he have the trademark tattoo?"

"Yep. It was across his rib, wrapped around his pectoral, went under his arm and trailed off to the back."

"So, same M.O. as the other deaths?"

"Yep. Other than that, he was the spitting image of healthiness. But there are two things we discovered, which may change how the department treats his case."

"What's that?"

"One, I ran his DNA in the database and got a hit on an ongoing case. AJ," she paused, her voice lower, "he's one of Angie Carmicle's three rapists."

"Fuck a duck!"

"Two, his DNA was also found in the Wheel House. He was there."

"Oh, shit..."

"Did you know he was Fasciata?"

"We suspected, but couldn't prove it. At least now we know the truth."

- - -- --- -----

"There's not much to tell you, AJ. Same M.O. as the other deaths. No clues at all except this." Peter held up an evidence bag.

"What is that?" She stared at the small vial of powder.

"It's crushed and dried columbine flower seeds. The lid has the number 'five' carved in the inside of it."

"Five, huh? What the hell are columbine seeds?"

"I know, right? I had to research it." He pulled up an internet window on his monitor and showed her.

"Columbine can be used medicinally. You can use small amounts of this powder for headaches, fevers, even love charms. But too much can cause internal bleeding and make you violently sick. It's poisonous in large doses. Now, these particular seeds were from this plant here, the Rocky Mountain Columbine."

He pulled up a picture of a white and periwinkle flower. She counted the petals.

"Heh. Five petals. And you said it's poisonous?"

"Yep, in large doses."

"It wasn't in the tox report though, right?"

"Nope, he didn't ingest any of it."

"Anything else?"

"Nope, other than what Cass already told you, that's it."

"Okay, thanks. I'm meeting with Conrad soon and I'll see what he thinks of it all."

- - -- --- -----

She sat across from her boss and peeked at the time on her phone. It was before lunchtime. She reiterated the details from Cassie and Peter.

"So now we've confirmation Frierson *and* Sotelo both raped Ms. Carmicle?"

"Yes, sir. We're looking for one more person."

"Have you spoken to Dr. Pinick? Can he determine who exactly are the next victims?"

"No, sir, he can't. I did talk to him on the phone yesterday and told him we have another victim. He said he'll wait to hear from me."

"And have you spoken to Copernicus?"

"Yes, sir. A little."

She paused.

"What is it, Jardine?"

"Sir, I told Copernicus I'd been searching for Rebecca's death certificate and couldn't find it. That's when he told me her name was changed on record to protect something."

"What's that?"

"To protect the *thing* that shall not be named."

She drew the initials on his desk and saw his eyebrows drop in surprise.

"What else has he told you?"

"A while ago he told me the Fasciata was responsible for the hit on Michael. He said Jose Perales drove the getaway car."

Conrad cocked his head slightly and leaned in. "Say that again, detective."

"The Fasciata killed Michael. And Rebecca. Copernicus said he's been doing extensive research and discovering the names of everyone who was responsible, including the shooters. That *thing*, the murders, the Fasciata—it's all connected, sir."

He gradually sat back and broke eye contact. He stared at the desk—she wondered if he stared at The Desk Scar—lost in his own thoughts. His fingers tapped nervously. She waited for him to respond. Finally, he rubbed his temples in frustration and shook his head.

"Jardine, you're to cease any more contact with Copernicus."

"Sir? Why?"

"You heard me. And I don't need to explain my actions to you, detective."

"But, sir—"

"No buts about it. No more communication until further notice." The tone of his voice was rigid.

"Sir, no, I—"

"Immediately, dammit!" He slammed his hand on the desk and she jumped in her chair. His reaction stunned her, much the same as Tony's the other day.

"Yes, sir," she finally whispered.

"Grab your things and go home."

"It's still ear—"

"Jardine! Just do it. We'll talk more tomorrow."

She nodded.

He dismissed her.

She grabbed her things and walked to her car, not

understanding what just happened with her boss.

Fuck. Why the hell would Conrad shut me down like that? What did I say to freak him out so bad? He's asking me NOT to speak to Copernicus again? I'm supposed to meet him tonight!

She sat in the driver's seat still deep in thought. Her stomach fluttered at the thought of meeting Copernicus. She knew he was Nick, from the kiss under the aurora, but he never confirmed nor denied it.

I can't NOT meet Copernicus. I have so many questions and need answers. Fuck!

She finally started the car and pulled out of the office parking lot.

Answers. Who can give me answers? Tony's out of the question. He's hardly spoken to me since the day Gigi went missing. I wonder who the woman was at his place? She knew Tony. Maybe she was Gigi's girlfriend. Maybe I can talk to her about Gigi's death.

After more mental debating, she decided to pay the mystery woman another visit.

- - -- --- -----

"Hello, can I help you?" The same attractive woman answered the door.

"Hi, I was here a while back with Tony. Do you remember?"

She stiffened and nodded. "Yeah. I remember."

"I wanted to ask you a few more questions if you don't mind."

"Actually, I do mind. I'm busy."

"It'll only take a few minutes."

"I can't talk to you." She leaned slightly and whispered. "You need to leave *now*, Ameena!"

AJ heard a man's voice from behind the door. It swung open and there stood Frankie. She did not expect to see him, and he appeared miffed at the disturbance.

"What're you doing here, detective?" Frankie's

monotone voice never gave away more emotion.

"I have additional questions regarding Sotelo's last day, and I was hoping to—"

"You need to leave. NOW!"

He looked at the woman. "Zoey, go back inside." Without hesitation, she did as she was told. He took a step out onto the porch where AJ stood. "Leave. Now."

Just then, Aggie came out and stood next to Frankie. While the latter did not intimidate her, fear surfaced from the former. She held her ground.

"Did you know Gigi was murdered? He was given a lethal dose of Prussian Black." She saw no reaction.

"Detective, I don't care," Frankie said. "He's a cop. They aren't a popular breed."

"He wasn't killed because he's a cop. He was killed because he's Fasciata, just like you." She got her reaction. Aggie stepped closer towards her. Frankie slapped his midsection and stopped him.

"Listen, bitch, get the fuck out of here," Aggie growled at her.

Before thinking her words through, she blurted to the menacing one, "I hope you're next, asshole." Aggie lunged forward, almost knocking her over, but Frankie grabbed and held him back. "In fact, I hope you're *both* next."

"Detective. LEAVE. NOW. Before *you're* next." Frankie dropped his arm from Aggie's midsection. As the menacing one took a step forward, AJ turned around and left.

"Place the call," she thought she overheard one of them say.

She got into her car and locked it.

"Jardine, you fucking idiot," she chided herself. "What the hell were you thinking to say that to them?"

She swallowed her fear and left quickly.

- - -- --- -----

I'm ready to meet you. ~nc

Where at? ~aj

Get in the car and head
east on Belmont Road
to Alton. Text me before
you reach the town. I'll
give you more instruction.
~nc

The text message came in shortly after eight.

She grabbed her coat and keys. "Momma, I'll be back later."

"Where are you going so late?"

"I'm meeting up with a friend in Alton."

"Okay, habibti, be careful. The roads are slick from the new snow."

"I will."

Ameena drove off and took the road as instructed. Her thoughts raced again. *Who is this guy? Can I trust him? Can I trust anyone nowadays? Is Copernicus Nick? He has to be! What if he's Tony? Could it be Michael?*

She drove down Belmont Road for several minutes and made it up one of the hills when her car stalled. She pulled over on the shoulder as all power flickered off. She sent Copernicus a text.

Am running late.
Car just died on
Belmont Road.
Looks like alternator.
~aj

As she sent the text, a cruiser pulled up behind her and flashed the lights.

Her phone rang from an unknown caller.

"Hello?"

"RUN! Get away from the car NOW!"

But it was too late.

- - -- --- -----

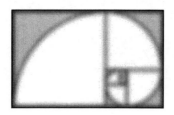

CHAPTER TWENTY-THREE: CAPTURED

Tuesday, March 22, 2022

AJ heard three voices: a calm voice giving instruction; a menacing voice that petrified her; and her own silent, inner voice screaming at her.

"Get out of the car. Now." It was Frankie. "If I see your hands move for a weapon, we'll empty two clips into you."

Stay calm. For fuck's sake, STAY CALM!

Blue and red lights flashed behind her. It appeared to be a police cruiser, but the men pointing guns at her were not the police. She did as she was instructed.

"Put your hands up where I can see them."

Stay calm, goddammit! Don't do anything stupid. He means what he said.

She held her hands up, keys in one and phone in the other. Her vision was impaired by the bright headlights shining on her, though she saw a menacing shadow approach her.

"You won't be needing these anymore, bitch!"

Aggie's rough hands ripped the items from her fingers and tossed them in the shadows.

"Turn around and face the car."

No no no no no! Stay focused! BREATHE! She closed her eyes, slowly turning her back to the men.

Aggie shoved her hard against the hood, pinning her head between the warm metal and his forearm. He forced her legs apart, offsetting her center of balance. He groped and fondled her, especially gripping intimate areas, as he searched for any other weapons. He smelled like cheap cigarettes and days' old deodorant. She wanted to throw up.

"She's clean."

"Cross your wrists above you."

Slow and steady. It's a kidnapping, not a hit. That's it. Deep breath.

She complied.

Aggie released her head and used the same hand to grip her hands together. He squeezed harder than necessary as he used his other hand to grab something from his pocket. His body pressed firmly against hers.

Zip! She opened her eyes to see zip ties binding her.

"She's good."

"Stand up and turn around."

Stay calm, Jardine. Do what they ask.

She slowly faced them as instructed. Frankie continued to point the gun at her.

"Walk slowly towards me."

Stay calm like him. Stay calm!

The flashing responder lights blinded her.

"Get in the back seat."

Deep breath. Don't do anything stupid. THINK!

She ducked in through the driver's side door and was suddenly shoved from behind. She fell on her stomach in the back seat.

As she scrambled to sit up and move out of the way, Aggie got in behind her and slammed the door. He grabbed her by the hair and twisted her head to look at him. The brutality in his eyes staring back at her made her want to unravel. Her inner voice and strength, at that moment, took flight and disappeared.

"You should've left when we told you to, you fucking bitch!"

"Aggie, cut it out."

Frankie sat in the driver's seat, pointing the gun at her.

"H-how did you know where to—"

Aggie interrupted her and pulled her up across his lap.

BAM! He smacked her head against the window, pressing her cheek into the glass.

"AGGIE! Cut it out."

"What? She deserved it! She fucking threatened me earlier."

Her lip and cheekbone smarted against the pain. She did not taste blood, but she knew the feeling would not dissipate anytime soon. Aggie kept her pinned against the window. Her head was twisted, and she could see the calm one.

Frankie put his gun down and glared solemnly at her. He picked up something in the passenger's front seat.

His focus alternated between her and the item in his hands. His voice remained cool and collective. "Detective Jardine. Understand you've crossed a line. You were warned earlier this year to back off. And you didn't. So, what happens later this evening is on you." He looked over to Aggie. "You got her?"

Aggie pulled her from the window and sat her on his lap facing Frankie. The menacing one's arms wrapped around and pinned her down. She felt one hand reach between her legs and grip her inner thigh.

Genuine, unadulterated fear took hold. And her inner voice came back to—

—*FIGHT DAMMIT!! Get away! They're going to kill you! RUN!!!*

In mere moments, she reared back and headbutted Aggie in the head. He released her to grab his face.

Frankie pulled back from her, in apparent shock from the sudden motion.

She scrambled across to the passenger side, grabbed the doorknob, and opened it. Aggie grabbed her and wrapped a thick arm around her neck. She was in a headlock before she could place a leg outside.

He yanked her back into his lap. His power lifted her off the seat, and she had no balance or way to escape.

She dug her nails into his forearm, but he increased the pressure. She began to lose consciousness from the crushing force around her neck. She grabbed his wrist and pulled his forearm down with all her strength, then twisted her head and jabbed her chin in the crook of his elbow so that she could breathe.

"Do you have her?"

"Mmm hmm."

Frankie stared at her.

Her heart raced from fear.

"Detective, this can go one of two ways. A. Aggie can tighten his headlock, make you pass out, and then rape you after I drug you. *Or* B. You can allow me to inject this, no struggle. You get to sleep for a little bit. Personally, I would prefer Option B, since our boss demanded that nothing happen to you. But Aggie here wants Option A. He had a lot of fun with Angie the last time this happened."

She knew he meant every word he said. She nodded in understanding. Frankie glanced at Aggie and nodded once. The menacing one released his grip enough for her to breathe and bring her hands down.

Aggie leaned in. "I was hoping you wanted Option A because I would have *so much fun* with you."

He squeezed one of her breasts with his free hand.

She froze in disgust.

"AGGIE!"

"What?"

"Leave her alone. Right, detective? Option B is what you wanted?"

She nodded her head rapidly. She desperately wanted to get away from Aggie.

"Extend your arm for me, please."

Stay calm. Whatever it is, try to fight it. Slow breathing. Slow your damn heartbeat, detective!

She did as Frankie instructed. He took a tourniquet and tied it around the middle of her left forearm. He played with the back of her hand.

Tap tap tap.

Tap tap.

Tap.

Tap.

"Not the back of the hand!"

"Shut up, bitch!" Aggie yanked her hair again.

"Aggie," Frankie scolded his partner, then looked at her.

"P-Please, I-I would rather it be in my elbow." Her eyes pleaded with him.

"Elbow it is."

He untied the tourniquet. Aggie repositioned himself, loosening his grip more. Frankie leaned in and retied the rubber band above her elbow.

Tap tap tap.

Tap tap.

Tap.

Tap.

She watched his every move, as he inserted the needle in the black liquid and filled the syringe with a small amount. He tapped the needle then stared at her. Suddenly, he reached up, touched a finger under her chin and gently forced her gaze to him.

His voice was quiet and monotonous. "If you try anything before I get this needle in your arm, I'll hunt down your beautiful little Jenna and let Aggie do to her what he did to Angie. Do you understand me, detective?"

Her stomach clinched from the fear building up again.

NOT JENNA! For fuck's sake, STAY CALM!

"Y-yes."

"Good."

He found the site on her arm and pressed the needle into her vein.

NO!!!

Panic!

The sting.

Then more panic.

She began to hyperventilate uncontrollably.

The dark venom-drug quickly traveled through her body.

"Detective, remain calm and it'll be more pleasant."

Her midsection went warm and her mind felt displaced from her body. Her hands and feet tingled. She held her hands up to study them; her fingers grew and shrunk in random patterns. Her jaw felt funny. She could feel Aggie's hot breath on her. Her body relaxed into the menacing one. She smiled from the effects of the drug.

"What," her words slowed to a soft slur, "did you give me?"

"Prussian Black." Frankie's words echoed in her mind as her brain tried to process what he said. "Not enough to kill you. Yet."

Her body drifted down into the seat from Aggie's release. She felt heavy and could not move. She heard a loud bang next to her. A few minutes later, she heard another loud bang in front of her. Voices echoed in a far distance and lights swirled around her.

She was losing consciousness from the drug, and she did not care. She enjoyed the pleasure-senses her body was introduced to. She felt no guilt—she felt nothing save the euphoria of the heroin making itself at home in her body.

The lights were beautiful. They continued to swirl and started changing color. They morphed into a kaleidoscope of wonder she had only seen a few times before: once up in the mountains and once in Maine. She smiled at the imagery as she drifted to sleep.

- - -- --- -----

She could not hear anything. Her arms and legs still felt heavy from the sedation. Her fingers and toes ached, as did her forehead. She tried to reach up to touch her temple, but her arms would not move. She twisted her wrists; something held them down.

She opened her eyes and squinted as her vision adjusted to the brightness around her. Her head ached more. The last thing she remembered was a wasp stung her.

No, that wasn't it. It's March, I think. No wasps. Not in March. What was it again? A needle!

Her forehead throbbed, and her temple stung. When she lifted her eyebrows and wrinkled her face, her skin felt tightened and constricted as if —

— Blood? But how?

Her brow burned. She forgot about the restraints and tried to use her hand to touch the wound but could not move.

What's wrong with my hands? Why do my fingers feel numb? Why is everything so foggy around me? Take another deep breath. Wake up, dammit!

She closed her eyes again.

She inhaled deeply.

Then exhaled.

Inhaled.

Exhaled.

The fog parted in her mind, though everything still felt out of focus. She looked back at her hands; her wrists were tied to the chair she sat in. She tried moving her legs; they were secured as well.

More deep inhales and exhales. More focusing.

This isn't fog. It's the room.

Panic set in as her eyes finally focused on the hazy polymer-covered walls.

IT'S A KILL ROOM!!!

Fear raged within her. She pulled and jerked the restraints, but she could not loosen them. She looked around from the ceiling to the floor, but everything was obscured from semi-translucent plastic.

Remember, dammit! If you can't escape right now, THINK! Clear your brain. Scan the place and remember the details!

She tried to focus. The walls beneath the plastic appeared an eggshell color. Trim surrounding the doors and windows appeared equally faded. She thought the ceiling appeared a dull yellow from years of cigarette smoke. The floors were hardwood.

The place is old. Could it be Gigi's house? No, his townhome is newer. A new Wheel House? Keep thinking, detective!

She twisted to see behind her. Through the room's doorway, she could make out a bar and cabinets. It could have been a kitchen.

The pain in her neck forced her back around.

She inhaled deeply to calm her mind. The smell of stale nicotine and static-riddled plastic filled her nostrils. She could smell coffee, Chinese food, and a slight hint of someone's aftershave. The combination of odors sickened her.

She tried to listen. There were no vehicles outside, no possible traffic along a busy road. She could hear the faint beat of music. There were voices in the other room, and she guessed they were talking about her. The words were mumbled, though, on occasion, she could hear the conversation when the voices were raised.

"Look, the Vassal passed the word to us. It's final."

I recognize that calm voice. It's Frankie.

"Fine. Let me taste her. Fuck her. Have a little fun before we kill her. Just give me the word, Frankie."

"You're a pig, asshole," came a woman's voice.

That sounds like the woman from Gigi's house.

"No, Aggie. Touch her and the Vassal will put a bullet in your head and toss you in the woods."

Oh, fuck! They're going to kill me!

She twisted her feet to free them, but instead, jerked the chair legs up. The wooden legs made a loud popping sound as they reconnected with the floor. The sound echoed in the empty room and made the voices go silent in the adjacent room.

With her back to the open door, she could not see the

three figures until they walked in and came around. AJ stared at her captors.

Frankie knelt next to her.

"How are you feeling, detective?" His tone was deceptively relaxing.

"My head hurts," she managed to say. "What happened? Am I bleeding?"

Frankie glared at Aggie. "See what you did to her face?"

"So? The fucking bitch head-butted me in the car and busted my lip."

"When he sees the blood and bruises, he's going to be fucking *pissed* at you."

Aggie squatted down close to her and glared at her. Her stomach knotted again from the fear. She hated the menacing one.

Don't let them see the fear. It feeds them and they have control over you. Sit up and push back, dammit! FIGHT!!! Don't let them get to you!

She sat up as straight as she could in the chair and stared back at the rough one. He did not like that.

"What are you staring at, bitch?"

"What do you want with me? Why am I here?" she demanded.

WHACK! Her right jaw and cheek took the brunt of a back hand.

"Shut up!" Aggie growled.

"Aggie!" Frankie yelled, as his fist smashed into the menacing one's face. "Sit down! The Vassal said don't leave a mark on her, you fucking idiot!"

Tears, from both the pain of the hit and her anger building, welled up. She attempted to shove them back down and stared into Aggie's eyes. She wanted to kill him.

"Fuck what the Vassal said! That was payback."

"Touch her again and I'll beat the shit out of you and make you EAT it!"

AJ heard a knock at the door and her heart leapt. The other three stiffened.

Yell for help! Scream! You can get away!

"Don't bother yelling or calling out for help, detective," Frankie said. "It won't help. Zoey, see who's at the door."

The woman's steps echoed through the room as she exited. Frankie and Aggie waited in silence. The sinister one kept staring at her until she looked away.

AJ heard multiple footsteps and knew Zoey was coming back with someone. She saw the men's demeanor change, as they stood up straighter.

"Vassal!" Aggie sounded surprised, something she did not expected to hear.

"Boss, we weren't expecting you." Frankie's voice cracked with concern. Again, something she did not expect.

There was an empty silence before AJ heard calculated, slow steps walk around her. She followed the threat until he—she assumed it was he—stopped in front of her. He held a gun in one hand.

He wore black on top of black: a long, black trench coat over a dark suit, leather gloves, and polished boots. His oval-shaped mask—constructed of thick mesh, fabric, and metal—perfectly disguised his face and any noticeable features. Other than an athletic build, his clothing camouflaged his identity.

The Vassal slowly crouched down and rested his gun-wielding hand on his knee. His mask came eye-level with her, and he leaned forward, then cocked his head. He moved like an alien mollusk protruding outward from its shell. His free hand slowly reached for her face and moved her hair back to see her bloodied forehead.

She recoiled from fear, but his touch was gentle. Her eyes pleaded with pain and anxiety.

He quickly stood up and turned to the others. With equal swiftness, he pointed the gun at Frankie's head.

"Boss! It was Aggie—"

BOOM!

Even with a suppressor, the gunshot echoed in the room and startled everyone.

"AAARGH! F-f-f-f-fuuck!"

The target: Aggie's upper arm. His shirt soaked the blood from the through-and-through wound. The Vassal continued to point the gun at Aggie; then he motioned with the weapon for the wounded man to leave the room. She hid her pleasure from the menacing one's pain.

"Zoey, go help that dumbass cleanup," Frankie commanded. "Wai-wai-wait!"

The Vassal turned the gun back on Frankie.

"Boss, I didn't know Aggie would knock her head against the wall bringing her in! He said it was payback. You know he's out of control sometimes!"

The Vassal lowered the weapon. He raised his free hand up to his neck and pressed something underneath the cloth.

"No. Marks. You. Had. SPE-CIF-IC. In-struc-tions."

She had heard that voice disguiser before — the night Angie was murdered.

"I'm sorry, Boss. Do you want me to take care of Aggie myself?"

"No. Do. What. I. Com-mand-ed."

"Yes, sir."

The Vassal returned his attention to her. He dropped down to her eye level again.

"What do you want from me?" She tried to sound defiant and strong.

"You. Had. Been. Warned. De-tec-tive. You. Should. Have. Backed. Off."

"I was doing my *job*!"

He reached over and touched her face.

"You. Have. Been. A. Good. De-tec-tive. We. Could. Have. Used. You."

She stared at the mask, appalled at the idea of working for the Fasciata.

"I'd *never* work for you. You've *killed* people. You killed my husband, you fucking bastard!"

"Yes. We. Did. But. So. Has. Some-one. Else. He. Has. Come. After. Us. Be-cause. Of. You."

"I don't know who he is! I've never met him in person!"

She tensed and twisted against her restraints, hoping to loosen them.

"Good. Bye. Jar-dine."

He stood up and looked at Frankie.

"Be. Quick. She's. Not. To. Suf-fer."

Frankie nodded and walked out of the room. The Vassal stood there for a few seconds before he walked away.

Oh, my gawd, they're going to kill me! Her face became warm as her blood pressure increased. *Calm down, dammit! CALM THE FUCK DOWN!*

The masked one walked to the door.

Without thinking, she yelled, "Wait! Please wait!"

There was silence, then methodic footsteps came closer to her from behind. She tried to rear her head back to see him, but the motion made her temple sting with pain again. She looked forward and cried from the fear and frustration.

"What. Do. You. Want?"

"Please!" She could no longer hide the fear in her voice. "Let me go before this escalates. I have two children who are already without a father. They need me! *Please!*"

She waited for an answer, any answer.

"Close. Your. Eyes."

She complied and waited, expecting to be shot. She sobbed hysterically as the fear consumed her. Her chest tightened from shallow breathing.

Then she heard him take a step closer. She heard the gun clunk softly on the floor behind her. She heard fabric brushing and tightening as he leaned closer to her. She heard him remove the mask and set it on the floor behind her. She heard him lean in from behind.

She never opened her eyes.

His breath warmed her neck and ear. His beard pricked her skin and she felt him gently kiss her on the jaw. His lips were smooth, cool, and comforting, and the sensation lasted for several seconds.

She kept her eyes closed.

She heard him move away and pick up the gun. She heard him exit the room. She heard her own sobs in the otherwise silent kill room.

- - -- --- -----

She heard several footsteps coming back.

Aggie carried a chair into the room and slammed it down in the corner in front of her. He sat and glared at her. The wound was freshly bandaged under his torn shirt.

Zoey stood there, arms crossed. She said nothing.

Frankie squatted down in front of her. He lifted her face up and they stared at each other. She studied his eyes, the contour of his nose, the freckles he had. She held his gaze until his fingers tightened slightly on her chin to emphasize what he said next.

"Detective Jardine, don't fight back. Don't try to escape. Or I *will* kill your daughter. Do you understand?"

She nodded.

"Good. Aggie will keep an eye on you while me and Zoey go run an errand. Understand?"

"Yes."

"And *if* you try to escape, Aggie will do things to you that will make you *beg* him for death. Will you try to escape?"

She quickly shook her head.

"Good." He stood up and glared at Aggie. "Don't touch her, got it?"

"Yeah, sure," he grumbled. The menacing one kept staring at her. She knew he lied.

Frankie peered down at her, and added, "If he harms you, I'll deal with him. Don't provoke him." He turned to Zoey. "Let's go get the product."

The couple walked out of the room and left.

She wiggled in her chair, readjusting her posture to ease her back pain. Her stomach muscles cramped.

Aggie glared at her for several minutes. She looked away

and remained quiet so as not to provoke him, but she knew it was a fruitless effort.

"Did you know they need me? They can't kill me. I'm too important to the Octave."

She did not react or say anything.

"Did you know I could do anything I wanted to you and just not give a fuck?"

She still did not react. She kept her head down and eyes closed, ignoring him.

"Did you hear what I said? I'm one of their top Merchants. And Frankie, there? He's the Fasciata Knight. Did you know that?"

No reaction.

"And that fine piece of ass, Zoey? She's our Craftsman. She took Chris's place."

AJ looked up when Aggie mentioned the professor's son.

"Oh, THAT got your attention, huh? Might as well tell you who your unknown friend has killed. It's not like you're gonna live to tell anyone, bitch."

He stood up and stretched, then walked over to the window. He peered through the blinds. With his back to her, she used the opportunity to twist her bindings and stretch the thick plastic. One of the zip ties gave just slightly.

"Yeah, good ole Chris was our heroin cook. He was in the process of training Zoey when he disappeared. We never knew what happened to him until your professor got involved. Dunno how he wound up in New York, though."

Aggie walked back to his chair and sat down, glaring at her again. He continued to spill secrets.

"Now, Damian was with us since the beginning. Damn, but he had one fucking mean streak to him! He was one of our Serfs, one of the best dealers we had. Him and Delarosa. Heh, Martín could bring in a lot of Peasants and pussy."

"Is that what Nathan Hull and Mary Fay were?"

"Shut up, bitch!"

He flew out of his chair and grabbed her arms, squeezing them into the wooden chair. He kept applying pressure until she screamed.

"STOP! You're hurting me!"

She tried to kick him, but the zip ties around her ankles prevented that. He squeezed harder for one final measure before he eventually released her.

"*I'm* talking, not you, you goddamn cunt. *Me, not* you!"

She nodded quickly and hoped he would back off. She turned away, avoiding eye contact again.

"You wanna know about the fucking married couple? Huh? They were loyal buyers. Shit stains of humanity *you* had the misfortunate of cleaning up. Yeah, they were Peasants, worked for us for the drugs and favors. They kept an eye out for law enforcement and took the heat for us when anything happened. Mary was a loose fuck, but Jose liked her. After the slut's husband turned up dead, Perales swept in. He got the spoils. Said she had a tight pussy. Wonder if you have a tight pussy, *detective*."

The bile returned to her mouth. She kept her eyes down. Another tear rolled down her cheek.

Aggie pulled out a pack of cigarettes from his pocket. As he lit a cigarette, he continued between drags, "Perales was a good Merchant. He'd transport and deliver the Prussian Black anywhere and everywhere. See, your friend might've taken out our Peasants and Serfs, but we're *still* fully operational."

He took several long drags in the silence.

Nathan and Mary were the Peasants. Damian and Martín were Serfs. She repeated the information over and over in her head and found it helped calm the anxiety and fear.

Chris and Zoey are the Craftsmen. Frankie's the Knight. Aggie's a Merchant. Jose's another Merchant. How many does this make in the Boston Octave?

"Ya know, Gigi and Carl were in our back pockets. They were decent Farmers, but Carl was a cowardly piece of shit. The ginger pussy tried to leave the Octave, but he was killed before he spilled. Haha! Guess it's blood he spilled. Stupid anal-loving dumbass…"

He took another drag and studied the embers. A vicious grin cut across his mouth. He stood up again and walked back over to her.

"Gigi. Now Gigi was gold. Did you know he was like a brother? Did you know that, stupid bitch?"

He dared her to talk. His shadow blocked the light as he towered over her.

She felt him lean closer into her personal space, and they locked eyes. Anger and malice combined with relentless mania staring back at her. The unadulterated fear and panic swept back through her.

"Did you hear me? I called you a bitch!"

She studied his face and noted the healed kink from an old broken nose. His eyebrows were thick and dark brown. His breath stunk, making her want to vomit. She remained quiet.

He grabbed her hair and pulled her head to the side.

"I called you a *bitch*." As he said the last word, he pressed the lit end of the cigarette into the soft skin of her neck near her collarbone.

The pain was worse than she imagined. She screamed and panted as she tried to calm back down.

"STOOOOP! I heard you!"

YOU FUCKER! I'll kill you as soon as I get free!

Her inner voice swung on the emotional pendulum again. Either panicking fear or boiling rage tried taking control, but she could not tell which one was winning.

He grabbed her throat and squeezed her trachea. The room darkened.

"I. Am. Your. *Death!*" He squeezed harder with each word then released her.

She gagged and coughed several times before finally blurting out, "FUCK YOU and your death threat!"

She tried to head-butt him but missed. When he reached for her throat again, she swung her head around and bit down on his forearm, tearing a chunk of flesh off. She spit the bloody mass out and smiled at her success.

"You bitch!"

He grabbed her hair again and jerked her head back. This time, he used his forearm against her neck, choking her again.

Her vocal chords ached from the crushing force. She started blacking out before he finally let go. She tried to regain her breath, but he punched her in the stomach. The pain caused her starved lungs to burn as she coughed and gasped for more air. She only managed shallow breaths.

She knew he enjoyed the torture.

"You're going to die tonight. And I'm going to enjoy watching your life leave your body."

"What do you want from me?" Her defiant voice rasped from the pain. The anger gave into fear again.

"You wanna know what I want?"

His eyes ate away at her nerve. He grinned, more malevolent than ever. He reached behind his back and pulled a knife out.

Shink! The blade opened. He twisted it in his hand, admiring the shine and sharpness. He traced the blade's sharp edge along her cheek and neck.

"Fuck," he whispered. "This is making me hard."

He rubbed and adjusted his pants with one hand while he kept the knife next to her ear.

Fear replaced all the rage.

"I." He guided the knife to her throat.

"Want." Down her chest, between her breasts.

"To." Firmly on her stomach, continuing south.

"Fuck." Into her side cutting her shirt and skin.

"You." Down her inner thigh, ripping through her jeans and burning her skin.

"*Up.*" He dug the knife in and opened her leg up. Warm blood soaked the denim.

She finally gave him what he wanted: her fear.

She tried to scream, but the vocal folds in her throat were bruised. Only a gargled noise came out. She wriggled her wrists from the ties and desperately tried to get away. She thought she could almost squeeze her wrist through one of the ties, but Aggie grabbed the back of her head, pulling her hair back. His mercy held her neck.

"Stop or I'll slit your throat, bitch!"

He swept the knife back up and pressed it above the cigarette burn. She closed her mouth and tried to regain her composure.

For fuck's sake, BREATHE! You're giving him what he wants! BREATHE, dammit!

He kept the blade at her throat for several seconds. Then he brought the knife down to her blouse, begging her to give him another reaction.

He slid one hand down, grabbed her shirt, and used the knife-wielding hand to slit the blouse open, exposing her bra and chest.

"Nice tits." He traced her breasts with the knife.

The sickness of the violation rose from her core. She kept her mouth and eyes closed, hoping not to instigate anything. It had the opposite effect.

Aggie wanted a reaction — *any* reaction — from her, so he pressed the knife harder into her skin.

She still did not react.

Like a predator with its prey, he toyed with her and kept pressing the knife into the inner side of her breast until her skin stung. She felt the metal cut through each layer of the epidermis, opening her up, making her bleed. The pain was intense, and the burning sent shocks through her. The pain became unbearable.

She opened her eyes to stare at him, and when he locked his gaze on her, he thrust and pushed quickly on the same location. The knife made another long opening. Blood soaked her bra as she tried to vocalize another scream. The tears fell.

"How about a matching pair of scars?" He continued taunting her with the knife in her other breast.

"NOO!" she tried to yell, jerking her restraints.

But he did not care. Another thrust-slice-remove motion

and she was given a mirrored laceration on her other breast. Blood trickled down her chest and stomach, soaking her shirt and pants. Her heart pounded, and her breath faltered again.

There was no anger. There was no inner voice. There was only maddening terror in her eyes.

And he loved it.

"How about matching scars down here?"

He placed the knife between her legs just as Frankie and Zoey walked in.

"What the fuck are you doing?" Frankie yelled.

Aggie stood up. "Just having some—"

BAM! WHACK!

Frankie pistol-whipped him until a tooth flew out. Aggie glared back, too stunned to do anything except spit blood on her.

"Go clean up!" Aggie left the room. Frankie looked at AJ. "I told you not to provoke him."

"I didn't! I tried to ignore him. It only pissed him off."

"Did he hit you?" She shook her head. "Good."

"H-he put his cigarette out on my n-neck and p-punched me in the stomach." She coughed with every other word.

"Where di—" Then Frankie saw the burn. "That fucker. The Boss didn't want your face messed up. I'll deal with Aggie later."

He gently brushed her hair back behind her ears. Then he took the knife Aggie dropped and cut away the rest of her sleeve.

"What are you doing?" she whispered.

Frankie squatted down and propped himself on his knees.

"Detective Jardine, we sent you a warning when we sabotaged your father's car. We thought you'd back off the Order. But you didn't."

He glanced over at Zoey and nodded.

The woman sat the bag on the floor and opened it. She pulled out a glass vial of black powder and tapped it to break up the compound. With a pair of small tongs, she held the vial in one hand, flicked a lighter with the other, and carefully melted the substance.

Frankie took a long rubber tube and wrapped it around AJ's upper arm. He repeated the process from earlier in the car, only this time she knew it would be a larger dose.

"So, we killed Angie and sent you another warning. But again, you did not listen."

He tapped her inner elbow, feeling for an immerging vein. Her blood pressure increased again, and she felt her heart tighten, then quicken.

"So, we killed your father."

Absolute anger fueled the fire within her as it overthrew the fear.

"YOU BASTARDS!" she yelled as loud as she could. "I'll kill you!"

She jerked violently in her chair and snapped the ties off her feet. She kicked at Frankie, but he easily moved out of the way.

He grabbed her face. "Stop. It's not going to help you."

He tapped her inner elbow one more time and continued to feel for the vein.

"We warned you yet again to back off."

Frankie motioned for Zoey and she brought over the warm vial.

"And yet again, you didn't listen to us."

He inserted a needle into the glass container, extracting the onyx liquid and filling the syringe until it could hold no more. Then he stared at her intently.

"You wouldn't—and won't—let this go."

He held the needle up and continued to stare at her.

"And now you must die."

FIGHT DAMMIT! FIGHT!

Fear and anger joined forces, pushing adrenaline through her body. As he brought the needle towards her arm, she jerked violently again, giving her left arm a sharp, sudden twist against the zip ties.

The restraint popped off and she sucker-punched him across his face a couple of times. The force knocked Frankie on his back.

Zoey ran over and tried to grab her while AJ struggled with the other zip tie on her wrist.

"Aggie!" Zoey called out.

Aggie came running into the room and put AJ back in a headlock. With one arm still strapped down and the other clawing Aggie's arm, her attention focused on remaining conscious.

"You fucking bitch," Frankie growled.

Pissed he had a split eyebrow and swollen jaw, Frankie clambered back up and stabbed AJ in the leg. He pushed every last drop of the drug into her thigh before the needle broke off inside her muscle.

A few seconds passed as she fought back, but the struggle lessened as the drug slowly took hold.

"*I'll kill you!* I'll kill you…"

Aggie kept her in a headlock until her body started to go limp. Frankie cut the last restraint off her wrist and she slumped in the chair. When Aggie let go of her neck, she slid out of the chair to a sitting position on the floor.

"I'll. Kill. You…"

"Good luck with that, bitch." She heard Aggie's voice and flopped her head back on the chair to stare at him.

Her body lost control faster than her mind.

Slow your heart rate, Jardine! Fight for fuck's sake! Eoghan! Jenna! Think of them! Live for THEM!

"The Boss won't be happy. The Prussian will take longer to kill her now," Frankie said.

"So? She deserves to die slow."

"Well, dumbass, we were supposed to make it look like it was that serial killer."

"Why not toss her in the water?" Zoey suggested. "She'll die quicker in the freezing water."

"Let's do it then. Aggie, pick her up and carry her."

"With pleasure. Can't wait to get rid of this bitch."

He bent over, lifted her limp arms over him and carried her on his shoulder like a feed sack.

"Fuck, she's getting blood all over me."

"You dipshit, you shouldn't've cut her up!" Frankie's voice echoed in her brain.

"Too bad I never got to tell her about Michael." Aggie's voice echoed everywhere.

"Whaaat abooout Muh-kull?" Her own voice resonated in her mind.

She could not lift her head anymore, but she could see Zoey and Frankie walking behind Aggie. The woman's face morphed and changed shape. The calm one's eyes bulged out to his nostrils.

She tried to take a deep breath, tried to fight the effects of the drug, but her mind finally caught up to her body.

She felt herself floating through the warmth of the room and into a cold freshness of the outside. She floated down the stairs to a sidewalk. The footsteps clopped and galloped like a horse-drawn carriage. Street lights danced like fairies on a midsummer's night.

She hallucinated—vividly—and could not stop the imagery around her.

Her torso burned, and her hands and feet went numb. But nothing hurt anymore. She felt no pain. She felt nothing at all.

She had no sense of time or space anymore. She thought she floated into a moving car. Or maybe it was a dark tunnel. She was light as air, though her limbs were dead weights. Feathers expanded out of her torso as bowling balls held her extremities. Her body was almost completely numb.

The floating finally stopped.

She heard what sounded like the roar and thunder of waves crashing on large rocks. She thought water spray flickered in the lighting. She thought the wind tickled her and spread her hair away from her head like exploding fireworks.

The street lights swirled a fiery orange and a man's terrorizing face stared at her. She did not like him. His menacing and malevolent persona morphed into hollow, darkened eye sockets.

A low growl reverberated from his mouth.

"I killed Michael…"

"Mii…chaell…"

"Miii…chaelll…"

"Miiiii…chaelllll…"

"Miiiiiiiii…chaellllllll…"

"Miiiiiiiiiiiii…chaelllllllllllll…"

The growl swirled everywhere around her, and her husband's name echoed within her body.

She watched as the eyeless shadows near her began to disappear. The sinister one was above her, but he disappeared. She fell away from the voices. Her body felt a sudden pressure as the movement stopped. She slammed into something hard. Then she slowly slipped lower into an encompassing chill.

The sky above her darkened. Slowly, the stars disappeared. Her hair moved like tentacles around her. Her shirt parted from her chest like a sting ray's wings. Her clothes held her limbs down like an anchor at the bottom of a rocky aquarium.

She started shaking.

Ice.

Cold.

So cold.

Why such coldness?

Sounds resonated again inside her.

Her husband's name echoed in her trapped mind.

"Mi…chael…"

"Mii…chaell…"

"Miii…chaelll…"

"Miii…chaelll…"

"Mii…chaell…"

"Mi…chael…"

"*Michael!*" she called out.

The stars reappeared around her as she felt the sky above her. She stood on the back porch of her house in San Antonio.

"*Michael?*"

"*I'm here, sweetheart.*"

Her husband rocked back and forth on their wooden porch swing.

"*Michael!*"

She ran over to him and pressed her body against his.

"*I've missed you! Why did you leave me? Eoghan misses you. And Jenna – she's growing up without you!*"

He wrapped his arms around her. She laid her head on his chest.

"*I had to go somewhere else, dear. I've missed you, baby.*"

"*Are you coming back to us?*"

She held him tightly.

"*No.*" His voice was gentle.

He rocked her back and forth, holding her for an infinite amount of time.

"*Why not? Where have you been all of these years?*"

"*I've been on the mountainside.*"

She looked up at him, confused.

"*What mountain? In the Hill Country? Here in Texas?*"

"*No, sweetheart. THIS ONE.*"

His last words echoed across the landscape. The porch swing stopped moving and became rigid. They still sat on the wooden surface of a bench and they still had a canopy above them. But it no longer appeared like their back porch. Her breath appeared in front of her as the temperature decreased. The glittering snow sparkled around her. The sky was dark, brilliantly clear, and glistened from all the stars.

"*Why is there snow in San Antonio?*"

"*We aren't home anymore, baby.*"

Michael stood up and walked away from the bench. He stood near a small two-posted fence with his back to her.

She walked over and stood next to him. They were on a mountainside. She could make out the pointy tops of pine trees around her; the branches on the deciduous ones were bare. The moon set at the horizon behind rolling waves of other mountaintops.

She felt a chill.

"This is where you need to be, Ameena."

"I don't understand. Michael. Where am I?"

He turned to her. Though he stood still, his body slowly glided away from her towards the horizon.

"The Northern Lights, Ameena."

"I don't understand!"

His silhouette blurred as his body became a dark shadowy speck on the horizon.

"Ameena, look for the Northern Lights. Find the aurora."

"Michael, don't leave me! MICHAEL!"

She tried to reach out and touch the shadow, but it broke into five morphing shapes as if a star exploded in different directions. The shapes took on frequencies of color and swirled across the entire sky.

"Ameena, go to the aurora. The Northern Lights will protect you. It's always been the aurora. I love you, baby."

"Michael!"

"Mi...chael..."

"Mii...chaell..."

"Miii...chaelll..."

The pieces of his shadow-self danced across the sky above her. They swirled and writhed around her. They took the shimmer of the starlight, incorporated the spectrum of gaseous colors. Nebulas, galaxies of spiraling vividness formed impossible shapes of ribbons.

The sky danced to Van Gogh!

It became the most beautiful aurora she had ever seen!

"Aaa...meeeeen...aaa..."

Her body floated towards the strings of reds and ribbons of oranges.

"Aa...meeen...aa..."

Michael's shadow-self faded into new shadows and white lights. The colors disappeared, and three dark shapes stood above her.

"A...meen...a..."

The white lights burned her! They were fire and breath and life, <u>and it hurt</u>! It was so painful! She did not want the pain anymore! She wanted the Van Gogh lights, not the pain!

"Ameena!"

The voice sounded familiar but foreign. The voice took her from Michael and the Northern Lights.

She floated on her side. A baseball bat hit her across her back. More pain!

The bat hit her again.

And again.

And again.

And again.

She rolled over. The stars were above her. White lights mixed with ribbons of aurora and stardust. Shapes merged into dark shadows again and blocked her view of the brush-stroked sky.

Scorching air rushed her mouth. She gasped and choked as her lungs expanded like hot air balloons. She gasped, choked, gasped, vomited liquid, repeated. Then she floated again.

She heard loud bangs and echoes around her. The noise snapped her spirit back into her body and she was aware of a car. The lights above her flashed and raced past her like a war horse galloping into hell.

She could not move. She could not escape.

Piano. She heard a piano playing. She found it odd.

Her head spun, her stomach tightened, and she gasped rapidly. She could not breath anymore and a black mass came for her.

The movements stopped, and she vaguely realized the car stopped. The back door flew open and a shadow lifted her head up. She felt a knife pierce her heart like a strange doctor stabbed her before surgery. Her heart halted, then leapt to life as medicine quickly coursed through her. Her lungs raged, demanding oxygen. She groaned and gasped repeatedly for air. She tasted cottony metal.

"Ameena!" She heard a woman yelling.

"Put the mask back on her!" She heard a second male voice. She almost recognized it, but her mind could not focus on the words or tone.

Air surged into her lungs, forcing its way in. The burning in her ribs subsided.

She still hallucinated. She still could not move.

Paralyzed.

The back seat caved in towards her and then pushed out away from her as if the vehicle breathed on its own. As air was forced into her lungs, the vehicle caved inward. As air exhaled, the car pushed outward. It repeated indefinitely.

She tried to focus her eyes, but blackness overtook her vision. The void created and filled with colors swishing and splashing in a whirlpool of movement. And the colors made playful ribbons of light around her again.

The Van Gogh lights surrounded her again. She tried to reach out and touch them.

"We need to keep going," the first man's voice echoed. The sound and distinct dialect vibrated in her mind. She knew safeness and comfort. "Keep the ventilator on her."

"I can't stabilize her here," the woman's voice echoed in return. "Ameena! Stay with us, dear. Stay with us!"

She thought a goddess commanded her.

The strangers' voices danced in her brain. Her breath eased, and her body relaxed. She could no longer keep her eyes open, as every muscle felt like leaded weights strapped to concrete. She wanted nothing more than to sleep with the lights.

She heard an engine roar to life and felt her body flying across the sky. She danced with every twist and turn of the road as she tangoed with Van Gogh.

She heard a piano again. It played with the darkness as

the stars set above her.

"Ameena!" The second man's voice pulled her back from her delusion. "Stay with me, Ameena! I'm so sorry. I'm so sorry. Ameena…"

She felt cold and warm, sheltered and exposed. She wanted to wake and sleep.

She took a deep breath and closed her eyes.

She wanted to dance with the painter just one more time.

Then, she drifted.

Into darkness.

- - -- --- -----

APPENDICES

THE JARDINE TRILOGY continues with ZEPH1RUM, Book Three in THE FIBONACCI SERIES.

A full appendix will be provided at the end of ZEPH1RUM, Book Three and the final part of this story.

This appendix will include the following:
A — Help Hotline & Information
B — List of Characters
C — Arabic Phrases & Pronunciations
D — Abbreviations & Definitions
E — Ameena's Family Tree
F — Excerpt from ZEPH1RUM

- - -- --- -----

A – HELP HOTLINES & INFORMATION

PTSD
Post-Traumatic Stress Disorder is a mental health condition that can be brought on by experiencing or seeing a terrifying and life-changing event. It can last for weeks or years. Simple triggers can bring back the memories.

If you think you suffer from PTSD, there is help. You are not alone out there.

Wounded Warrior Homes
www.woundedwarriorhomes.org/ptsd
Phone: 1-866-382-2287

National Institute of Mental Health
www.nimh.nih.gov/health/topics/post-traumatic-stress-disorder-ptsd/index.shtml
Phone: 1-866-615-6464

U.S. Department of Veteran Affairs
www.ptsd.va.gov/
Contact: ncptsd@va.gov
PTSD Information Voice Mail: 1-802-296-6300

SUICIDE

If someone you know is having feelings of hopelessness, depression, or suicidal thoughts, please talk to them. Acknowledge them. Just listen to what they have to say.

If you are having suicidal thoughts, please reach out to someone. Someone will hear you.

National Suicide Prevention Lifeline
www.suicidepreventionlifeline.org/
Phone: 1-800-273-8255 or 1-800-273-TALK

Crisis Text Line
https://www.crisistextline.org/suicide
Text CONNECT to 741741 in the United States.

United States suicide hotlines by state:
http://www.suicide.org/suicide-hotlines.html

International Bipolar Foundation and a list of international suicide hotlines:
http://ibpf.org/resource/list-international-suicide-hotlines

DRUG ADDICTION

Drug addiction can and does affect families and communities. If you know someone who has a problem, or if you are an addict and trying to get clean, there is help for you.

Drug Abuse Hotlines
https://drugabuse.com/library/drug-abuse-hotlines/
Phone: 1-877-820-1646

Substance Abuse and Mental Health Services Administration (SAMHSA)
https://www.samhsa.gov/find-help/national-helpline
Phone: 1-800-662-4357 or 1-800-662-HELP

Heroin Hotline – **Recovery is Possible**
https://heroin.net/heroin-hotline/
Phone: 1-877-749-9324

- - -- --- -----

AJ's close friend. Getting married to Nadine

Chris. Computer technician at the toll road office.

Chris Pinick. [Pen-ik] Boston Octave member, a Craftsman. Tentacle tattoo on neck and right arm/shoulder. Raymond Pinick's son.

Conrad McMillan. [Kahn-rad Mik-Mil-un] I.S.B. Deputy Director and AJ's boss.

Copernicus. Mysterious hacker by the handle, NCPoland1543.

Costello. [Kuh-stell-oh] Labrador retriever mix. The Andrewson's goofy and clumsy dog.

Damian Winters. Boston Octave member, a Serf. Tentacle tattoo on inner and back right thigh.

Dana. Longtime girlfriend of Nabih Jardine.

Derek. Eoghan's best friend and abuse victim. Son of Nancy. Moved in with the Andrewsons and has become part of the family.

Elizabeth "Lizzy" Jardine. Daughter of Arif and Katherine Jardine, Jenna's cousin. Brother is William.

Ellie. I.S.B. receptionist and one of AJ's friends in the Bureau.

Eoghan Hawthorne. [Ee-guhn] Son of Michael Hawthorne and Ameena Jardine. Older brother to Jenna.

Ernest Andrewson. AJ's stepfather, Jamilla's husband. Scottish American with heavy Rhode Island accent.

Faruq Jardine. [Fah-rook] Son of Paden Jardine and Jamilla Andrewson. AJ's younger brother, the oldest of her three full-brothers. (Faruq means 'knows the truth'.) Married to Ghada. Father of Hakim, Houda, and Hani Jardine.

Fasciata Order. [Fah-see-ah-tah or Fah-shee-ah-tah] One of the Five Orders under the drug king, Hapalo Chaelena. Controls Prussian Black heroin in the North American continent.

Francesco "Frankie" Marino. [Fran-ses-koh Mar-een-oh] Boston Octave member, the Knight. Octopus head/skull tattoo across entire back. The calm one.

Ghada Jardine. [Ghah-duh] Faruq's wife. Mother of

Hakim, Houda, and Hani.

<u>Giovani "Gigi" Sotelo</u>. [Gee-oh-vah-nee Soh-tell-oh] Boston Octave member, a Farmer. Tentacle tattoo on left rib. State trooper.

<u>Greg Montgomery</u>. Another detective at I.S.B. AJ's coworker, dating Becky.

<u>Hakim Jardine</u>. [Hah-keem] Son of Faruq and Ghada Jardine. Older brother to Houda and Hani.

<u>Hani Jardine</u>. [Han-ee] Son of Faruq and Ghada Jardine. Baby brother to Hakim and Houda.

<u>Hapalo Chlaena</u>. [Huh-pall-oh Chlay-nuh] Drug King of the Five Orders, including the Fasciata. No one has ever seen him/her.

<u>Houda Jardine</u>. [Hoo-duh] Daughter of Faruq and Ghada Jardine. Sister to Hakim and Hani.

<u>Jamilla Andrewson</u>. [Jah-mee-lah] Lebanese mother. Current wife to Ernest Andrewson. Ex-wife of Paden Jardine. Had four children with Paden: Ameena, Faruq, Arif, and Nabih. Grandmother of: Eoghan and Jenna Hawthorne; Hakim, Houda, and Hani Jardine; and William and Elizabeth Jardine.

<u>Jenna Beth Hawthorne</u>. Daughter of Michael Hawthorne and Ameena Jardine. Baby sister of Eoghan. Born premature with birth asphyxia which has caused an autism spectrum disorder.

<u>Jesse</u>. AKA "Baby Face." Coroner's assistant.

<u>Jose "Mudo" Perales</u>. [Moo-doh] Boston Octave member, a Merchant. Tentacle tattoo on inner and back left thigh. ('Mudo' means speech-impaired.)

<u>Katherine "Kat" Jardine</u>. Arif's wife. Mother of William and Elizabeth.

<u>Katie Smith</u>. Reporter from New Hampshire.

<u>Lady Lusca</u>. [Loos-kah] The name Valda Bigollo gave one of the blue-lined octopuses. "Lusca" is a mythological creature/urban legend, a Caribbean sea monster and gigantic octopus.

Larsson Clancy. Agent Aserbbo's supervisor. Longtime friend of Deputy Director Conrad McMillan.

Loki. AKA Holloski Steward Mahoney. Tattoo artist at The House of Skulls Tattoo and Piercing Shop.

Martín Delarosa. [Mar-teen Duh-lah-row-sah] Boston Octave member, a Serf. Tentacle tattoo on inner and back right thigh.

Mary Fay. Boston Octave member, a Peasant. Tentacle tattoo on upper left arm/shoulder. Married to Nathan Hull.

Michael Hawthorne. AJ's husband. Former F.B.I. undercover agent and Julie McCaffrey's partner. Father of Eoghan and Jenna Hawthorne.

Nabih Jardine. [Nah-beeh] Son of Paden Jardine and Jamilla Andrewson. AJ's younger brother, the youngest of her three full-brothers. (Nabih means 'smart'). Dating Dana.

Nadine. Cassandra Owen's girlfriend and fiancée.

Nancy. Derek's mother.

Nathan Hull. Boston Octave member, a Peasant. Tentacle tattoo on upper left arm/shoulder. Married to Mary Fay.

Nick (Nikterio). British guy AJ kissed in the White Mountains.

Paden Jardine. [Pay-den] AJ's biological father. Jamilla's ex-husband and Patricia's current husband. Scottish American father to: Ameena, Faruq, Arif, Nabih, Eunan, and Quinn.

Peter Yates. Forensics lab technician. One of AJ's best friends.

Dr. Raymond Norbert Pinick. [Pen-ik] Professor teaching C.A.D. at a technology institute in New Hampshire. Father to Chris Pinick. Cracked the Code.

Rebecca. Copernicus's wife, murdered by the Fasciata.

Dr. Tarakini Amin. [Tair-ah-key-nee Ah-meen] Lead C.S.I. of the more violent crime scenes. Indian-American.

Taylor Rion. Carl Frierson's boss at the A.T.F.

Tiffany Devry. I.S.B. employee. AJ's coworker and office

nemesis.

<u>Valda Bigollo</u>. [Vall-duh Bee-go-low] C.E.O. of research facilities specializing in octopus venom antidotes. From the Dominican Republic.

<u>William "Will" Ernest Jardine</u>. Son of Ari and Kat Jardine. Brother of Elizabeth.

<u>Zoey</u>. [Zoe-ee Sore-ee-ah-no] Boston Octave member, a Craftsman. Tentacle tattoo on neck and right arm/shoulder.

- - -- --- -----

C – ARABIC PHRASES & PRONUNCIATIONS

Ana bahebak. [ah-na ba-eh-bahk] I love you

Alhamdulillah. [al-hahm-doo-li-lah] Praise be to Allah (God)

Allah U'Akbar. [ah-lah oo awk-bar] Allah (God) is Great

Anaa aasif. [an-uh eh-siff] I'm sorry

Bismillah al Rahman al Rahim. [biss-meh-la all rah-mahn all rah-heem] In the name of Allah (God), the Beneficent, the Merciful

Habibi. [ha-bee-bee] Dear, sweetheart, loved one – when spoken to a male

Habibti. [ha-beeb-tee] Dear, sweetheart, loved one – when spoken to a female

Inshallah. [een-sha-lah] If Allah (God) wills it

Khamsa. [khahm-sa] (The 'kh' is said with the back of the throat) Five

Lah. [La-ah] No

Ma'a as-salaama. [ma-ah ahs-sah-lah-mah] Goodbye

Mabruk. [ma-brook] Congratulations

Salam alaikum. [suh-lahm ah-lay-koom] Peace be upon you

Sukran. [su-krahn or shoo-krahn] Thank you

Ta'ala hon. [tah-all-ah hone] Come here

Tayta. [tay-tuh] Nickname for Grandma

- - -- --- -----

D – ABBREVIATIONS & DEFINITIONS

APB. All Police Bulletin

ATF. Alcohol, Tobacco, and Firearms

ATV. All-terrain vehicle

BOLO. Be on the look out

CAD. Computer-aided drafting

CCTB. UK's video surveillance

CFT. Computer Forensics Team

CI. Confidential informant

COD. Cause of Death

CODIS. Combined DNA Index System.

CSI. Crime scene investigation

DB. Dead body

DEA. Drug Enforcement Administration

DTF. Drug Task Force

ECU. Engine control unit

EMI. Electromagnetic interference

EMS. Emergency Medical Services

EMP. Electromagnetic pulse; used to disrupt electronics and wireless communications

ETA. Estimated time of arrival

FBI. Federal Bureau of Investigation

FDA. Food and Drug Administration

GPS. Global positioning system

ICU. Intensive care unit

ID. Identification

IES. Computer term

IP. Internet Protocol; similar to a postal system of addresses for computers

ISB. Investigative Services Bureau

ISO. The sensitivity of a camera sensor to light

IT. Information technology

Kp index. Scale used to measure geomagnetic storm intensities

ME. Medical examiner

MO. Modus operandi, or Method of Operation; a

criminal's signature

OD. Overdose

PD. Police Department

PPE. Personal protection equipment

Puta. Spanish insult meaning prostitute or slut

RICO. Racketeer Influenced and Corrupt Organizations Act

RN. Registered nurse

SWAT. Special Weapons and Tactics

Tonneau. A hard or soft cover used to protect the cargo bed in a pickup truck

TOD. Time of death

TOR. The Onion Router, software used for the darknet

Tox. Short for toxicology

TTX. Tetrodotoxin, a neurotoxin found in some marine animals, including the blue-ringed octopus.

Vic. Short for victim

VR. Virtual reality

Weta. Spanish insult for white girl

- - -- --- -----

E — AMEENA'S FAMILY TREE

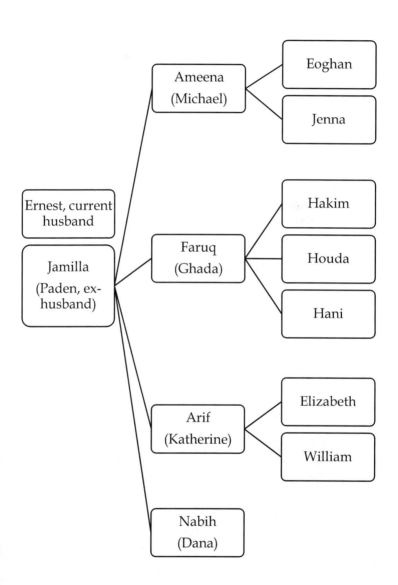

F — EXCERPT FROM ZEPH1RUM

"What would you like me to do?" His voice was quiet with concern.

She shrugged in frustration. "Compared to what you HAVE done so far? YOU'VE killed the last of HIS family. And HE helps the same organization that killed YOUR family. I'll show you what you've done so far!"

She grabbed his arm and dragged him to her room. She pulled out her dresser drawer, collected several items, and tossed them on the bed towards him.

"This! This is what you've done! Teasing me with death quotes and gifts over the years." She pointed at the papers and the kinetic mobile. "Look at this!" She picked up one of the cards and waved it at him. "And what the FUCK are these numbers?"

He smiled. "Love, I told you. They're —"

"—Breadcrumbs? No! Stop!" She paced back and forth. "You know as much as HE does and are as MUTE as he is. How am I supposed to choose between the secrets and deceit? How am I supposed to choose a vigilante serial killer or a partner who's a goddamn double agent? Huh? HOW?"

He walked over to the bed and sat down on the edge. He continued to grin. He was so oddly quiet and calm, it unnerved her. He studied her as she studied him. She could not read his mind. She could not figure out why he was smiling ear to ear as she paced back and forth.

"WHAT?" she finally yelled at him.

"You remind me of a caged tiger, pacing back and forth. How beautiful would all your glory be unleashed on the Fasciata?"

- - -- --- -----

ABOUT THE AUTHOR

Karma Lei Angelo is a new, emerging author and the mastermind behind THE FIBONACCI SERIES universe. She creates very real, down-to-earth characters and weaves them together effortlessly through the stories. She provides as realistic a setting as possible to emerge the readers right into each scene. And she's unapologetic for it.

Originally from Texas, she grew up on a farm just outside the town of Paris. In 1994, she moved to San Antonio and lived there for nearly two decades, working in the civil engineering field for a majority of that time. Following her mom's and maternal uncle's deaths in 2012, and then her father's death in 2015, Karma walked away from her engineering career and Masters' degree pursuit. She turned her focus to her family and finding a new career path: writing.

It was her daughter's interest in the F.B.I. and The X-Files in early 2016 which planted the idea to write a mystery suspense thriller. That book began as one novel, then morphed into THE JARDINE TRILOGY. That trilogy eventually became the twenty-six-book endeavor known as THE FIBONACCI SERIES, a project in the works spanning several years.

Karma also brings decades of engineering, CAD, and math experience to the table, building her characters' worlds with elaborate and interesting concepts. She's a strong supporter and advocate for STEAM (Science, Technology, Engineering, Art, and Math) fields, and she's not afraid to challenge readers beyond a linear cookie-cutter, action-packed read.

She encourages readers to participate and try to solve the mysteries, even leaving dozens of "Easter eggs" throughout the chapters. And she doesn't limit the mystery to just the story inside the book. Clues for what comes next can be found in the appendices, images, and even the outside book jackets of the printed copies.

In her spare time, Karma enjoys reading, gardening, crocheting, traveling, and anything she can manage to fit into her busy schedule. Karma currently resides in rural Belmont, New Hampshire, with her family, pets, and a lot of wildlife.

She looks forward to engaging you all the way to the endgame!

- - -- --- -----